MEMORIAL TO THE DUCHESS

Alice, only child of Thomas and Matilda Chaucer, was destined to a rich inheritance, but not even her ambitious father could have imagined the events which would advance her position and fortunes. As the wife of William de la Pole, Duke of Suffolk, she became second only to the Queen of England.

This well-written and historically authentic first novel traces her eventful life from childhood at the beginning of the fifteenth century to her death seventy years later. She saw the accession of three more kings.

Henry V brought to England the glory of Agincourt and by his untimely death left a nursling infant on the throne. The long minority encouraged opportunism among the barons and broke down effective government. Henry VI grew up under the shadow of ambitious, self-seeking men. His weakness of purpose destroyed the last of the old chivalry towards the crown and made of it a mere trophy in a contest at arms. Finally Edward IV won it and wore it for the House of York.

These were restless and dangerous times. It took courage, cunning and a cool head to live through them. Widowed at the height of her husband's power and attainted of treason by the Yorkists, Alice might have become their tragic victim. But, as the author shows, she was a woman of purpose, endowed with wit as well as beauty. She mastered the politics of the time and the men who made them, guarding her son's inheritance with a jealous pride and dying in her own good time.

**Also by the same author,
and available in Coronet Books:**

The Athelsons

Memorial to the Duchess

Jocelyn Kettle

CORONET BOOKS
Hodder Paperbacks Ltd., London

Copyright © 1968 by Jocelyn Kettle
First published by Herbert
Jenkins Ltd., 1968
Coronet edition 1974

For my mother, E.M.W.

This book is sold subject to the condition that
it shall not, by way of trade or otherwise, be
lent, re-sold, hired out or otherwise circulated
without the publisher's prior consent in any
form of binding or cover other than that in
which this is published and, without a similar
condition including this condition being
imposed on the subsequent purchaser.

Printed and bound in Great Britain for
Coronet Books, Hodder Paperbacks Ltd,
St. Paul's House, Warwick Lane,
London, EC4P 4AH
by Hunt Barnard Printing Ltd,
Aylesbury, Bucks.

ISBN 0 340 18813 8

The House of de la Pole showing the Beaufort connection

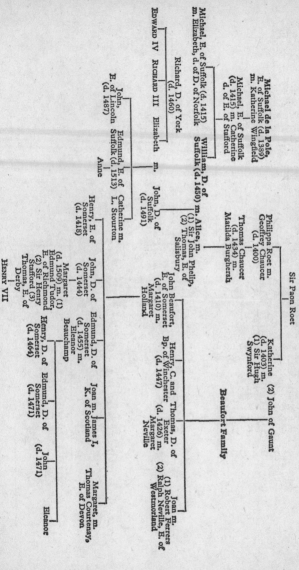

EDWARD III (d. 1377) m. Philippa of Hainault

Edward of Woodstock (d. 1376) — Isabella — Lionel, D. of Clarence (d. 1368) — John of Gaunt D. of Lancaster (d. 1399) m. (1) Blanche of Lancaster (d. 1369) (2) Constance of Castile (d. 1394) (3) Katherine Swynford (d. 1403) — Edmund of Langley, D. of York (d. 1402) — Mary — Thomas of Woodstock D. of Gloucester

RICHARD II (d. 1399) — Philippa (d. 1355) m. Edmund Mortimer 3rd E. of March (d. 1381) — Philippa — HENRY IV (d. 1413) m. (1) Mary Bohun (2) Joan of Navarre — Elizabeth — Catherine — Edward D. of York (d. 1415) m. Philippa co-Heiress of L. Mohun — Constance m. Thomas, E. of Gloucester (q.v.) — Richard D. of Conisburgh (d. 1415) m. Anne Mortimer — Anne

Edmund — Elizabeth — Roger Mortimer (d. 1398) E. of March — HENRY V (d. 1422) m. Catherine of France — Thomas, D. of Clarence (d. 1421) — John, D. of Bedford (d. 1435) — Humphrey, D. of Gloucester (d. 1447) — Blanche — Philippa

Edmund, E. of March (d. 1425) — Anne, m. Richard of Conisburgh (q.v.) — Eleanor

Richard, D. of York (d. 1460) m. Cicely Neville — HENRY VI (d. 1471) m. Margaret of Anjou

Edward (d. 1471) m. Anne Neville

EDWARD IV (d. 1483) m. Elizabeth Wydeville — George, D. of Clarence (d. 1478) — RICHARD III m. Anne Neville — Anne — Elizabeth, m. John, D. of Suffolk — Margaret

Edward (d. 1484)

EDWARD V (d. 1483) — Richard, D. of York (d. 1483) — Elizabeth (d. 1503) m. HENRY VII

FOREWORD

THE PURPOSE of this book is to reconstruct the life of the woman born Alice Chaucer, who later became Alice de la Pole, Duchess of Suffolk. In endeavouring to tell her story I have not disturbed the chronological sequence of events, nor changed the circumstances of any incident for which reliable historical sources offer a record. Where I have quoted extracts from documents such as the last letter of William de la Pole to his son, also his Will, and the authorisation given him by Henry VI when he was appointed to escort Margaret of Anjou to England, I have modernised the language slightly.

Alice was destined both by inheritance and marital alliance to live her seventy-one years in intimate association with the men and women who struggled about the pinnacle of power in fifteenth century England. Thomas Carlyle described history as 'the essence of innumerable biographies' and I have tried to relate some of the episodes of this exciting period as they affected individuals rather than the whole nation.

One or two observations might be helpful to the reader who is not familiar with the social conditions and customs of this century. In regard to the marriage arranged for Alice by her father when she was only ten years old, this was in no sense a proper marriage as we understand it – although the parties were styled 'husband' and 'wife' – but rather a preliminary contract in which terms would be agreed and the settlement of property arranged. It was binding to a limited extent but not indissoluble – a similar child 'marriage' contracted between Alice's son, John, and Margaret Beaufort was later cancelled for political reasons. No marriage could be formally completed below the legal age of consent which was then twelve years. It is interesting to note that at this time, marriage for the nobility was not considered to be a matter for the church. The poor and the middle class might go there to exchange their vows, but among the aristocracy it was an affair of clerks and lengthy negotiations, culminating in the meticulous language of the law and the flourish of s.gnatures. Perhaps this is not surprising when one remembers that it was a period in which heiresses were handled like real estate and a grant of wardship was a valuable asset.

The materialism of the fifteenth century is far from being the only characteristic which gives it an affinity to our own times, absent from the intervening periods. It was a century racked by war and its economic consequences. Old feudal loyalties and moral standards were being swept away, and while men still paid lip-service to their religious faith, this too was beginning to be called into question. There were labour disputes – a legacy of the Black Death which had depleted manpower – and wages were high. Taxes were also climbing and everyone blamed the government.

Successive statesmen struggled to evolve policies which would be the ultimate solution to problems both at home and in Europe, unable to accept the simple truth that there could never be a total answer for a progressive civilisation.

The people of fifteenth century England were vital, sanguine and humorous. They expressed themselves in a vivid, forthright language and their vices, like their virtues, were uncomplicated by the refinements which would make our twentieth century seem as unbelievably degenerate to them as theirs may sometimes appear cruel and bloody to us.

I should like to thank Mr. Charles Toase, senior reference librarian of the London Borough of Merton for his valuable assistance in my research.

CHAPTER ONE

'WILL BYLTON, Will Bylton! Are you there, Will?' The clear, high voice of a child echoed up the crumbling staircase of a derelict tower, which stood across the courtyard from the manor-house at Ewelme in Oxfordshire.

For years Thomas Chaucer had been saying the old tower must be pulled down because it was unsafe. But its slender, pointed turret was the first glimpse he had of home, when he turned off the road from London. Then he would urge his company to gather up their weary horses and make some speed over the last mile or so to the village, eager to be in that fair manor which he took such pride and pleasure in possessing.

So, though under sentence of destruction, the tower continued to stand where it had stood for centuries, and because the manor servants no longer dared to go there, it became a favourite hiding place for Alice, Thomas Chaucer's well-beloved and only child.

Alice knew that if she was seen visiting the tower she would be whipped. It had been forbidden ground to her since she took her first toddling steps about the courtyard. But there was no better place to escape a scold or avoid a tiresome duty.

Only Will Bylton was permitted to share the secret of her retreat and on this particular day important guests were expected at the manor-house, so he would surely be using the turret window as a look-out post.

She called again and this time the freckled face of an eleven-year-old boy appeared round a bend in the stairs and presented itself for her reassurance.

9

'Well I am here and I should think every one of your father's servants will know it too, when you have done hallooing down there. I have told you times-a-number not to call from the foot of the stairs. Why do you not come up and see if I am here, idle-bones?'

Another day Alice would not have let that pass unchallenged. But on this occasion she confined herself to a muttered threat of boiling Will's head in a cauldron and, gathering up her skirts to avoid the dust, ran lightly up the stairs.

'What do you here at this hour, then? Surely you should be helping your mother make ready to receive Sir John Phelip!' Will had meant to make the observation mocking and indifferent, but instead he sounded sulky and hurt.

'I am come to watch for my husband. From here I shall be able to see the pennons as his riders cross the old stone bridge.' The reply had a new self-conscious dignity. It was something after all, when one was but ten years old, to have been asked in marriage by a knight who was close friend to the young soldier-king, Henry V.

Alice knelt on the stone window seat and peered out at the dusk stealing over the sad November fields. He must come soon. He would be riding hard, urging his men to a good pace, not wanting to be benighted on an unfamiliar road. Or would he have fallen in with his father's party along the way? Aye, that seemed likely. Her father had originally sent word that he would arrive in Oxfordshire the previous day, and the Saints alone knew what had kept him! What a state her mother had been in since yesternight, anxiously awaiting the silver dishes and chargeours which he was to bring with him, to say nothing of the costly new tapestry from the hall of their London house, signed by the weaver and inscribed with the date, 1414. And the fine fur bed-rugs and rare wines just arrived from the Rhine and Gascony.

Still seeing no sign of horsemen, Alice finally left the window and turned her thoughtful gaze on the boy beside her. Will Bylton was the son of their neighbour and friend, Nicholas Bylton, a witty and scholarly gentleman whose preoccupation with philosophy and literature had caused him to neglect the interests of his modest property. Will was an only child and, since his mother died bearing him, father and son had leaned much upon Alice's mother for guidance in the past eleven years.

Alice and Will had grown almost like brother and sister, sharing their games and physicked by the same hands for their childish ailments. Often in infancy they had been bathed together by Gundred, who was nurse to Alice. Sometimes they had been tucked into the same cradle. Came a day when they rode their first ponies side by side, and later, with the ready approval of Thomas Chaucer, who saw no reason why his daughter should not be educated as well as if she were a boy, they studied their lessons together under Nicholas Bylton's gentle and enlightened tutorship.

But although Alice knew her father valued Nicholas Bylton as a friend and enjoyed a bond with him in their shared appreciation of the poetry of her grandfather, Geoffrey Chaucer, she was equally well aware that her association with Will would never be permitted beyond childhood. As soon as she had been able to understand anything, she had understood that she was heiress to her father's fortune and had a duty to him and to her Chaucer heritage to marry as he thought fitting in their mutual interests.

Nevertheless she was woman-child enough to sense that Will resented Sir John Phelip's intrusion into their life. So now she glided gracefully into a dance step and concluded it by asking: 'Do you think this gown becomes me, Master Will?'

'You are tricked out well enough, I suppose.'

'Oh Will!' Alice's face fell. 'Is that all you have to say?'

'If you want courtly compliments you had better wait until Sir John comes. You will get them then, I doubt not.'

He looked at Alice, a year younger than he, yet as tall and seeming taller because she was so slender. But he looked in vain for the girl he knew. This young woman with the demurely folded hands and the strange secret tawny-green eyes set with oddly dark brows and lashes seemed suddenly remote to him.

'I do not know what you want to marry for and go off and leave Ewelme and me and everything,' he blurted out.

Alice was surprised. 'But it cannot be a true marriage until I am twelve and I will not be going away – oh, not for a long

11

while yet. I have to marry someone or else I shall grow to look like Gundred.'

'Women do not turn ugly because they are unwed, silly ninny. Who told you that?'

'My mother says it is so. But anyway I want to marry Sir John, and I want you to be pleased about it too.' Alice was beginning to feel ill-treated. 'Sir John is bringing me a white palfrey, a snow white palfrey, for my very own.' This did not seem to make much impression and she went on: 'We are having such a splendid banquet tomorrow – your father will be there and in fact he may well come to supper this night too, only that is to be nothing remarkable . . . and oh Will! I am to be called the Lady Alice now, only think of it . . . my mother says so . . . But Gundred and the other servants will not remember and keep calling me Mistress Alice . . . I am so vexed! I tell them to have a care of it, but they only laugh. Very soon I will be able to beat them when they are insolent and then they will see!'

'I think you are a vain, selfish girl with ill manners and no heart. I do not know why you should want to beat the good people who serve you right well, aye, and love you too. My father has taught you to know better than that. My father says no one has the right to use the lash simply because they are ill-pleased with servants. And I shall *not* call you "lady" for you are none such by nature.'

Very red in the face at the conclusion of this outburst, Will swung on his heel and stumped off down the stairs, sending clouds of stone-dust into the air as he went and causing a minor avalanche of loose fragments. 'And you may ride your white palfrey to the devil,' he shouted back over his shoulder.

He left Alice fighting back tears – she must remember not to redden her eyes. Finally cold anger numbed the pain of the cruel words. Very well, so Will Bylton might turn against her if he pleased. She would make him rue the harsh words by-and-by.

Suddenly Alice became aware of a rhythmic drumming that grew louder and ran to the window, exclaiming impatiently at her own folly to be taken unawares. Already the riders were streaming up the lane, their flying torches making a pretty sight, born as if by magic through the gloom. She had meant to see them in good time and be back at the house before they dismounted. That was impossible now. She would have to creep round behind the stables and up the outside staircase to the servants' dormitory. From there she might reach the gallery unseen, if her luck held.

It was no easy task, though. Alice skirted the cobbled court-yard hesitantly, trying to remember in the darkness where was grass and where was mire. Men's voices called and lads ran to help riders dismount. Several times she had to duck the beam of swinging lanterns and once she caught sight of her father, a big, impressive, purple-clad figure astride Crécy, his favourite grey charger. He was shouting jovial threats to the stablemen above the stamp of hooves. 'Please God he does not see me or he will not be so merry,' Alice prayed earnestly. How angry he would be if he caught her, careless for her dignity, skulking round the stables, unattended in the dark.

At last she reached the house and was soon slipping through the panelled door which led from the dormitories to the gallery. She made haste to her room to leave her cloak, to shake the folds of her dove grey, velvet gown and arrange its long, full sleeves so that the pink silk, embroidered linings were shown to their best advantage. A final look in her mirror – one made of real glass and set in wrought silver, which her father had bought from the princely stock of an eastern merchant. The reflection of her pale, pointed face was satisfying, framed by two thick braids which gleamed, nearer silver than flaxen, in the candlelight. No tell-tale smudges or cobwebs. She settled the circlet of tiny pearls over her pink gauze veil and exchanged her hide slippers for a daintier pair in grey velvet.

The gallery ran along two sides of the hall. The first arm of it, screened from below by a lattice of carved wood, made it easy for anyone above to look down without being seen. Peering through the spokes of a Katherine wheel, her father's heraldic device from the arms of Roet, Alice saw the group around the huge log burning fiercely on the stone-flagged hearth. Her father, taller than any man there, stood like a

Colossus astride one of his hounds, turned sideways to the blaze and smoothing the fine wool of his rich ankle-length robe over one slowly toasting thigh. His fine head, which was uncovered at the moment to show his short-cut, greying, black hair, was bent as he listened to something his wife, Matilda, was saying, so that one could not see the thick dark brows meeting across the prominent nose, nor the keen eyes which sometimes gave him the look of one of his own falcons, nor the close-trimmed beard.

But where was Sir John? Had he not arrived after all? There was a man there receiving much deference from those around him as he took up the conversation, but there seemed little of the soldier about him. He was slender almost to the point of elegance and not above middle height. In a pleated knee-length surcoat of dark green velvet he looked more like one of her father's merchant friends than a fighting man. Alice smiled to herself to think that she had pictured him always in heavy armour. But that was ridiculous – a knight did not wear armour save for battle or a tournament as she very well knew.

Thinking it was more than time to put in an appearance, Alice gathered the folds of her dress carefully in one hand and, lifting her chin, turned down the second half of the gallery. They saw her under the lights of the wall sconces on the staircase.

'Aah-hah!' commented her father.

'At last!' said her mother on a note of exasperation.

The stranger in dark-green velvet detached himself at once from the fireside and came to meet her at the foot of the stairs.

'My lady wife?' he enquired gently taking her hand. 'How does my lady?'

Alice was trying desperately to keep her hand steady in his. She was very nearly successful but lost the battle with her voice which, instead of being calm and cool as she wished, came out a breathless whisper.

'I thank you. I am in good health, my lord, as . . . as I have been p-praying you are also.'

Sir John led her to the fire.

'Well,' said her father gruffly, trying hard not to look pleased at what he saw when he gazed on his daughter. 'And where do

14

you think you were, mistress, when you should have been waiting with your mother to greet our guests and your betrothed?'

'I was working on a piece of embroidery, father, and did not mark the hour,' Alice lied.

'A likely tale. I never saw you apply yourself to your needle so diligently in all your life. Head stuck in one of my books, more like,' her father snorted. 'Do you know Sir John this girl of mine is for ever taking my books and going off to read them somewhere in secret, while her mother hunts high and low to chase her to the still-room.'

The lady Matilda, clearly thinking this was little recommendation for a wife, hastened to add that Alice was quick to learn when she did apply herself to housewifely duties.

'Well, well, she has time enough before she needs think of keeping house. I like a well-informed mind and a lively discourse in a pretty woman,' put in Sir John, with a kindly smile at Alice.

'Aye, but good food counts for more than converse at times,' said Thomas. 'Come, lady wife, are we to stand here for ever drinking spiced ale, or have your cooks not a morsel of food to offer us?'

It was a true country supper party such as Thomas Chaucer liked to preside over. Tomorrow was time enough for a show of stateliness to honour and impress his son-in-law. While they ate trout scented with herbs and stuffed with toasted nuts, pigeon pie and cuts from a fine, fat goose, the talk was general and such as might include and entertain the women. Matilda was longing to hear how the young king looked, she told Sir John.

'My husband says nothing but that he will "do well", is "comely" and "has a good presence". Do tell us more. It is long since I saw the young prince and I hear he is much changed.'

'Why, yes he is changed – and yet again not so. The same boyish enthusiasm still shows through every now and then. But since he was crowned king a new sternness has settled on his face and his eye warms less readily . . . He is a man all Englishmen will gladly follow, I think.' Sir John spoke in the hesitating way of one who explores his own thoughts. 'When he talks of his ambitions for England . . . well . . .

15

maybe it is simply that one senses he could be a ruthless enemy. He seems to need no one close. Even with those who serve and advise him there is a reserve in his manner. High-principled, knightly, dedicated . . . these are all words one might use to describe him . . . For the rest, I do not think he is exactly what women would call handsome, though he has a fine manly face and regular features. He is broad in the shoulder and narrow in the hip and wears his hair cropped as I do . . . And that, ladies, is all I can tell you.'

'It is well. I can see him vividly now,' said Alice softly.

'Yes indeed, Sir John,' smiled her mother, 'you have given a far fairer and fuller account than my husband could be made to part with. But this king certainly does not sound like the wild young Hal who used to plague his father so and often shocked the worthy London citizens with his pranks.'

Thomas Chaucer was probably better acquainted with the new king than any of those present, but he chose not to comment as he sat staring before him and toying with the stem of a silver goblet. That he enjoyed the royal favour was known to them all. He had been made Chief Butler of England only two days after Henry V came to the throne in March of the previous year. The appointment was the first on the Patent Roll of the new reign. He had held the same post under the young king's father, but that was no precedent for him retaining it on the accession, and the appointment was a credit both to Henry V's astuteness in sizing up the men who served him and Chaucer's unimpeachable reputation.

The politician was deep in the nature of the man, however, and discretion was deep in the nature of this politician. Thomas was not likely to pass opinions on the man who hired him, nor abuse the confidence placed in him by using his proximity to the king as an opportunity to furnish his guests with colourful cameos of the royal private life. He might seem a bluff and hearty squire in his own hall, but those who knew him in Westminster, as the Speaker of the Commons, held him to be a close-mouthed man with busy and sometimes devious thoughts.

After a while talk turned on the prospect of war with France. John Arundel, Matilda's brother-in-law, asked Sir John if he had any idea when the army would sail.

'Why, matters are not so forward as that! But our good host is more privy to the king's mind than I; you should ask him. For my own part I think another delegation will be bound for France soon, bent on peaceful negotiation. I know nothing of outright war as yet.'

'But they do say that the king intends to demand not only that Charles gives him his daughter Catherine in marriage but also grants him full and independent sovereignty in Normandy, Touraine, Maine and Anjou as well as Brittany, Flanders and Aquitaine,' put in the voice of Thomas Carew, a City wine merchant. As he was known to be almost as well informed as he was rich, the company gave him its full attention – all that is except for his host who seemed absorbed in spying down the ear of a great bay hound which leaned against his knee.

'It would be hard to imagine Charles VI agreeing to such terms as those,' said Nicholas Bylton surprised.

'No, by God's teeth, he will not. Harry knows what he's about, never fear. And the hour could not be riper nor sweeter for his interests, with the Armagnacs and the Burgundians at each other's throats,' Carew replied. 'If he wants war, and I believe he does, now is the best of times to force it on the French. What say you Thomas Chaucer?'

'I say we have sown many sons in the fields of France and the harvest has been a long time coming,' said Thomas quietly. And he did not even look up.

*   *   *

The days of Sir John's visit passed all too quickly for Alice, with rides on her white palfrey while she listened to Sir John's talk of battles past and future, and such gallantries as matched her years. Then there were the hunts, and the long merry meals, when minstrels and strolling mummers earned their meat and a night's shelter.

On the morning when Sir John was to leave, Alice rose while it was still dark. Skipping anxiously back and forth between the frozen window panes and the hastily stirred fire on her bedroom hearth she was sure she would never be ready.

'Oh! make haste do, Gundred! Why you have not even brought my robe from the closet yet. They are leaving at first light, you know. Would you have me keep them waiting? What are you about, old crone? Devil fly away with my hair – it is alive, for it will not braid! Mother of Heaven, do you go to work backwards that you take so long, Gundred?'

'Mistress Alice, pray save your breath to cool your meat. Great-lady airs do not sit well on you while you are still the size for a spanking. You have time enough,' said Gundred calmly as she continued to go about the task of dressing her fretful charge at her own speed. In the end she was satisfied with her handiwork.

Alice in a gown and cloak of holly green velvet, the furred hood just resting over her pale hair, which had been subdued at last and neatly braided and coiled, was careful to walk, not run, downstairs. In the bleak hall the travellers were huddled round the hearth, mugs of hot ale steaming in their hands. The first logs of the day were just beginning to catch on the hot embers which had been bedded down in ash through the night, and Matilda was promising a box on the ears to the lad who had slept beyond his time and neglected to stir the fire earlier. Thomas thought retribution should not be delayed and booted the boy on his backside to the amusement of the company.

Sir John disentangled himself from four enthusiastic hounds, whose life-long adherence he had just purchased with the remains of a platter of cold meats, and drew Alice to one side. With a firm hand beneath her chin he tilted her head up so that he could look down directly into her eyes.

'Well, my lady, no tears for your departing husband, I see.' Alice was dismayed – no, indeed, here was a fine thing, she knew herself to be looking not wan and pale but in the best of health with the frost stinging a rosy colour into her cheeks. 'Nay Alice, I only tease you, child. I would not really have you moping and mowing. But listen, it may be many months before I come to see you again. It may even be more than a year, I cannot say. If we go to war I shall have many

18

matters to attend to before leaving England and that will keep me from Oxfordshire. Yet you will know that I am thinking of you. When I return mayhap you will be of an age for our marriage contract to be completed. In the meantime I shall be seeing your father in London and he will tell me how you grow in loveliness, stateliness, obedience and virtue. Pray for me and I will write to you whenever I am able.'

'I will, my lord. I will think of you often and especially when I ride Minerva . . . oh yes, I had not told you, I decided on a name for the palfrey at last. You say you prize wisdom – at least you like my grandfather's words about wisdom and women – and Minerva was wise. Do you like the name?'

'Yes indeed, it is well chosen.' Then turning from her with a smile Sir John went to take a last leave of her parents while a great bustle broke out around them and everyone began hurrying servants to bring the horses round and secure packs.

At last Sir John's own company, and some of Thomas Chaucer's friends, who were also journeying back to London, were mounted. With their servants riding to the front and rear, the little cavalcade moved off as the first pale light was opening up a path among the morning stars.

'God-speed, God go with you. Adieu! Adieu!' The cries hung echoing in the frozen air and they were gone, cloaks streaming behind them and hooves fading from a clatter to a steady drumming as they left the paved courtyard and cantered down the lane away from the manor.

The big hall seemed empty and desolate now that most of the guests were gone. Thomas Chaucer and the rest would leave tomorrow, then all would be as it had been before. Only the dull days of winter would be hard to bear after the excitement, thought Alice. Matilda was behind her saying brightly and not without relief: 'Well, well. So he is away, my love. Never mind. Come to the still-room and you and I will try a fine new recipe I have for making sweetmeats from dried rose petals. If it is good we will make a great store for Christmas.'

Alice thought longingly of a book by the fire in the winter parlour – the turret room would be out of the question now the really cold weather had set in.

'Yes, let us try the recipe. Do let us!' she said at last, slipping her hand into her mother's, rather self-consciously because it was not her way to display affection. Matilda was surprised and pleased. She chattered on about how she had the recipe from Gundred's sister, who worked for Lady Katherine Hardynge. Alice wondered what Will was doing.

CHAPTER TWO

THE HARVEST of 1424 promised to be a good one, the best for close on ten years the villagers were saying. And that set them harking back to another year – 1415 – when plenteous early rain fed the fields and the long, golden days of a high summer, ripened and dried them to perfection. Ah, but that had nearly been a disaster! They remembered and shook their heads. For many a stalwart farmer's son and many a field hand was missing that harvest-time – gone across the sea to fight for King Harry who wanted half France as well as England.

It had been a near thing in Ewelme, as in other English villages, to get the fields cleared before they spoiled. The men who had stayed at home worked in teams on each other's land, putting in back-breaking hours before it was done. And when Thomas Chaucer rode home from the war, with his twelve men-at-arms and thirty-seven bowmen – everyone of them safe though some not so sound as they set out – all talking of the horrors of Harfleur and the glory of Agincourt, he had found his manor prospering.

This orgy of reminiscence into which the whole village suddenly seemed to have plunged had a depressing effect on Alice. It reminded her that she had been betrothed then and now here she was, nearing twenty and still unwed. Poor John Phelip had died at Harfleur, not gallantly in the press of battle, but shivering and vomiting with the flux, which came like an unseen enemy on the breath of the marshy ground where the besieging English army was encamped. It had been a wretched end for a man in his prime.

21

Many more fine soldiers had shared this miserable fate, Alice remembered. Yet in the end the depleted army had marched on from Harfleur with high courage, looking to find an elusive French chivalry and thrash out for all time the issue of King Harry's Angevin inheritance. The dauphin had bided his time. Only when the tired force of six thousand Englishmen turned their march through Normandy, towards the sea, did he move at last and set down the might of his army of fifty thousand men across the road that led to Calais.

Henry V was desperately outnumbered and he had been out-manoeuvred. But two assets still remained to him – his ability to fire the men who followed him with a belligerent devotion, and the superb marksmanship of his bowmen. Moreover it was clear to every one of his soldiers that the only road home would have to be hacked through the enemy.

On the morning of the feast of St. Crispin, the twenty-fifth day of October 1415, these circumstances had been enough to give him victory. And the French, who had taken up their stand on a narrow neck of land between two woods surrounding the villages of Agincourt on the one side and Tramecourt on the other, had ended the day struggling helplessly upon the bodies of their own dead and wounded, impeded by heavy armour, defeated ultimately by their own ill-directed numerical strength, and unable to deploy on the confined battle-ground they had chosen.

It had been a moral conquest as well as a physical one. It seemed to prove to the French soldiery that eight of them could not match the fighting power of one Englishman, and when Henry led a second expedition to France at the end of July, 1417, the awesome repute of his army helped to break down the resistance which lay between him and the achievement of the Treaty of Troyes.

The treaty had given Henry the French princess, Catherine of Valois, as a wife, and promised the crown of France to him and his heirs when his father-in-law, Charles VI, died. Meanwhile in view of Charles' ill-health, Henry was to act as Regent of France, and he set out to reduce the territory still under the control of the disinherited dauphin.

But with the triumph of his great design in his grasp, Henry had died of a fever at Bois-de-Vincennes on the last day of August, 1422. Charles VI outlived him by two months. The crown of France, which Henry V had come so close to wearing, passed instead to his son, an infant of ten months.

Henry VI was two years old now and being brought up in a world of official nursemaids and royal uncles since he had been taken out of the care of his French mother. The country faced the long years of a minority ahead and looked to men like John, Duke of Bedford, and Humphrey, Duke of Gloucester, the brothers of the late king, and Henry Beaufort, Bishop of Winchester, who was a half-brother of the late king's father, Henry IV, to steer the affairs of the nation. It was a time of opportunity, of new ideas, of waiting for the good times to come, when England would see some return for the money she had poured into France. The future was uncertain, but it was challenging and exciting and Alice wanted an active part in it.

Restless in her own company, on a serene day when not even a cloud varied the monotony of the blue horizon, Alice rode over to the Byltons' house. Will always made cheerful company and it was cooler up the road towards Swyncombe.

There was no one about in the stableyard, but the sound of Will's tuneless whistle floated through the creeper-covered archway leading to the garden. Alice slid from Minerva's back, and followed it.

'Whatever are you at now?'

Will was on his hands and knees amid a curious assortment of metal dishes and scoops and there was a great deal of water about the place in jars, in pails, but principally on Will himself.

'I am trying to make a water clock. It is a means of telling the time used for many centuries in far eastern lands. The dishes are balanced at different levels and spill from one to another in a given ... '

'Oh pray spare me a treatise in applied mathematics! Or is it some more exotic science? You know I understand nothing of such things.'

'Ah but that is where you are wrong. You limit the exercise of your mind too much to literature and philosophy. Virgil says ... '

23

'I did not ride over to hear you quote Virgil, either,' Alice interrupted flatly. 'When you have finished bathing in your water clock perhaps you will offer me a cordial. It is a thirsty day.'

Will bowed mockingly and went to do her bidding When he returned he found Alice seated against the trunk of a tree, her eyes closed.

'I watered Minerva for you. I cannot think why young Luke is not about in the yard.' He sat beside her. 'And here is your cordial . . . What a harvest it will be if this weather holds, eh? Will you loop up your skirts and come help us with the oats in Down Meadow? No, you are too much a woman for such caperings now, I think,' Will teased. 'But I mind a time when you did. It was the summer before Agincourt, remember?'

'Oh for mercy's sake, "remember, remember" that is all anyone is saying these days. Must you be at it too. It plagues me to death, all this looking over the shoulder.'

'Why, here is a piece of ill-nature. What's to do?'

'Oh Will, I am sorry to be so sharp. I do not know what is the matter with me. I seem to have the glooms . . . I keep thinking of John Phelip.'

'Well do not tell me you have been mourning over him for I'll not believe it. He was twenty years older than you and twice a widower. And you only knew him a short time and then he was dead!'

'Yes, but I was nearly his bride and things might have been so different if he had lived. As it is I grow old unwed.'

'If that's all that troubles you I will offer for you myself,' replied Will gaily, but his eyes were serious. Alice caught the look in them and stood up.

'Spinsterhood is no light matter for a woman,' she said with mock severity.

'Who treats it lightly? I am very serious. You know that I love you; couldn't you be happy with me?' He uncoiled his lanky six feet and stood looking down into her cool, tawny-green eyes.

'Such thoughts have never been spoken between us . . Wh-what are you saying? What has love to do with marriage . . . ? You are gone moon-mad!'

A slight breeze stirred her veil and made it float around them. There was the heavy-sweet scent of lime-trees in the air and a hush in the bird-song. It was such a moment as remains suspended for ever in experience. Then Alice took his hand and turned him about towards the house to break the spell.

'Come, let us go look for your father and talk of other things. You know I must take a husband whose fortune matches mine. You have been reading too many romances,' she said gently.

'But if you wanted to marry me your father would not refuse you, surely? He loves you right well.' Will knew his cause was hopeless but felt that having come so far he must pursue it to the end.

'Aye, he loves me because he knows he can trust me to do his bidding.' They were nearing the house and she turned to look at him, still holding his hand. 'Will, I value that love and would do nothing to forfeit it. In many matters I resemble my father who has treated me more like a son than a daughter. He often discusses policy and matters of State with me as you well know. Do you really think I would be suited to live quietly as your wife? Do you really think he would be happy to see his ambitions for me end here in Ewelme where they began?'

'But if you were happy . . .'

'Would I be? Who can say? One is impelled along a certain road in life by what one is. Sometimes we see a byway and think it might be good to turn along there. But are we really free to make a choice or is it already made for us?'

'That is all so much talk to me,' growled Will. 'The truth is you do not love me as I love you. If you did you would have your way and wed me. I know it. Because there is strength in you, far from womanly!'

'I love you like my own brother, dear gentle-hearted Will.'

They continued towards the house in silence. Nicholas Bylton, emerging suddenly from a low archway, nearly collided with them.

'Bless my soul! I had no idea you had come a-visiting, Alice my dear! But hurry both of you, there is something to do up the lane. I was looking from the window of my chamber and saw a crowd of villagers approaching. They appear to be driving someone before them with sticks. Whatever can it mean?'

They could hear angry voices and tramping feet passing round the front of the house and now the chant of 'Witch! Witch!' was distinguishable. In a minute Alice had gathered up the folds of her blue kirtle and ran to the stableyard, catching up Minerva's reins and swinging herself into the saddle almost before Will and his father had collected their wits enough to follow her. There was no time to waste getting a horse from the stables so Will ran after her.

Catching up with the straggling band of villagers, Alice slapped Minerva's rump and urged her through them shouting 'Clear a way there!' She was recognised and the crowd had come to a shambling halt by the time she reached the front rank and turned Minerva sideways-on, barring their progress in the narrow lane.

She noted with relief that they were all youngsters taking part and their leader troublesome Ben Clutch. Of course, it would be. Tom Clutch kept the Saracen's Head and served good ale, but he had much to plague him with a scolding wife and this bullying son who was always up to some mischief, Alice reflected. The victim of Ben's vicious sport today was poor Adeliza Crookback.

'Now,' said Alice coolly, in the sheepish silence which followed her appearance, 'what goes forward here?'

No one seemed willing to answer and uneasily shuffling feet stirred up the dust of the lane, while the sun blazed down upon them. She noticed with disgust how the sweat rolled down Ben's red and sullen face, how they had tied Adeliza's hands brutally behind her stooped, mis-shapen back. She saw that Will and Nicholas had now come up and were waiting to see if she had need of them. Finally she found the unwilling eye of Hugh Bythorn and riveted it. Hugh was one of the older lads, she knew, and not ill-natured, though slow and easily led.

'My lady, this here's Adeliza whoon all say is a witch,' he managed to get out at last. 'Ben Clutch says witches bleed black and we'm going to stone her to show the truth of it.'

'Indeed.' She turned to Ben.

'Aye, it's right enough. We're going to show her how we deal with witches in Ewelme.' He eyed Alice defiantly.

'I had not thought we dealt with them at all,' said Alice levelly. 'I do not recall any witch-hunt in Ewelme in my life-time and I am two years older than you.'

Some of the children giggled. Ben Clutch was not popular and most of them followed him out of fear. But with his baleful eye upon them reminding them that he would still be there when the Lady Alice rode away, they rallied, persisting that the witch must be stoned.

Alice saw their mood and took a decision. 'Well we cannot turn loose an untried witch it seems. Untie the girl and let her come here to me. I will test her.'

Will could not understand what she intended to do and moved to join her in front of the wavering rabble. Ben Clutch was not pleased to have his leadership usurped, but Hugh Bythorn accepted Alice's conduct of the affair without question and promptly unbound Adeliza, pushing her forward roughly.

'Come here, Adeliza,' Alice ordered. When she was close by the palfrey the girl raised her face, pushing back a weight of tangled black hair as she did so. Alice was struck with wonder at the delicate beauty of her countenance. But the girl's eyes were wary and hostile.

Alice leaned down to her under pretext of grasping her wrist and whispered: 'Do not be afraid. Trust me. This will hurt but little. Stones could break your head.'

Adeliza nodded her understanding and Alice uncoiled her small riding whip from about the high pommel of her saddle and brought it down sharply across the girl's forearm. The thin weal welled scarlet.

Alice motioned the onlookers closer and Adeliza extended her arm disdainfully for all to see.

'So!' said Alice, deliberately making the word thunderous with anger, 'Adeliza Crookback is no more a witch than I am. How dare you accuse her falsely, Ben Clutch. How dare you lead a violent mob against this innocent girl whose only crime is that an accident of birth twisted her body. It was

27

you – all of you – with your taunts through the years of her childhood, who drove her to live alone in a ruined cottage on the edge of the common. I am tempted, Ben Clutch, to see how you bleed. But we will wait until my father comes next to Ewelme. Now go home and think shame over this day's work.'

'I will ride back with them and tell Ben Clutch's sire what has taken place here,' said Nicholas Bylton. He had found his truant stable-lad among the witch-hunters and dispatched him to saddle his bay while Alice was talking.

Much subdued the children followed Nicholas and the sullen Ben in orderly procession down the lane, the boys tugging forelocks and the girls bobbing curtsies at Alice as they passed. It was only when the last retreating back disappeared beyond the winding hedgerows that Alice and Will noticed Adeliza had slipped away without a word.

'Phew!' breathed Will. 'What a to-do. You handled them very well I thought . . . It was like watching the judgment of Solomon. I was nearly in awe of you myself!'

'If you make mock of me I shall set about you too,' said Alice, laughing. 'I am in just the mood for it.'

'That Adeliza's a strange creature, though,' Will mused. 'She did not seem much afraid . . . more resigned.'

'I do not think her strange. I like her,' replied Alice simply.

'Like her? I did not think you knew her.'

'Nor do I. But I like what I have heard of her. She comes up this way to gather grasses and wild plants, I believe. She uses them to dose sick animals and, I may say, her cures are very effective. Well, I must be on my way. Mother will be looking for me. It's been a very eventful day,' she added lightly. And Will knew she was thinking not only of the witch-hunt but of what had happened earlier between them.

*　　　*　　　*

The ensuing weeks kept Will occupied with matters of business. It was necessary to recruit casual labour from among his father's tenants to bring home their own modest produce and in addition he had a duty to take a paternal interest in the harvesting of acres under lease.

Nicholas was tending to retreat more and more into his library and could scarcely ever be brought to talk seriously with Will about their finances.

'I really do believe we must own the most unproductive acres in Oxfordshire, or possibly England,' he assured Will. 'The land was never rich and it has been overworked, the pasture is scrubby and we seem to have a knack of taking on the most unlucky men to farm it. Their promising beasts are stricken with the cough before they reach maturity. If they do survive either their cows are barren or their bulls impotent. Their likeliest offspring take the fever or fall down a well . . . and their best looking womenfolk run off with pedlars.'

'Perhaps if we were to take a closer interest in the estate we might be able to improve it,' Will said pointedly.

'My dear and only son! I thought I had taught you that the age of miracles is past – that is if it ever existed, which I doubt. What do you expect me to do? Should I *breathe* on the crops to make them multiply or would you recommend that I kiss the cattle to ward off evil spirits? No, giving our farms closer attention will simply depress me. I leave it all to you. It will be yours one day so you may do with it what you please. You could try paying a visit to Adeliza Crookback. Since the whole village believes she is a witch and she resides in one of our cottages, she ought to do what she can to cast some spells in our favour.'

Will had no more aptitude for building a fortune than his father. But he did discover in himself a certain instinct for farming and his advice on the care of sick animals, together with intelligent guesses at future produce demand, were beginning to pull things into a brighter position. Meanwhile he organised a volunteer labour force among the tenants so they could help each other with harvesting and repairs whenever possible, praised their progress, and dealt as constructively with their problems as he could.

When at last he found himself with a free day he decided to do as curiosity had been prompting since the incident of the witch-hunt. His father's little joke apart – he would indeed go to see Adeliza.

*　　　*　　　*

Adeliza Crookback had been born to a cottager's daughter. Her mother, comely but unwed, never looked on her for she died exhausted in the struggle of giving birth to the premature, mis-shapen babe. Her grand-sire looked with loathing at the fruit of his own child's folly and his first instinct was to smother the infant. But being a superstitious man he could not bring himself to it and instead gave Adeliza into the care of her aunt.

This goodwife was not actively cruel to her. Indeed, out of respect for her deformity she beat her less often than she did her own offspring. But she had no love to spare for her either. And she resented having another mouth to feed when already all went hungry six days out of seven. Adeliza's uncle had been quite fond of his pretty sister, and for her memory's sake tolerated the deformed brat sired on her by some itinerant farm labourer. He put bread in her mouth and would have thought it asking a good deal that he should give her affection into the bargain.

Adeliza was still a little child when she came to understand that life offered her a simple choice. Because she was a freak she could either be scorned as an imbecile, or she could be feared as a child of darkness, a daughter on whom the devil had set his mark, a witch.

She grew up with one shoulder raised hideously high and a hump on her back, but she also grew with a strange elfin beauty of countenance and a lively intelligence. So because the villagers and common-dwellers could not treat her as a fool, they knew not how to treat her, until, at sixteen years of age, she went to live alone in a ruined cottage on the boundary of the Bylton property. Then they felt they had her measure. Many said they had known it ever since she was a baby. Neighbours, who had assisted at the birth, recalled suddenly how there had been the clear print of a hoof on the mother's belly. Others remembered that the child had chuckled

30

in her cradle while they went about the task of composing her mother's body in death.

There was speculation about the lame dog which suddenly went to live with Adeliza. No one had seen it in the neighbourhood before. Was it her familiar? When a crow with a broken wing joined her household it added the final touch to her reputation.

Young men and women began to go to her for charms and love potions. She told them she knew nothing of such things, though she would sometimes give them the benefit of some brisk advice. But her denials were unavailing. If what they so earnestly desired in their hearts came about they were convinced that Adeliza had worked a charm for them. If it did not they blamed themselves for the paltriness of what they offered her. Perhaps the milk they pressed upon her had been none too fresh after all; next time it would be better to take two dozen eggs or a length of homespun.

Soon farmers were asking her to take spells off sick animals. Like many who feel the rejection of their own kind, Adeliza was drawn to other creatures and discovered in herself an intuitive skill in diagnosing their complaints. She saw how free ranging animals sought out certain plants to cure their ailments and hasten the healing of wounds, and made good use of what they taught her. So her reputation grew.

Though the years seemed to increase the awkwardness of her twisted body, they left her face practically unchanged. Her eyes became more remote and wary and her voice softened from long communion with her pets. But she was familiar to the Ewelme villagers, who did not fear and hate her as they would an outsider believed to have the same powers.

Nevertheless Adeliza knew that one day they might come for her across the waste with stones and pitchforks in their hands. A disaster like flood or fire, an epidemic could be her death warrant. Even some lesser tragedy – the accidental death of a child or the firing of a well-stocked barn by lightning – might claim her victim, too.

When Will rode up to Adeliza's cottage he found her crooning to a prostrate goose, which watched her with soulful eyes from the depth of a basket of woven reeds. His first inclination

31

was to laugh, but Adeliza was so serious and intent upon what she was doing that instead he knelt beside her and asked what ailed the bird.

'I think she's just unhappy,' said Adeliza simply.

'Oh! come now,' Will laughed. 'What do you imagine can grieve the heart of a goose?'

'I do not know. She is a grey goose and perhaps she always longed to be a white one. She is draggle-feathered and perhaps she wants to be sleek and plump. Or it may be she is pining for a gander who pays her no attention. Who should know what troubles the heart of a goose. Or,' she looked directly at him for the first time, 'of a man for that matter.'

Will felt a little uneasy. He was not sure himself why he had come to see Adeliza and yet all at once he had the uncanny sensation that she knew.

'It is strange you should ride this way today. The lady Alice was here an hour since.'

Will was startled. 'Lady Alice? Why whatever had she to do with you?'

'Ah! she has ridden this way several times lately. We like to talk. She is a strong woman. A fine woman, that one.'

'What do you talk about?' Will was intrigued. 'Never tell me she comes to buy a spell or ask you to read her future for I will not believe it.'

'No, the lady Alice does not think any man or woman can see the future unrolled like a parchment before them on the table. What is not written cannot be known, she says.'

'But you do not agree with her, eh Adeliza? There would hardly come so many hopeful customers to your door if it was known you subscribed to such heresy! So you debate the supernatural do you?'

'I could do without them coming to my door,' Adeliza said sharply. 'I do not boast of powers beyond other folk.' She turned away offended by Will's clumsy raillery and would have gone into the cottage and shut the door. But Will, seeing he had wounded a sensitivity he did not even suspect, hastened before her and barred the way.

'No, stay, Adeliza. I beg pardon for my ill-mannered jest. I am like an ox in a bluebell wood.' He steered her firmly away from the door. 'Come, sit down here beside your love-lorn goose. I am curious to know more about you. We have never talked before and I want to know why Alice Chaucer comes to see you.'

'How can I say what brings her?' Adeliza shrugged, not to be so easily mollified. 'Perhaps she comes to gape like all the rest of you.'

'No, Alice would not come for such a purpose. She must like you Adeliza.'

Adeliza smiled then, and her smile was a slow-dawning, gladdening thing to watch. It began with a softening of the chiselled planes of her face, curved at the corners of her mouth and finally revealed unusually pretty teeth.

'Why, when you smile, you are quite beautiful,' said Will slapping his thigh with approval.

'Fiddle-de-dee. I am an old witch.'

'How old?'

'I was born old. I was born a hundred years old. So now I am one-hundred-and-twenty. Does that satisfy you, young man? Or have you further prying to do while you are here?'

'Spin a spell for me, Adeliza. Make me rich or make me happy . . . or turn this grey goose into a beautiful swan,' said Will leaning back against the trunk of a crab-apple tree as crooked as its owner.

This time Adeliza was not offended. She was beginning to understand the gentle nature behind the teasing tone.

'I do not think you will ever be rich and we all have joy in some measure. As for a spell which would change my poor draggled goose into a swan . . . why do you think if I had such a power I should not have used it on myself before this time?' The words were reflective rather than bitter.

'But you do have some power, something that sustains you in this lonely life you lead? Besides there are so many tales told about you among the villagers and the tenants. Did you not lure the soul back into Ned Throsser's black stallion? And how about Ann Clutch, the innkeeper's thorny-tongued wife? She was a veritable shrew until Tom Clutch paid you to drive the devil out of her. This past sennight I hear she is as meek

3   33

as an old ewe. Come Adeliza, tell me your secrets. They shall be safe with me.'

'Hah!' Adeliza snorted. 'So you believe, do you?'

'A little perhaps.'

'To think a son of Nicholas Bylton could have so little wit! Why Ned Throsser's stallion needed a dose of my herbal horse cure and a hot poultice and Ann Clutch needed to be told she was driving her good husband into the ready-and-waiting arms of Murella Swarth. Good sense is the only charm, you see. Yet I do sometimes have a sort of vision . . . ' Adeliza went on turning aside and dropping her voice as if she had suddenly forgotten Will's presence and was questioning herself. 'Sometimes I seem to find a scene growing about a person while I look at them. Often it is shadowy, no more than an impression of what might be. At other times it is clear and sharp, so clear I feel it must be real. Is this a power or do I simply think "Such-and-such a thing may happen to this person" and so create the scene in my mind?' Adeliza sighed and, turning to look Will levelly in the eyes, added: 'One grows strange living alone you know. There are times when I talk to the wind. When it whines under the door or growls in the chimney I say, "Well, well, come along in then and don't make such a to-do about it" and if it stirs the rushes on the floor and carries them in a sudden flurry to the hearth-stone I say "Now that's enough of your games. Take a warming do and be still".'

'Adeliza, what do you see in the future for the lady Alice?' Will had been listening intently and now the question he had meant to ask casually came out sharp and anxious.

'Alice Chaucer's future has naught to do with you. She has great strength and people endowed with strength of the spirit always find a use for it. Perhaps they even bring about events where they will have most need of it. Who can tell? But now you must go. You are both so young and vigorous and between you you have made me feel very weary.'

Will took his dismissal meekly and collected his grazing horse. For some reason he felt he must bow before he rode slowly away, leaving Adeliza standing looking after him, shading her eyes against the late afternoon sun. Will understood

34

now why Alice visited the lonely cottage on the edge of the waste. Adeliza might be the child of poverty and ignorance, and it seemed ridiculous to compare her with Alice, but some quality in these two women had surely come from the same mould.

*　　*　　*

Alice usually revelled in the slumbrous days when the countryside unfolded the last and best of its beauty, but that year they seemed to pass unbearably slow. She began to feel boredom like a progressive sickness sapping away all vitality until it required a conscious effort of will to go about simple duties.

Her father should have been home at harvest-time but urgent business had detained him in London. Casual visitors were rare, and as Matilda managed the household affairs, Alice had little to do but keep an eye on the tenants.

Even Will had been too busy to come calling for weeks past, and when they did meet both were uneasily aware of the declaration of love that had been made in an unguarded moment. It infuriated Alice to think she had led him on to say those words, and she longed for them to be unspoken.

It had been in order to give some direction to an afternoon's ride that she decided to call on Adeliza for the first time. Any company, it seemed, would be more entertaining than her own restless throughts. But she had been amazed and charmed by the refreshing personality she encountered. It was impossible to explain, yet somehow just talking to Adeliza made her feel livelier and more hopeful.

After one of these visits, and in a mood for getting things done, Alice turned Minerva's head towards the village smithy. She had been intending a gift for her father – a wrought device of his and her mother's arms to set above the great carved door of the manor – and it seemed a good time to give her instructions to Matt Bowman.

She found him, leaning on his mighty hammer at the entrance to the forge. He was enjoying the spectacle of Tom

Clutch – round as he was merry – trying to catch the ragged child who served him as potboy.

'When I have done cuffing you, you will wish you had never seen that pie, let alone etten it,' panted Tom, as the boy ducked and weaved before him.

'First you have to catch him! You should have etten less pie yourself, Tom,' Matt laughed. 'Why, here is Lady Alice come to watch your sport. Good-day to you, milady. Have you work for me, then?'

While Alice told him what she required, her eyes wandered by chance into the cavern of the forge. A young man was standing in the glow of a brazier of fresh coals, and following the direction of her glance Matt asked leave to present his nephew, who had come to take up apprenticeship with him.

The youth came forward shyly, blinking at the sun. Shyly, but not – Alice noticed with pleasure – awkwardly. Here was no shuffling of the feet nor rolling of the head, common symptoms of unease among the local lads. Alice looked him over coolly, deciding that his natural grace must arise from the perfect proportions of his splendid body. He was a veritable young Thor.

Matt was saying ' . . . and so having no son of my own it suits me right well to have Stephen here and I hope one day he will be allowed to serve you in my place. Aye, but it were a sad thing, his father and mother both, to be taken by the plague betwixt sunrise and sunset on the same day.'

'Ill-chance,' said Alice.

'But not uncommon for it seldom takes less than two from a family. Stephen has his sister here with him and that is all his kin save me. With my Molly dead, I am sure I do not know how I shall make out with the lass.'

'How old is she?' Alice asked, and tried not to be aware of the open admiration of the younger man's continued stare.

'Turned sixteen just.'

'Why, what's to do then Matt? She will be married and off your hands before you know it.' To Alice's surprise Matt looked uneasy and Stephen, she felt without looking at him, had tensed. Something must be amiss with the girl. She turned deliberately to Stephen. 'Where is your sister now? Perhaps

I can discover if there is something useful she could do in my service.'

Stephen looked uncertain and the same doubt touched Matt's face, but after a slight pause he jerked his thumb towards the cottage alongside the forge. 'Fetch her, Stephen.'

While they waited Matt, whose responsibility it was to drill the men of the village in archery, talked about their improved standard, which he hoped to demonstrate when her father next visited the butts. Alice checked Minerva, who had begun to sidle restlessly, and eased herself on the pillion saddle. She had not intended to make so long a stop but now there was nothing for it except to see her impulse through. She could have exclaimed in impatience and ridden away, but Matt Bowman was a proud man and a loyal servant to her father. She could not bring herself to hurt his feelings.

At last the cottage door opened and Stephen stepped out, beckoning impatiently to the shadowy figure who hesitated behind him. Then with downbent head came a young woman. But what a woman! Alice could not suppress a startled gasp as she beheld this sister of a giant – a giantess. The girl came shambling towards her, fully six feet tall and bitterly conscious of her own ungainliness. Moreover, as she walked, she dragged one foot slightly.

Alice was appalled to think how she had committed herself. Her mother would scarcely welcome so awkward a female, and one slowed by a limp as well, among her maids. And Matt Bowman's niece ought to rank higher than the kitchen too.

'This is Cecily, my lady,' said Matt apologetically. Alice felt trapped.

'Look at me, Cecily,' she said at last, addressing the top of a starched cap. The girl looked up and, as Alice suspected, she was extremely plain. The strong features which became her powerful brother were faithfully reproduced to the detriment of the woman. Here the thick brow and long, straight nose were at a sad disadvantage. But the face was an honest and wholesome one for all that and the expression in the dark eyes which met hers reminded Alice of a deerhound she had once been very attached to.

'Can you sew, Cecily?'

37

'Oh yes, my lady.'

'How would you like to enter my service and take charge of my robes? Gundred, my old nurse, grows slow with years and cannot do as she should.'

'I . . . I should be honoured, my lady, to serve . . . serve you,' was the uncertain reply.

'Aye, lass, you would be fortunate indeed to dwell at the manor and be about the lady Alice. Shall she bring her things and come tomorrow morning, my lady?' Matt beamed his gratitude.

'Yes. That will be well.'

'Beg pardon, my lady,' Stephen interrupted suddenly. 'But may I just have a word aside with my sister?'

'Why, of course,' said Alice surprised.

Stephen led his sister a few yards off and holding her by the arm appeared to question her anxiously. Cecily nodded vigorously. They returned.

'Yes, she will come tomorrow. I had to make sure she was not afraid to take the post. She would not like to say, you know. But she has never been out to service.' Stephen flushed slightly at having intervened.

'That is settled then,' said Alice with an indulgent smile for his brotherly care. She raised her hand and nodded to Matt as she urged Minerva off down the street.

Oh well, perhaps she would be able to do something with the girl. What her mother would say, – and Gundred – she could well imagine. But she had made her decision so there was an end of it.

The next morning Alice was in the still-room watching her mother prepare a fragrant water for washing the hands. She would not have been there only she wished to put her mother in an agreeable frame of mind to receive Cecily into her household.

Matilda, following her custom whenever she managed to get Alice as a captive audience, was carefully describing each action she performed, although her daughter could see quite well what she was about if she had a mind to do so.

'Now I think that is long enough for the sage to have boiled. I will strain it off so, and set the water aside to cool.'

Drying her hands on her apron she turned to Alice and added: 'Gundred will not like this, you know.'

'What, the herb-water?' Alice teased, pretending to be astonished.

'Of course not,' snapped her mother. 'I speak of Bowman's niece coming as your maid. And why you should want to choose a freakish girl as this one sounds I cannot understand.'

'She is not a freak, mother. She is just over-tall and has a slight limp. But when I have improved her a little she will be quite presentable.'

'Well, she sounds freakish to me! Gundred will certainly make her life a misery – she is very jealous of anyone else doing things about you, you know. Why, I remember when I recovered from your birth and wished to rock you or croon to you she positively drove me away. The only one she would tolerate near you was the wet nurse and she would not have let her by if she could have fed you yourself. It was most vexing. Of course, it would never have come about if I had not taken the fever and been so weak for six months after you were born . . . Ah! this is cool enough now. Shall I add camomile or marjoram? Or maybe rosemary would be better? Which do you prefer, Alice?'

'Oh . . . rosemary. But mother, Gundred is old and truly she grows lazy. She does not bestir herself to mend, press and hang my robes as she should.'

'Now I will just boil this up again, adding these laurel leaves . . . Yes, well I have warned you. But you will do as you please. Your father will be sure to say you are right, so how should I protest?' Matilda concluded in a mildly aggrieved tone.

'But mother, I want you to say I am right, too. It is your household into which I bring the girl.'

This diplomacy did not fail and Matilda patted her daughter's arm and said more graciously: 'There, then I do not object, child.'

By the time Cecily arrived, Alice had gone through an edgy interview with Gundred and had a deal to do arranging for her maid to be given a space at one end of the women servants' dormitory.

Matt Bowman brought his niece to the kitchen entrance, gave her an encouraging push and disappeared. Cecily was so overcome at being left alone to face the open-mouthed amazement of the cook and the mockery of the scullions that she was quite unable to make herself intelligible about her mission and oddly enough it was Gundred who rescued her.

Gundred, a small neat spinster in her late fifties, of forbidding aspect and little humour, had never had any interest in life except Alice. She did not often unburden her soul to anyone but, resentful at the advent of Cecily, she felt the need of a sympathetic ear. She was on her way to see cook, the only member of the staff it would not be beneath her to confide in, and behold there was the usurper, standing like a maypole – though not nearly so pretty as one, Gundred decided with relish – surrounded by jeering spit-boys and giggling laundresses.

'You must be Matt Bowman's niece, come to serve the lady Alice.' Gundred bit the words off sharply and was conscious of waiting ears. She thought carefully – her own status depended very much on her conduct of this public encounter – before adding: 'The lady Alice told me she had engaged you to assist me. Come, I will take you to her.'

Cecily was grateful to escape from her tormentors and limped meekly after Gundred. Blessedly she was unaware that two of the scullions limped painfully after her as far as the door.

Alice was in her bedchamber. It was a large, pleasant room, much improved by the oriel window, which her father had recently given his builders instructions to add, partly to please his daughter and partly because he thought it made a counterbalance on the frontage to the other second storey oriel in the winter parlour.

She dismissed Gundred firmly and, finding she could not speak to Cecily without developing a crick in the back of her neck, bid her to take a foot-stool and sit.

'Now, I will explain your duties and then we will talk about you. My robes, cloaks, furs and shoes are kept in the closet between this room and the foot of the stairs which lead to the dormitory where you will sleep. They are your respon-

40

sibility from now on and you will see that they are kept clean, are hung to air, each in turn, that they are pressed when necessary and that the hems are always well brushed. In this coffer are underskirts, hose and such-like, and the other coffer at the foot of the bed holds my jewels, veils and chapeaux. You will do all the necessary mending, supervise any goffering or starching that may be done upon my apparel and you may also take it upon yourself to remind me when the catch of a necklet becomes loose or the links of a girdle are broken.'

Cecily attended closely to this recital and, thinking with pleasure of the delicacy of the tasks she would perform, lost her dazed look and became quite animated.

'Oh yes, my lady. Indeed my fingers are more nimble than one . . . one would think.'

'I am sure they are,' said Alice kindly. 'Now as to your appearance, we must do something about that, too. We must transform you at once, for as my maid your status in this household will be high, and you will often have to come to me in the presence of company.'

Cecily paled visibly. 'My lady . . . oh, alas, I could not . . . not before many people.' She wrung her hands in her agitation. 'They laugh, you see.'

'They shall not laugh if I have anything to say about it,' Alice replied firmly. 'Indeed, why should they laugh? If you hold your head up and look them coolly in the eye you will diminish them. Think of yourself as a tall elegant tree among so many shrubs. Come, we will both stand up and you shall walk towards me, so, across the room.'

Alice was rather enjoying herself. Having Cecily to brace up had given her an occupation she could enjoy.

Cecily tried, but not very bravely. 'Oh dear, it is useless, my lady. I drag this foot, you see.'

'I see that perfectly well. What is the matter with it? Raise your skirts and let me see.'

'My father's hammer fell upon it when I was a tiny child – he was a smith too, like Uncle Matt. The bones were broken and did not mend as they should.' She displayed a large shapeless member bearing little relation to a foot as far as Alice could observe.

'Well, we can do nothing to heal that so you must walk more slowly and the hesitation will be less noticeable. Come now, try again. Very slowly towards me . . . the chin just a little higher. Fold your hands together level with your waist, so. There, that is unbelievably better. You see, when you advance slowly your skirts are concealing the foot and that pace matches your stately build. All we have yet to do is dress your hair more softly, find you a more becoming style of coif and set you to work sewing yourself some new dresses. I have ells of dark grey lawn here which will suit admirably.'

The transformation of Cecily was not completed in a trice, but it was well begun.

As the days went by Alice came to prize her maid's diligence and the strong personal loyalty which soon became apparent. She also began to understand Cecily's gentle yet dogged nature. She was not altogether surprised when the sound of hot words reached her ears one day, and she came upon Gundred and Cecily, locked in seemingly mortal struggle over a green velvet gown, which looked to be getting much the worst of the encounter.

Regrettably the scene was taking place on the main stairway and was watched with enjoyment by servants in the hall below. Ah well, thought Alice, it had to come, and perhaps the audience was not such a bad thing either if Cecily was to be established in her rightful place in the household.

'What is the meaning of this brawl?' Alice asked icily from the head of the stairs. Cecily was silent, but Gundred had much to say. Her resentment had been festering and now she blurted out incautiously: 'Cecily Wryfoot is much above herself. She says this robe must be pressed and I say it is not necessary. She defies me and is taking it down to the laundry-room. How dare she! How dare she go against my orders!'

'Your orders, Gundred? I was not aware you had hired Cecily! I give her her orders and they are to keep my raiment in readiness for me to wear. If she thinks the green velvet needs pressing then it must be pressed.' Alice's voice was dangerously quiet but jealousy made Gundred rash.

'The maids have enough to do about the laundry-room

without dancing attendance on Mistress Wryfoot at her every whim.

'Gundred, you are insolent,' said Alice. The hall below held its breath. 'And what is this name of Wryfoot you have coined? My personal maid is Cecily Bowman and she must have respect or, by God, all will suffer for it!'

Gundred was beside herself. She would never survive such public humiliation. 'Alice how can you set this chit over me – I who nursed you when . . . '

'When I was a child, Gundred,' Alice cut in sharply. 'But I am not a nursling now.'

The habit of arguing back to her young mistress died hard and Gundred, feeling the ground slipping from beneath her feet, made one last attempt.

'Your father would not like this manner in you. I have grown old in your service . . . '

'Perhaps too old,' was the deceptively gentle reply. 'Perhaps it is time he pensioned you and let you return to the home of your family.'

At that Gundred was utterly vanquished. Casting herself in anguish at Alice's feet she cried: 'No, no, do not send me away, Mistress! I had hoped to die at Ewelme when my time comes. Do not send me from you.' The harsh old face was rivered by tears.

'Well, well,' said Alice more gently, 'it need not come to that. But in future you will let my maid do her work unhindered. Come Cecily, I have a task for you now. You shall press that ill-used gown later.' Unhurriedly she led the way back to her bedchamber.

When they were safely inside Cecily cried: 'Oh my lady, I am so sorry that such trouble should have come about through my doing. I know Gundred does not like me but . . . '

'Never mind, child. It was not only on your account that I had to put Gundred in her place. She has disregarded my orders and thwarted my wishes ever since I can remember. One may understand how it comes about as she had me in her charge from a baby. But I could not permit her to flout my authority any longer.'

'But she must love you so,' said Cecily still close to tears.

'Love? Yes in her own way I suppose she does. The way of some people's love is power and Gundred has had much pleasure in compelling me to do as she said. When I was very small she used to beat me for the slightest and most innocent disobedience. Yet on other occasions she would lie to protect me from my father's just anger. That is a strange, rather ill-judged kind of love, do you not think?'

'She beat you?' gasped Cecily appalled. 'I did not know gently-born girls were ever beaten!'

'Did you not? Mayhap you think we are born well-behaved eh? Well, that is a good thought. Pray cherish it!' Alice concluded dryly.

CHAPTER THREE

It was the end of August when Thomas Chaucer rode home to Ewelme. He appeared in hearty spirits and after greeting Matilda and Alice told them to come to the winter parlour as soon as the company supped. 'I have important news to relate,' he said, and would add nothing more to this tantalising statement despite all entreaty.

Alice, puzzling while she watched him eat, had decided her father meant to tell them of some high appointment. So when the family drew together in private she was taken completely unawares, for leaning back in his high, carved chair with a satisfied smile, Thomas Chaucer asked his wife casually: 'How do you think Alice will like being Countess of Salisbury?'

It pleased him to tell it this way and see them rendered speechless. But only for an instant. Then he was overwhelmed by questions so there was scarcely breathing space for the answers.

'Well, well!' Matilda exclaimed over and over again. 'And when did all this come about? Why did you tell me nothing in your letters? Are you at the point of exchanging contracts?'

'When is the wedding to take place? Shall I see my lord of Salisbury soon?' Alice took over the interrogation from her mother.

'Quietly, quietly now. They will hear you both in Henley,' Thomas Chaucer said laughing at the excitement he had created. 'Firstly, I did not tell you earlier because I wanted to surprise you. Furthermore, Salisbury is only in England for a short visit and must return to France next month so you will be married in two weeks' time. All is arranged . . . '

45

'All arranged,' Matilda almost shouted. 'What is arranged, my lord? Never say they will be married here, for nothing is arranged at all! You do not think I can make preparations for a marriage feast and ready a suitable wardrobe for our daughter in a fourteen-night!'

'No, of course I do not. They will be married at our house in Westminster and preparations there are well ahead. You need only fret over the clothes – I know there are two dower chests already full to overflowing. You have been tucking things into them, like the provident little squirrel you are, these many years.' He reached out and gave her veil a playful tug.

Alice realised that the match her father had made for her was a brilliant one but she could not help the slight note of misgiving in her voice as she said: 'Then I shall not meet Salisbury until my wedding day?'

'No. It is unfortunate that all must be done in such haste and I would have wished that you could know him a little first. But as commander of our army in France he cannot spare time for courtship. He has a glorious military record, as you know, and his future opportunities must be boundless. In all ways I believe Thomas Montacute to be a man worthy of you, Alice.'

Matilda was eager for every detail of her daughter's future husband but, thinking it would be tactful to leave Alice alone with her father, declared herself ready for bed.

When they were alone Alice took a stool at her father's feet. She sat, encircling her knees with her arms in an unconscious attitude of childhood, and gazed unseeing before her for several minutes without speaking. Thomas watched her with a look of tenderness.

'What are you thinking, my child?'

'I am thinking you and I will not sit like this often again.'

'No. And that troubles you?'

'Very deeply.' Alice looked up, her eyes wistful as if she had already passed beyond the present and was looking back at it.

'Alice, my beloved daughter, we are so very close, you and I. You understand how much I want to see you advanced in the world. You will like to be married and have a home to

46

run and children to occupy you, will you not? Your mother has written me that you have been in low spirits of late. She seemed to think you were pining for a mate.' Thomas' voice took on its habitually dry note at the last remark.

'Well mayhap she is right in that,' Alice smiled wryly. 'It is no dream of mine to end my days a maid.'

'I should hope not.'

'There,' Alice raised a brighter smile and patted her father's hand, 'I am recovering from the suddenness of it all now. Do you think me ungrateful. I understand the trouble you have been at to make such a splendid marriage for me. Now tell me more about Salisbury. What does he look like?'

'He seems a well-looking man to me, tall, strongly-built, with clear-cut features and a lofty brow. I cannot know how a woman's fancy runs but there is nothing about him to displease.' Alice nodded and her father went on: 'Let me see now . . . he is thirty-six years of age and is a widower. His first wife was Eleanor, a daughter of Thomas, Earl of Kent, and by her he has one child – your namesake – Alice. I believe she is about your own age too.'

'And he wants a son?'

'I am sure he does.'

'What of his temper?'

'He is a proud man, very authoritative in manner, very controlled. His wit will please you I think.'

Alice reflected, with an inward sigh, that these qualities inspired admiration rather than affection, but she merely observed: 'It is no wonder my lord Bedford thinks so highly of him.'

She knew, for her father had given her some instruction on affairs in France, that Salisbury's military leadership and flair for strategy had played a vital part in maintaining the hard-won English possessions in France.

'Aye, indeed, he does.' Thomas Chaucer looked grave as he added: 'I do not know where Bedford would be without him. Of course he is himself a fine general in the field but, as Regent in France, he needs to be able to delegate the leadership of the army. The volume of administrative work he has to cope with must be overwhelming. I have not had a chance to talk with you for some time but I hear disquieting news from France. Philip of Burgundy is giving trouble again. I do not see how Bedford can hold him to the terms of our alliance indefinitely.'

'But if the alliance fails we shall never hold France, shall we? You have always said it was vital for us to have the help of Burgundy in keeping so large a territory subdued.'

Alice thought of John, Duke of Bedford, striving to hold together two kingdoms for his nephew, Henry VI, acting as Regent in France and all the time worrying what his headstrong brother, Humphrey of Gloucester, was up to as Protector of England. It seemed too cruel that all his efforts to fulfil the trust that had been willed to him should end in bitter failure.

'Aye, I have spoken so and believe it still,' her father agreed. 'But you may soon judge the position for yourself. Salisbury wants you to return to France with him.'

'To France!' Alice exclaimed excitedly.

'Yes. But you need have no fears. You will be safe in Paris with the Duchess of Bedford, when Salisbury is in the field.'

'Oh, I am not at all afraid. Why the worst that could befall me is that I be taken hostage by the dauphin's army and no doubt you would ransom me,' said Alice laughing.

'If need be I would rob the exchequer to that end,' promised her father with mock solemnity. It was a joke but they knew the underlying truth of it.

'I will bid you good night now, father. You must be tired and my mother will be impatient to hear all you have told me about Thomas Montacute.'

He embraced her and, in a rare show of tenderness, stroked her cheek with his finger. 'Sleep sweetly, my Alice,' he said. When she had left him Thomas Chaucer lingered a few moments alone, crossing to the window to look out at a windswept moon. 'Bone of my bone, blood of my blood,' he muttered leaning his forehead against the fist which struck the latticed panes.

* * *

During the next few days the courtyard of the manor rang with the stamp of impatient hooves while packhorses waited to be relieved of their burdens or eyed with resentment the rump of their master's mount, which they would soon follow on the weary road back to London. For Thomas Chaucer had had the foresight to arrange that silk merchants, furriers, dealers in precious gems and workers in gold should follow him home to parade their wares for his wife and daughter.

The great hall, no longer bare and stately, was cluttered with bales and pouches. Bolts of silk and velvet, fashionable damask and satin were sent skating down the banqueting board as merchants flung out lengths of their most beguiling shades. Here and there tangles of miniver lay by dark pools of sable, as if improbably lustrous-coated animals slept amidst the bustle.

Nicholas Bylton and Will were among the first to hear of the approaching marriage. Alice tried to avoid seeing the sadness in Will's eyes, while his mouth smiled congratulations.

'I will come back home again soon, you may be sure,' she promised. And for the first time recollected with misgiving that she would need her husband's permission to do so.

Perversely, because she was soon to be parted from Matilda, Alice felt she had never been so close to her. Eagerly she drew comfort from her mother's own reassuring experience of marriage.

'I was a young heiress, as you know, and when my father died the king gave me in marriage to Thomas. I was so afraid that I should be forced to take an ugly, old man to be my husband, I wept for joy when I saw Thomas, strong and straight and handsome. And I do not need to tell you what a good husband he has been to me and how happy he has made me!'

'Have you, mother, have you truly been happy?' Alice snatched hold of her mother's hands and held them tight that she might look closely into her eyes for the answer.

Matilda was startled by the sudden passion in her daughter, usually so cool and controlled, and felt compelled to strict honesty. 'Why . . . of . . . of course I have been happy. I will not say there was never a time when I displeased your father. I know in many ways I am slow to understand such things as

4   49

our country's affairs when he tries to explain them to me. Perhaps he has been a little impatient. But then he has always had you. I have thanked the Holy Mother that I was able to give him a clever daughter, though not . . . not a son.'

Alice did not want to hear Matilda humble herself. She had known her father speak sharply to her mother on many occasions, when over-anxiety caused her to bustle about him too much or her little superstitions offended his incredulous good sense. She said firmly: 'I believe my father thinks you the very queen of housewives! He is for ever telling me that I should attend more closely to the way you run our home and keep your accounts.'

'Is he indeed? Well imagine that! I have thought sometimes he did not make much matter of such things.' Matilda flushed with pleasure. 'But,' she added generously, 'you have no need to fear. You will find running a home will come naturally to you. You have watched me at it and everything comes easily to my Alice! Only think what a wife you will make a great man like Salisbury. At his side constantly, able to understand what is going on about you and watch his interests like a second pair of eyes.'

'Why, mother,' Alice protested laughing, 'you have never been wont to speak such flattery before. I am your troublesome Alice, remember, riding Minerva to the devil and not able to make a syllabub!'

'Ah no! If I have chided you . . . well that is a mother's part . . . but I am proud of you. I am glad Salisbury is a man in his prime. You are mature for your years. You need an older man, one you can look up to and respect. Indeed, I am sure this is going to be a good marriage.'

The days of preparation passed busily and happily. Only one slight disagreement occurred – between Alice and her father – and that was over Cecily. Thomas Chaucer held Matt Bowman in high esteem and he did not disapprove of his daughter having taken Cecily under her protection. But he opposed the idea of the girl accompanying Alice to France as her personal maid.

'She is not at all suitable for such a post. Why the chit is a humble village lass and it will demean your dignity as

Countess of Salisbury to have her attend upon you closely. Some poor relative of the Burghersh's, your mother's family, would be more the thing. Have you no cousin, Matilda, who would be glad of such a position?'

'I have racked my mind with trying to think of one,' his wife assured him, 'but the only cousins I can recall are mothers of large families and could not be spared even for a short while.'

'Mayhap Salisbury will have one on his side, then.'

'No!' said Alice determinedly. 'If I am to leave my home and family behind and go across the sea with this stranger husband I will take someone with me who is loyal to me, and me alone!'

'What is this nonsensical talk of loyalties, girl?' her father snapped impatiently. 'You are going to wed with Salisbury not wage war on him.'

'I know that, father. But Cecily is a good-hearted girl and serves me well. I can trust her and I want to take her with me. It is just a little thing to ask, surely? I shall be less homesick for Ewelme when I may talk to her about it. I will dress her richly and bid her speak seldom and no one shall know her background . . . Why, I can pass her off as a member of our family.'

'Not my family,' said Thomas stoutly. But he was beginning to allow himself to be persuaded, and it only needed Matilda to add her entreaties that Alice be given her own way, for him to admit grudgingly that Cecily was not without a certain dignity of stature. 'That name Bowman will never do, though! Wait, I have it. Give it French intonation, call it Beaumain and everyone may be fooled into thinking her family of Norman origin!' Thomas chuckled, pleased with his own ingenuity.

'Beaumain it shall be!' said Alice and hurried off to tutor Cecily.

Before Thomas Chaucer returned to London he went with his daughter on their customary tour of the manor. Tenants and villagers expected it of them, and on this occasion it was fitting that Alice should make her farewells, while receiving congratulations on the news of her forthcoming marriage. At

51

the same time her father was able to look into the affairs of Ewelme. Dick Tearle, the bailiff, had always seemed an honest man, fair in dealings between master and tenants. But Thomas liked to hear complaints and answers at first hand before taking decisions. Never let a grumble turn into a rumble of discontent, was one of his favourite sayings.

Alice knew it was this almost paternal attitude towards his tenants which made him such a popular landlord, not only in Ewelme but all his manors, and she thought, with a sigh, how much she was going to miss the warm and loyal response which always greeted them among their own people.

Though there was little enough baggage room to spare Alice insisted on taking most of the humble keepsakes which the villagers had thrust into her hands as she rode among them. There was the medallion Jeremy Thatchitt had fashioned for Minerva's brow. That reminded her too that she was leaving Minerva behind in Will's care until she returned to England. She would miss the old palfrey, but better that than risk her breaking a leg if they had a rough crossing. And there was the silken purse stitched by Goodwife Bowdie's careful hands. She remembered those hands fashioning gingerbread men for her when she was a child and how the neat fingers deftly placed split hazel nuts for the eyes. The handsome gilt buckle was from Tom Clutch. Well there was money in ale to be sure. Holy Saints, but her father had had a word to say to Ben Clutch about his persecution of Adeliza! Tom Clutch had already given the lad a sound beating, however, so the matter was left there . . . And there was Adeliza's gift. She had walked the longways from her cottage to the manor to put it into Alice's hands. It was devised like a book, made of thin sheets of bark with wild flowers, leaves and sprays of berries pressed between them. It had the scent of the copses and the hills and the meadows about Ewelme.

*   *   *

It seemed impossible that all could be made ready in time but at last Alice and Matilda reached London, with a day to spare before the marriage feast. Matilda was not a woman to give way to nervous fancies, but travelling with such a rich baggage train was an experience she would not care to repeat. And she told Thomas so roundly, the minute they arrived.

'But what of the men I sent to guard you? Fourteen strong-armed fellows, everyone hand-picked. And there were the servants you brought besides. It would have been a fool-hardy band of robbers who dared assault such a company.'

'Oh, mother has seen a cut-throat looking from behind every bush we passed,' Alice laughed. 'Pray let us unburden ourselves at once. Cecily and I are wearing all my finest jewellery tucked in our bodices and we are scratched to death!'

Thomas chuckled and slapped his wife on the rump with hearty discourtesy. 'That was your idea, eh my Mald? And what have you down the bosom of your attire I should like to know?'

'Leave off, husband do. And before the servants all gawping . . .'

'Go on, mother, tell him!'

'I will not. You are all making enough mock of me as it is.' Matilda was pink with her exertions to keep Thomas' hands from her gown and laughing despite herself. 'Very well, if you must know, I have the keys to every piece of luggage we travelled with and two pouches of gold! And mighty un-comfortable they are.'

They had no sooner washed off the dust of the journey and taken some meat when a loud knocking was heard at the door and Thomas Montacute strode into the hall. Alice was dismayed to be caught unawares in a loose woollen robe, with her hair hanging in braids. It did not occur to her that this simple, innocent attire added to the piquant quality of her beauty.

Even Thomas Chaucer, in the act of ladling mulled wine for the informal family party, was taken by surprise. He had not thought that a man like Salisbury would be so impatient for a glimpse of his bride that he would come before the hour they had arranged on the following day. However, he greeted his son-in-law graciously and presented him first to Matilda – who was thanking heaven that she at least had not sacrificed dignity to comfort and was clothed elegantly enough in tawny damask – and then to Alice.

'I want you to know, Lady Alice,' Salisbury told her at once, 'that I am right pleased with what my eyes behold.' He had her hand locked firmly in his and continued to smile down upon her while he asked Thomas Chaucer: 'May I speak with my bride apart?' But he did not even wait for Thomas to gesture assent before drawing Alice to the window recess.

Alice thought: 'He is accustomed to have his own way. It would not occur to him that anyone might refuse him.' She wished he would not look at her quite so intently and lowered her eyes so that she might be more composed.

'I heard report of you, Alice, some while ago. It was said you were like a lovely, pale lily-of-the-woods. But they who told it were wrong. Your burnished beauty makes me think of the blade of a sword caught in candlelight. I find you exciting to look upon and . . . ' He broke off and added more lightly: 'I must try to earn half as much favour in your eyes.'

'My lord you do me great honour in saying these things.' Alice felt herself blushing. 'I am sure you will make me a good husband.'

'I would rather make you a good and loving wife,' he answered and then they both laughed and were at once more comfortable and at ease.

'And tell me, my lord, will you train with kindness or chastisement?' asked Alice, keeping her eyes demurely lowered. 'I understand both answer with dogs and bears. Which method would you say was most effective with women?'

'I shall not reveal to you my methods with wives until after we are wedded,' this whispered over her bowed head as her father approached to say jovially: 'Well and what is my minx telling you, my lord? That she is good and dutiful? She is no such thing. I shall be glad to be rid of her!'

*   *   *

The marriage feast was sumptuous. Thomas Chaucer had ordered no expense spared to ensure the guests were well filled and well entertained. One elaborate dish succeeded another, eighteen principal courses to say nothing of the side dishes, sauces and sweetmeats.

In breathtaking succession serving boys presented prime ducks roasted whole in golden pastry crust, boar's head in aspic, venison highly spiced in the old Norman way and prepared from a cherished recipe handed down by the women of Matilda's family with love and pride, an enormous carp stuffed with smaller fresh-water fish, glazed and decorated capons perching regally in overawed circles of attentive quails, syllabubs, fruits drenched in rich cordials, pyramids of tiny melting cakes and gigantic cheeses, snowy and young or slumbrous and mellow. And goblets and tankards were for ever refilled with delicate and costly wines or foaming ale.

Alice sat in one of her father's great pine chairs, eating and drinking little, and listening more than she spoke. The Byltons were among the guests and Will found his eyes drawn to her whenever he could take his attention from two offensively cheerful neighbours. He thought he had never seen her look more beautiful or more remote.

Although the feast went on for more than six hours it could not be long enough for Alice. When they were mid-way through the parade of dishes she was aware of her mother's eyes upon her, signalling that she would withdraw whenever Alice wished it. Alice shook her head vigorously in Matilda's direction and was then appalled to find by her bridegroom's amused expression that he had seen this exchange.

Alice felt it becoming increasingly warm. Soon she would make her way up the long hall to the stairs. Her mother would lead her by the hand and the other important women guests would follow in procession. All the men would see her climb those stairs and would know she was going to the elaborately hung guest chamber where she and Salisbury would lie this night and the next. There she would be unrobed and made ready for bed. Like a sheep being shorn for a pagan sacrifice, she thought a little hysterically. Would this experience of bedding with a man be terrible? She wished she knew more about it. From gossip and events which occurred in the household she was aware that what took place was physical. She

55

had reached the conclusion that some women enjoyed it, too. But others shook their heads and sighed over it as a duty and a martyrdom.

Intimidated by her mother's discouraging silence on the subject she had only essayed one question about what would be expected of her. 'You will do whatever your husband requires of you,' was Matilda's unenlightening reply.

The hall was beginning to grow restive when Alice finally nodded to her mother who positively leapt to take her daughter's hand – 'Before I change my mind,' thought Alice with a wry, inward smile. The withdrawal from the full company was as much an ordeal as Alice had imagined. The clamour and the music fell away until there was scarcely a whisper. In the silence, the rustling of the gowns of the women who followed her and the muffled pad of their light velvet shoes was a sinister accompaniment to her progress. At last she reached the guest chamber and it was sanctuary of a kind. There was Cecily waiting with the glorious new furred bed-robe ready on the bed and all the candles burning before the looking-glass where she would uncoil and brush her mistress's hair.

Out of consideration for Alice's sheltered upbringing and because she herself was too fastidious to relish it, Matilda quelled the bawdy talk which some of the women had come expressly to enjoy. They withdrew into twittering groups while Matilda helped Cecily remove Alice's heavy pink silk robe and when all was ready she sent one of the Burghersh matrons to tell Thomas Chaucer he might bring the bridegroom.

Naked beneath the furred robe, Alice shivered, although the night was mild and the room close from the scores of candles which burned and the crowd of women who had pressed in. She made an uncertain move to climb into the vast velvet-hung bed, but Matilda put out her hand to stay her.

'You wait beside the bed, child,' she said.

'Lady Mother, all the people . . . when . . . when do they go away?' Alice had never felt so unsure of herself, so dependent on her mother's superior knowledge.

'When your husband is with you, then we bid you "good night" and go.' Matilda felt a great tenderness for Alice at this moment, but because it was not their custom to demonstrate their feelings for one another she was at a loss to know what gesture might comfort her daughter without being too extravagant for the occasion.

Now they heard the men coming. There was a heavy tramp upon the stairs and much loud laughter. Matilda leaned close to Alice's ear and whispered: 'Have no fear. I have not disliked your father's attentions. Thomas Montacute is not such a man as will make a rough lover.'

Then the men were filling the low doorway, clamouring for a glimpse of the bride. Alice, holding her fur robe close about her, dared to raise her eyes and was astonished to see her bridegroom similarly attired in a furred bed-robe. It had not occurred to her that he would be quite so ready for bed. It left less time in hand than she had hoped.

Alice was aware the men were making jokes but spared understanding by a nervous pounding of her pulse which deafened her ears. The women were saluting her one by one and departing. And for a brief second Alice recognised Will's face in the crowd at the door before he turned and fought his way out.

At last her mother and father were genially urging their guests below stairs for more refreshment, Matilda mercifully pinching out candles as she went. The door closed and Alice, no longer able to stand, sank down on the side of the bed. She could not look at her husband. She was aware of him snuffing more candles until only two remained beside the bed. She knew that he threw open the window to let a soft refreshing night breeze into the darkened room and finally he was handing her one of the twin silver goblets of spiced wine – their pledging cup – and sitting beside her.

Thomas Montacute took her hand and held it while they drank the soothing draught. Alice began to feel a little better and at last managed to say: 'I thought they would never go away.'

'Well, they are gone now. We must think ourselves fortunate at least that we are living in an age of greater delicacy than our grandparents. Then it was not unusual for fathers of both bride and groom to wait behind the hangings of the bed until the marriage had been duly consummated! It was considered a necessary precaution against any attempt at annulment if the alliance proved . . . disappointing.'

Salisbury rose, as if to put an end to further discussion. 'Are you not weary and anxious to rest now, my fair bride?'

Alice, hoping to delay the moment of getting into bed, answered, falsely bright: 'Oh no, indeed, I am not at all tired.'

'Splendid,' said Thomas Montacute swinging her up in his arms and dextrously losing her robe in the process. 'That is exactly what I wanted to hear.'

*   *   *

The sun had already climbed high over the spires of London town when Alice finally opened her eyes in response to Cecily's urgent hand on her shoulder.

'My lady, oh my lady! Make haste. All the company are risen and coming to bid you good-day. Here is your robe. Let me brush your hair a little. I knew you would not wish them to take you unawares.'

'You did well. I will rouse my lord.' Alice turned to her peacefully sleeping husband. 'My lord, awake! Unwelcome callers are on their way.'

Thomas Montacute stirred reluctantly. 'What's to do? Ho! our guests are coming to make some sport are they?'

Noisy whispers and scurryings were heard outside and Thomas had just time to snatch his own robe and thrust his arms into the sleeves before the door was thrown open and a crowd of beaming faces peered round it.

'Why, they are both awake – we hoped to catch you still a-sleeping.'

'See them there, so proper and with my lady's maid to watch fair play. But we know what you have been at.'

'What say we toss them in a blanket?'

'Aye, a good thought.'

Thomas protested, laughing, but it was to no avail and as the men made first for him Alice jumped out of bed and ran for the door. The women, excited by the rough good humour

58

of the men, tried to stop her. But she charged through them. None of the men dared lay hands on her so she was able to escape along the gallery to the robing-room.

'What a madcap hunting party and with me as the quarry, too,' she gasped once safe inside. 'Holy Mother! I did not know gentlefolk took so much licence with a marrying. They become as crude as labourers working among farm beasts. Now bestir yourself Cecily to help me bath and dress.'

Alice was coiling her hair in a severe knot to go under one of her new, tall chapeaux when her mother tapped on the door. She greeted Alice with a kiss and then watched her closely as she asked: 'Well, and how do you like your wifely state?'

Her daughter smiled mischievously. 'It seems to me when women talk they make much of a small matter. Behold I am neither broken in spirit nor changed in heart.'

'Oh Alice, Alice,' Matilda shook her head wonderingly. 'I can never understand you. Last night you seemed as timid as a wild coney and this morning you are cock-a-hoop. Salisbury would not like to hear you dismiss the consummation of your marriage as small matter. Men like to feel they are at their most puissant in the bedchamber.'

'Some men, mayhap. I believe my lord would prefer his victories on the battlefield.'

It was on the tip of Matilda's tongue to say something encouraging about the way love would grow with the years of mutual loyalty and the shared duty of parenthood. But her daughter's face was turned away from her, and before she could choose the right words Alice changed the subject by asking: 'Is this not an enchantment of a head covering? See, mother, the veil is supported on thin wire so that it appears to drift above the steeple crown as if by magic. When I purchased it from Master Dessoisons he promised me it was the very latest fashion among ladies of the Burgundian court. He whispered to me that in France the eyebrows are plucked and also the temples so that not a single hair shows upon the face!'

'In truth is it so?' gasped Matilda. 'Surely that is extreme. Indeed, Alice, I should not do any such thing if I were you.

Salisbury might very well dislike your appearance when you are in . . . in private with him,' she concluded delicately.

'No, I shall not ape fashion so far as that. It might have but brief life and I will not be taken unawares with bald temples at a time when the hair is shown once more. Now we had best go down and see to our guests. I am sure there are many nursing sore heads this day!'

Matilda had intended to find another opportunity for a talk with Alice. But the hours sped away in ordering affairs about the house. Before she knew it she was watching her daughter ride away beside the man who was the new master of her destiny.

*   *   *

The house Thomas Montacute had taken in Paris was small but pleasantly appointed, and conveniently close to the Hôtel des Tournelles on the Place des Vosges, where John, Duke of Bedford, and his duchess, Anne of Burgundy, were in residence. Alice liked it at once and set about refurbishing the rooms with costly tapestries and hangings.

Salisbury was pleased with her taste and indulgent of her whims and the newly-weds spent a few harmonious days settling in. Then a round of entertaining began such as Alice had never encountered in her years of leisurely living at Ewelme. Occasional visits to London and gentle progresses around the family's properties had seemed exciting events in those days. Now she was suddenly snatched into the arduous masque staged by an exiled nobility to keep up its spirits in a hostile land.

Soon after their arrival Salisbury escorted Alice to the Hôtel des Tournelles for her presentation. The Duke of Bedford, who received Alice with every kindness and spoke warmly of her father, was much as Alice had imagined him. A grandson of John of Gaunt, for whom he was named, he had failed to inherit the good looks which usually marked Lancastrian descendants. He was a massive man over six feet in height and heavily built, with a prominent nose and small, deep-set eyes. But he had his compensations in character and ability. Alice knew his administrative talent and diplomatic achievements were the wonder of Europe. In addition he had proved himself a just and honest ruler of Paris and northern France on behalf of his nephew the infant king, Henry VI.

But no report had prepared her for the impact of his duchess. Anne of Burgundy was a year older than Alice. Most people called her plain; indeed it was said the Parisians seeing her for the first time, riding through the streets with her mother and sisters, had labelled them 'laides comme des chouettes' – 'ugly as screech-owls'. Yet she had the gaiety, the high spirits and the self-assurance of one who was beautiful. She was certainly the most flamboyant young woman Alice had ever met.

'Ah but how you are beautiful! You and I are both novice in this matter of marriage, eh? We must be friends therefore and comfort each other when our husbands are ferocious, n'est-ce pas?' This greeting began with a shriek and a pounce overwhelming Alice in an aura of sweet, flowery scent as she found herself clasped in Anne's hands. The duchess concluded it with a side-long, provocative glance at her affectionately grinning husband. Alice was aware of Salisbury disapproving such want of dignity and did her best to maintain her own poise. But it was not easy with Anne leaping about her like a friendly puppy.

'Wait until my brother Philip sees you! He will desire a close acquaintance you may be sure. John, mon cher, you should permit la belle comtesse Alice . . . how you say . . . negotiate with Philip. He will give her all Burgundy! Mais non, perhaps not Burgundy,' Anne corrected herself laughing. 'But he will wish a strong alliance with her!'

Salisbury made it apparent neither by word nor look, but Alice sensed he bitterly resented these light-hearted jests made by his commander's wife. Almost as soon as he could decently take his leave he escorted her firmly away, and because she was learning to understand him it did not surprise her when he re-opened the subject abruptly the same evening.

'Philip of Burgundy is expected to arrive in Paris tomorrow.'

'Yes, no one talks of anything else. I understand he is coming in a great rage because Gloucester is preparing to invade Hainault but I do not understand why. Please will you explain it to me, my lord?'

'I do not wish to discuss politics with you,' Salisbury replied coldly. 'I wish to warn you to comport yourself with care. The Duchess of Bedford has been reared with very free manners it seems to me and after what she had to say this day I do not believe she will stop short of embarrassing you in his company.'

'Oh, indeed, I did not heed what she said. Her tongue runs along with her in a harmless way because she is so lively.'

'She is ungoverned!' said Salisbury sternly. 'Bedford permits her too much tether. He is clearly besotted with her, though it is beyond one to understand why. However, that is nothing to us.' He paused to sip Rhenish wine from a crystal goblet which Alice had taken pains to procure for him as a love-token. It did not serve as any softening reminder and he continued in the same unrelenting tone. 'I chose this house for you so that you might be close to the Regent's court and under its protection when I am with the army. But I do not want you to come under the influence of Anne of Burgundy. You will be called to wait upon her from time to time, that is unavoidable, only pray do not allow her to cultivate you as a friend. There are a number of women in the English community here who would be ideal companions for you. So choose your friends carefully. That is all I have to say.'

Alice had set down her embroidery when her husband began to speak and when he finished she bowed her head meekly over it once more, simply saying: 'It shall be as you wish, my lord.'

It did not occur to Salisbury to look for any undercurrent in this forbearing and dutiful reply. It seemed natural to him that his wife should lean on his better judgment. After all, she was but an innocent girl brought up quietly by her mother in the country. He was pleased with her close attention to his advice.

*   *   *

The weather became exceptionally warm for late October and as Salisbury's house had only a small paved courtyard,

Alice was glad to accept the thoughtful invitation Bedford had sent her, to walk in the gardens of the Hôtel de Tournelles whenever she chose.

She was sitting with Cecily in one of the pleasant arbours two days later, admiring the romantic façade of the building with its forest of tiny turrets, and thinking how wise Bedford had been to make his home there instead of the gloomy Hôtel Saint Pol. The official residence of the kings of France, with its oppressive ceilings and its memories of tragic royalty could never have been a happy home. Suddenly, Alice was startled to hear her husband's voice close at hand. In another instant he had turned the corner of a dense hedge, which screened the arbour, and she saw that he was talking earnestly to the Regent, who led Anne of Burgundy by the hand. Behind them walked a number of men whom Alice recognised as Bedford's closest government aides, and there was also a sprinkling of military talent – but no woman, save Anne, not even any attendant.

Guessing that an informal conference of some kind was taking place, Alice signalled to Cecily to collect her embroidery and prepared to withdraw.

Salisbury acknowledged her with the chilly formality he always showed in public, but Bedford and his wife greeted her pleasantly and urged her to stay.

'Indeed I shall be glad to have your company,' Anne insisted. 'You see how I am situated – the only woman among all these men. It is an outrage! Come, we will sit together over there.'

Alice looked enquiringly at her husband, who intervened.

'I am sure my lady appreciates your courtesy. But she will not choose to intrude when matters of state are to be discussed.' He turned to Alice: 'We will meet at supper, then.'

'No, we pray you, do not dismiss so fair a flower from our garden. We have no secrets which we cannot entrust to the wife of Salisbury!'

Bedford's kindly protest was not well received, but Salisbury bowed his submission reluctantly and escorted Alice back to the curved stone seat she had vacated. As he bent over her hand he whispered: 'You should have left at once. Why were you so tardy? You know I dislike you to flaunt yourself in men's company, where subjects discussed are unsuitable for your ears.'

'Why, my lord, do you mean the talk will be such as to make me blush?' Alice asked innocently.

'You know what I mean. There are aspects of war and politics which ought to make any lady of delicacy blush.' He left her angrily.

Anne, who had tactfully delayed taking her seat beside Alice, rolled her eyes expressively as she moved across the grass to join her.

'Mon dieu! What a barbarian your husband is, petite – I do not comprehend how you have the tolerance for him. Forget him and we will listen to the scandals that will be talked of Jacqueline of Hainault. Pah! She is wild, that one. One moment! Attendez! The so handsome Suffolk is staring at you.' Anne had seized hold of her hand and was squeezing it hard.

'No, no! I cannot look at him, it would be immodest,' Alice protested smiling down at her hands upon her lap.

'Oh, can you not?' Anne was disappointed. 'Then I will watch him for you!'

Some little distance away Bedford was saying: 'Those of you who were not present will have heard by now of the unfortunate scene which Philip of Burgundy created when he burst in upon me yesterday. He blames me for not having restrained my brother of Gloucester. I am sure I do not know what he expected me to do. I cannot prevent Gloucester – after all he is Protector of England – from marrying any woman he chooses, no matter how irregular the union may seem. Nor can I forbid him to help Jacqueline of Hainault regain her property . . . '

Anne hissed in Alice's ear: 'Jacqueline of Hainault's true husband is positively feeble-minded and impotent into the bargain so they say, you know.'

'Her true husband? But is she not married to Humphrey of Gloucester now? I had thought that was why he was going to help her invade the low countries and reclaim her inheritance.'

'How can she be married to him? My brother united her with our cousin, John of Brabant.'

'Did she not get an annulment?'

'I do not believe it for one, and nor does my lord,' Anne said disapprovingly. 'However, no matter the rights and wrongs of the marriage, the so – how do you say? I must make better my English –'

'Let us speak French then.'

'No, for when we visit your country I wish to show myself sympathique – er, "reckless", that is the word I desired – the so reckless Gloucester has already damaged the alliance between England and Burgundy, by threatening to march into territory which my bother wishes to control through Jacqueline. Ah, what is my lord saying now?'

But it was Suffolk who spoke next: 'If Philip of Burgundy is prepared to negotiate with the dauphin on any matter, it means he no longer considers an alliance with England of uppermost importance?'

'Exactly!' Bedford agreed. 'He feels secure enough to stand mid-way between us. We can only hope that he will not want to risk an open breach with me for fear I declare war on him and send an army to help Humphrey take Hainault.'

Alice sat, absorbed in the discussion, so that she did not notice the advancing hour nor how chilly it had grown since the sun began to fall. But Anne had started to shiver beside her and soon contrived to attract her husband's attention, whereupon he brought the discussion to an abrupt conclusion.

Salisbury was immersed in Bedford's problems as he escorted Alice back to their house. When she asked his pardon for any displeasure her presence had caused him, he seemed to have forgotten his anger and simply said: 'Well, well, you had your way on this occasion. Only remember in future that when you are not in my bed or at my table, I prefer you to be in your solar.'

Alice sighed forlornly. Married to Salisbury she might just as well have been living in the twelfth century.

*　　*　　*

On the surface, relations between the English and Burgundian courts appeared to be as good as ever and lavish hospitalities were exchanged. But underlying them all, and only partly submerged by civilities, were strong feelings of mistrust and rivalry.

A fête of exceptional splendour had been planned as a climax to all the earlier entertainments and even the widowed Queen Isabel of France, mother of the dauphin, who lived as a recluse in the echoing loneliness of the Saint Pol, was persuaded to attend.

Alice had been at great pains to choose a gown that would not pass undistinguished in the glittering assembly and finally decided on cloth of silver. The huge sleeves were full from the elbow and thrown back to reveal linings of coral velvet. The robe was boldly designed after the style of a tabard, slashed to the thigh on each side of the skirt to show the same coral velvet and she wore with it a rolled headdress of silver tissue, set low on the centre of her brow and curving back steeply. A dyer, skilled at his craft, had contrived to match the exotic coral shade to dip a length of diaphanous silk. No one had ever seen a veil of such magnificent hue before and, knowing that her appearance was strikingly elegant, Alice enjoyed the stares of the women and the warm approval in the eyes of the men as Salisbury led her forward to make her curtsy to the Duke of Bedford.

'Why, how radiant and lovely is your lady, Salisbury,' the Regent greeted them affably. 'My Anne is hoping you will both sit alongside her to help in the arduous task of entertaining the queen. But just at this moment I have lost sight of her in the crowd. I think she has gone in search of her brother.'

As he spoke the press about the canopied dais where they were standing opened to form a pathway and Anne came towards them, swept along in the encircling arm of Philip of Burgundy.

Alice looked at him intently. She had heard many conflicting reports, for some found him charming and others thought him unstable, even depraved. She was eager to form her own impression and thought him well-looking as he approached. His bearing was easy, manly rather than graceful, and he made good use of a flashing smile. As he drew nearer she saw that he had thick fair hair and that his eyes were piercingly bold under slanting bushy brows. Unhappily they were at that instant directed full into her own frank stare and the awareness that he had caught her appraising him threw Alice into confusion.

Anne, following the direction of her brother's glance, saw at once who had caught his attention. Aware of Salisbury disapproving in the background, she felt urged to gentle mischief and beckoned Alice forward to make her curtsy.

Philip was entranced. Accustomed to easy success with women, he sensed cool resistance behind Alice's pale Anglo-Saxon beauty, even while her tawny eyes watched him with devastating attention. He was not fooled by the blatant scrutiny. Previous experience of Englishwomen had taught him that this was not necessarily an invitation. It was different with the women of his own country, where the sun put fire into the blood. Dieu, but there would be fire behind those eyes or he knew nothing.

'Madame!' He kissed her hand, the back and then the palm. 'But you are ravissante, like a rare jewel . . . no . . . like a star. Ah, but a star is at a great éloignement – distance – and you are here, are you not?' He threaded her hand through his arm. 'You shall stay beside me to enhance my pleasure. Your husband will not be so ungenerous as to deny me.' He saluted Salisbury casually and led Alice to a seat on the dais.

Alice saw a thunderous scowl collect on Salisbury's face and signalled her helplessness to him. But he did nothing to intervene.

At first she enjoyed Philip's gracefully phrased compliments and entertaining conversation. But while they watched a performance of miming, Alice became slightly discomforted by his inclination to lean his arm about her chair and breathe hot whispers in her ear. She found herself laughing often, defensively. When she became aware that Salisbury had taken up a position standing close behind them, she began to feel a creeping chill of apprehension where a few minutes before she had felt herself blushing warmly.

Anne, seated on her brother's left arm, grew alarmed at

67

the situation developing before her, and did what she could to draw his attention away from Alice. But Philip would not be distracted. He was beginning to believe what he wished to believe – that Alice was encouraging his advances and that Salisbury, being so much older than his bride, was a complaisant husband who would not object to his wife's dalliance with a princely ally.

Sensing a flutter in Alice's voice as she parried his more outrageous flatteries and seeing her breasts rise and fall rapidly, he mistook these symptoms of anxiety for excitement and decided to advance their flirtation a stage further. He laid his hand upon the slender curve of her thigh outlined beneath the silver tissue of her gown and in that instant felt her freeze as Salisbury's voice roared out as in a battle-cry: 'Enough!'

Philip swung round in his chair and found himself looking up into Salisbury's furious countenance.

'How dare you make so free with my wife!' Salisbury thundered.

Alice and Anne rose anxiously and Bedford, noticing the disturbance, came quickly to Salisbury's side.

'Come, my lords, what is the meaning of this unseemly exchange?' he said sternly.

'This Prince of Burgundy has left his honour where he stabled his horse,' rapped Salisbury. 'His advances to my wife have been unseemly ever since he set eyes on her. But now I can keep silence no longer for he begins to put his hands upon her. It is beyond toleration.'

Bedford saw Salisbury's fingers curl around the hilt of his sword and hastened to restrain him. 'God in Heaven, remember where you are! Rash action will cause far greater harm than whatever has occurred to offend you. What precisely did happen, anyway?' he concluded irritably, throwing the question at his wife. Anne stood on tip-toe to whisper in his ear. Then, turning to Salisbury, said in gentle entreaty: 'My lord, pray do not make a fracas here. You are greatly distressing your wife. Philip shall see you in private and ask your pardon.'

'I shall not,' countered Philip, rising angrily. 'One would think I had ravished his wife. Does he understand nothing of the courtly homage a civilised man may choose to pay a beautiful, married woman?'

Alice felt sick with humiliation but she managed to keep her chin defiantly high.

She heard Salisbury proclaim to the anxious nobles gathered around: 'Behold this prince whose lusts are so great he cannot contain himself. Do you ask me to serve alongside such a man? I will rather offer my sword to Gloucester's service and war against the interest of Burgundy in Hainault!'

Bedford was appalled at the thought of losing his best general over such a tiresome incident and did his best to soothe Salisbury. But it was to no avail, and resolving to give him time to cool his anger, gravely nodded his permission for Salisbury to withdraw.

Alice was scarcely able to look up as she passed through the silent throng with her husband's hand clamped like a vice about her wrist. She had a fleeting impression of Queen Isabel enquiring querulously what it was all about and of one pair of eyes smiling encouragingly into hers. They belonged, she recollected late, to William de la Pole, Earl of Suffolk.

Salisbury said no word to her until they were within their own home. But when she would have left him in the hall he detained her with a heavily formal: 'Well, madame?'

She stopped at the foot of the stairs and turned to face him: 'I have nothing to say, my lord.'

'What! Have you no words to say in defence of your conduct, no pardon to ask?'

'My conduct does not need defending, I think,' Alice looked more composed than she felt and she went on bravely: 'I did not encourage Philip of Burgundy to dally with me. I am aware of his ill-repute with women and would have avoided his attentions if I could have done so without causing a stir. As it was I thought best to suffer them until I could find a time to slip away without giving offence.'

'I will have you know it gave me great offence that you suffered his advances at all! And you need not play the innocent for I heard you laugh, aye, and saw you look right pleased at what he had to say.' Salisbury unbuckled his sword and threw it with a clatter upon the table. Alice was so tense she winced

69

at the noise but her husband went on relentlessly. 'Perhaps you are overly-young and inexperienced for life about a court of mixed nationalities where customs and manners are varied. I cannot guard your honour when I am with the army. Perhaps I had better send you back to England!'

'My honour was never in danger, sir, until you spoke out and drew all eyes upon us.' The injustice of Salisbury's attitude stirred Alice's anger until she forgot her vulnerable position as a wife, and answered him back like a man. 'Send me home if you choose and make tongues wag the more. It will be a rare scandal!' She moved towards him suddenly and stood looking up, her eyes narrowed and her voice low. 'Do you know what they will say? They will say Bedford's greatest commander is cuckolded and sends his bride to hide her shame in the country. Is that what you want?'

For an instant she thought he would strike her but suddenly some of the anger ebbed from him. He shook his head impatiently. 'No, no. There is reason in what you say. I will not send you home, this time. But in future you will hold yourself more aloof. Now go to your chamber.'

Alice turned to leave him and felt Salisbury move up close behind her. His hands gripped her shoulders and pulled her back so that she was forced to lean against him for a moment. 'You have a formidable pride, Alice. And a haughty temper. Do not turn these qualities on me again. You try my self-control too far.'

He released her. She climbed the stairway slowly and did not look back.

Later she told Cecily what had taken place and found comfort in her loyal indignation. Cecily had changed during her service with Alice. She had gained poise and confidence, conquered the broad vowels which would have betrayed her humble background, and as Alice's confidante, was beginning to understand that wealth and position carried with them responsibilities which she could previously never have imagined.

'What a misfortunate thing that my lord should have spoken out before everyone!' Cecily concluded.

'It was a madness! My god, but I was told Salisbury was a man whose pride would accept no compromise. He is indeed.

He will trip over this pride yet and be undone. It will certainly not serve the advancement of his career if he cannot temper resentment for ambition's sake,' said Alice bitterly.

Ye even while Alice raged against her husband, she was already beginning to understand him better and to accept that the ideal partnership she had dreamed of in marriage could never be realised. Moreover, Thomas Montacute's anger, rash and sudden as it was when his pride was touched, soon spent itself and he was too great-spirited to carry a grudge. She liked him the better for that and was pleased when he confided to her that he had made a gracious peace with Bedford and withdrawn his vow never to fight on the same side as Burgundy again.

*　　*　　*

Only two days after the unpleasant scene at the fête, news came that Gloucester had landed with his invasion force at Calais. Five thousand men were preparing to march on Hainault and Philip of Burgundy, bringing the celebrations in Paris to an ungracious end, hurried north. There was a rumour in the New Year that Philip had challenged Gloucester to single combat as an alternative to war, and Salisbury related it to Alice with scorn. She agreed with him that it was a flamboyant gesture but could not resist pointing out two notable precedents. Louis of Orleans had sent a similar challenge to Henry IV and Henry V had offered to meet the dauphin alone before Agincourt.

Alice was often summoned to attend Anne of Burgundy and, despite Salisbury's disapproval, the two young wives became close friends. Through this association, Alice began to see that understanding politics was a question of understanding the people with the power to create policy. It was, for example, easier to predict Philip of Burgundy's actions with his sister Anne, to interpret his character, which she knew and understood so well. And Bedford's and Philip's feelings for each other, which influenced the relationship and destinies of their two countries, were in turn influenced by the young woman they each loved in their own way and who loved them.

71

Being so much in Anne's company Alice was among the first to get diplomatic news. When Humphrey of Gloucester, finding the conquest of the Low Countries a harder task than he expected, lost some of his ardour for Jacqueline and switched his affections to Jeanne de Marigny, wife of Jacqueline's equerry, Anne could not resist telling Alice. Then as the months passed by there was talk of Humphrey taking a new love – this time one of Jacqueline's ladies-in-waiting, the beautiful Eleanor Cobham. Finally, in April of 1425, Humphrey returned to England, allegedly to collect reinforcements, and his Eleanor went with him.

Once Gloucester had left Hainault, Bedford went to work to patch the strained alliance with Burgundy and spirits in the British colony rose.

The army was on the move again, too. When operations had come to a standstill in the previous autumn, the greater part of Maine and Anjou had been overrun. The logical objective was now Le Mans and as spring warmed to summer Salisbury led an army, strengthened by fresh reinforcements from England, to capture the town.

Alice watched him ride away with uncertain emotions. There was relief because she would have some respite from his energetic prosecution of the task of begetting a male heir; there was regret, because she feared his efforts had so far been unavailing and she was eager to prove herself a fruitful wife. There were some slight misgivings, because she was not sure what difficulties might present themselves while she was unprotected and far from home; and there was pride in the splendid appearance he presented on his elaborately dressed charger, pride in the way his captains sprang to answer the authority in his brief commands.

Soon she was hearing of his victories. All Burgundian troops had been withdrawn from active service but even with a depleted force at his disposal Salisbury could not fail it seemed. By the end of the first week in August, Le Mans was in English hands, and he turned north. As the months went by he accepted the surrender of every garrison which stood between his army and the total conquest of Maine.

Meanwhile Alice adapted herself to her new life. Marriage

and rank gave her freedom to enjoy the social round of the court and the company was stimulating at best and diverting even at its most trivial.

But her new routine was soon to be disrupted. Bedford received alarming news from England. His brother, Humphrey of Gloucester, not content with the damage he had done to the Anglo-Burgundian alliance by his opportunism in Hainault, had on his return to his own country, attempted to seize complete power. Civil war threatened and Bedford stayed only to make arrangements for the government of France in his absence, before setting out for England.

'You had better come with us,' Anne told Alice. 'My lord is making Philip co-president of the council to govern while we are away and Salisbury will not like you left under his protection! And you cannot possibly join your husband campaigning in Maine.'

Alice was writing to Salisbury for instructions when his messenger arrived. He had heard from Bedford of the crisis at home and told her: 'There is no question but that you must accompany them to London. I will write you further when we see how matters stand. It may be fitting for you to return to Paris in the train of my lady of Bedford but in the event of any unforeseen difficulty you can consult your father.'

He added more warmly, the memory of her having softened him as he wrote: 'I would you might have joined me for I miss your company sorely and had thought with pleasure of you waiting for me in Paris at the end of this campaign. I commend you unto God's keeping and urge you to make my own continued success a cause in your daily prayers.'

CHAPTER FOUR

THE ROYAL Christmas was to be spent at Eltham Palace. Alice had not expected to have any part in it and was looking forward to keeping the feast with her mother and father at their London house. But the Duchess of Bedford and fate had, it seemed, decided otherwise.

'My dear friend, I certainly will not permit you to remove yourself from me at such a time,' Anne said warmly, but with sufficient firmness of tone to show Alice that it was as much a command as a pressing invitation. 'I need you to help me raise a little joy in this cold, damp island. The ladies of court here have the look farouche . . . grim . . . n'est-ce pas? One cannot contemplate making a fête with them. I shall die of boredom if you abandon me to their company.'

So with a good grace Alice made arrangements to convey her wardrobe and a limited number of her household to apartments at Eltham. She sent a regretful message to her father. His disappointment at least would be outweighed by the compliment of the royal invitation. And as it chanced his reply brought the news that he had been called to Taunton on urgent business, while Matilda must needs hasten to the bedside of her favourite aunt. A family reunion would have been out of the question anyway.

With Alice to help her, Anne of Burgundy threw herself with customary enthusiasm into making the festivities memorable for the serious, docile child who was Henry VI. She confided to Alice that her husband wished to soothe public alarm by making his visit seem as domestic as possible. Many would guess the true reason for his hurried return. But others, re-assured by his presence, might be less inclined to panic if they saw he was prepared to relax and spend Christmas getting to know his four-year-old nephew before tackling the political problems which had arisen between his brother, Humphrey of Gloucester, and his uncle, Henry Beaufort, Bishop of Winchester.

But inside the Palace walls it seemed, not all the deliberate gaiety could overcome the wary look in the eyes of men who had much at stake. Alice, coming upon some who pondered in the dim stone galleries, where her gliding velvet slippers gave no warning, watched how they drew affability across their faces as a woman might use a veil. Once, as she sat in a shadowed archway of the great hall, Beaufort himself passed close by, his ecclesiastical robes spreading across the floor. As he raised his hand in graceful benediction to those who made a way for him, she caught the dull glint of chain mail beneath the rich cloth of his office. He might trust the care of his soul to his God but it seemed that he preferred to make his own provisions for his mortal being.

Only Bedford showed no sign of stress, working quietly to heal the quarrel between Gloucester and Beaufort and re-unite the two hostile parties which their enmity had created among the lords and members of the Commons.

Alice admired his astuteness in handling men. She noticed that he did not summon those he wanted to see but preferred to let them find him with his royal nephew, lulled by story-telling on his knee, the flaxen head drooping upon his arm. Across the body of the sleeping king, the duke talked and listened, soothed and bargained with the men who balanced power in England. In order not to disturb the child, they whispered. And that must be to Bedford's advantage, Alice smiled to herself. One could not make angry demands in an undertone.

She had, too, an opportunity to study the boy, Henry him-self. He was a pretty child with a quaint self-conscious dignity and an understanding far beyond his age. He was obedient to those appointed to govern his training and day-to-day life, and his nurses and tutors had no complaint to make of him.

75

Yet Alice, striving to find in him the king he might become, felt misgiving. She would have been reassured to see a brief spark of rebellion in his eye, the stamp of a foot or a toy broken in rage. Men of the House of Lancaster had all the mark of spirit and singular courage in boyhood. Had Henry's father perchance done an ill day's work when he mingled his blood with that of the Valois line?

Henry was not a confiding child but it chanced that one afternoon he joined Alice on the deep, velvet-cushioned window seat in the solar. Perhaps he chose Alice's company because she was reading an elaborately decorated Book of Hours belonging to Anne of Burgundy, and this seemed to him a more interesting occupation than the working of an altar cloth in gold thread and pearls, which was engaging the attention of the duchess and other ladies of the household.

For a time Henry was content to lean against Alice's knee looking at the richly coloured designs bordering the pages and illuminating the letters. Finally he pointed one out:

'That is my favourite letter . . . B for B-Bedford. He is my favourite uncle.' He twisted a brilliant ruby which overwhelmed one small finger. 'He gave me this ring.'

'I know. Is that why he is your favourite uncle, because he gives you handsome presents?' Alice teased gently.

'No! I like him because . . . because he is quiet . . . and . . . and good. He does not roar and toss me up in the air like Uncle Gloucester.' Henry scowled and then added with just a touch of petulance: 'We do not like being thrown about like a sack of barley.'

Alice forbore to laugh at this evidence of the hurt royal pride and asked curiously: 'Is your Uncle of Gloucester not good – apart from the rough play he makes with you?'

Henry's baby-smooth forehead wrinkled in consideration before he answered. 'No he is not good. He is very rude to my great-uncle Beaufort, and that means he is rude to Holy Church! Great-uncle Beaufort is Bishop of Winchester, you know,' he explained kindly.

'Yes, I know very well,' Alice smiled slightly.

'Then Uncle Humphrey has been doing very wrong things among my people, also. He made the riots happen. Perhaps it

76

is the devil in him. Do you think that is what it is, lady Alice?'

'Indeed I do not! And you must not say such things of one of your father's brothers.'

Alice did not speak of Henry's confidence to anyone. But what he had told her lingered in her mind and she pondered what game Beaufort was playing. It must be he who was influencing the boy's mind against Gloucester, and if so how self-interested were his motives?

*   *   *

On the tenth day of January the Duke of Bedford made his official entry into London. Thomas Chaucer was among those summoned to meet him and at last, when the ceremonies were over, Alice found herself riding with reckless excitement through the twisting, cobbled streets to their town house. She raced Cecily into the courtyard and slid from the saddle into her father's waiting arms.

'Dear father! How well you look! I swear you are not aged by one hair in these many months. Months do I say? It seems like years!'

'Alas I cannot say the same for you,' Thomas Chaucer chuckled. 'You have aged a great deal. It is no longer a girl but a woman, all of twenty-one years, I see before me. But come away in, child, come away in. I have a hearty supper set for you . . . And Cecily, too, greetings. I scarcely recognise you, you are become so elegant.'

Soon they were seated in the great carved chairs, so dear and familiar to Alice that her fingers had to be constantly caressing the leaping lions which formed the arm-rests. The fire blazed and spluttered upon the hearth, and when Cecily left them early, pleading weariness, father and daughter settled down in companionable ease.

'Matilda was much distressed that she could not accompany me. But as I sent you word, your aunt is taken very ill and your mother felt she must go to her first. She will come to London as soon as maybe.'

'I long to see her! How does she look?'

'As handsome as ever. She carries her years as lightly as

77

I.' Thomas bowed mockingly. 'Ah, but a man is blessed to have two beautiful women in his life as I have.'

For a time they continued to exchange the gossip of court and manor, the political scene at home and in France.

Then her father asked her abruptly: 'How are you finding life with Salisbury, my child? Does he make you happy? I have felt that in your letters you left much unsaid, but you must confide in me freely now.'

'He has been exceedingly kind and attentive to my comfort, father. You need have no doubt, but that he is a good husband and cares for me well.'

'That is no answer. Come, out with it! I see trouble in your eyes.'

Reluctantly then she told him of the unhappy meeting with Philip of Burgundy and as he listened without comment, only nodding an assurance of close attention, went on to describe her husband's unfavourable reaction to any interest she showed in politics and his discouragement of her friendship with Anne of Burgundy.

Thomas Chaucer was scowling heavily when she finished speaking.

'From what you tell me, it appears I have ill-matched you, my daughter,' he said at last. 'I had not thought Thomas Montacute would make such a high-handed husband. But leaving that aside, I fear that out of my great love and pride in you, has come a harm. I have been sadly at fault.'

'Oh no, father. You must not blame yourself for the man Salisbury is!'

'Indeed I do not. I blame myself for the woman you are. I have trained you to be an equal partner for an ambitious man and I see now that it is not the way to rear a daughter so she be happy. I have always had the feeling that if a woman is a fit creature to beget a man's heirs then she is a fit partner for him in every way. She must, however, be educated for the role and methinks few men are yet able to appreciate wit and learning in a wife. They want only grace, manners and beauty and begrudge the independence that understanding might bestow upon your sex. In time it may come, but I

78

believe I have condemned you to dwell in a prison by letting in just enough light for you to see the bars.'

'If it is as you say, still I am glad not to live out my life in darkness.' Alice leaned towards her father, anxious to reassure him. 'Besides Salisbury may change his outlook, as I grow older and gain status as the mother of his children.'

'Ah yes.' Thomas Chaucer stabbed a finger at her to point his words. 'Where are these grandchildren of mine? Your mother has been anticipating them hourly ever since your wedding day! And for my part I think you are taking your time about it!'

Alice blushed slightly and hung down her head. 'Well, Salisbury would not consider taking me on campaign with him and now here I am in England.'

'And he in France! When does he expect to see you again? Bedford's business here will keep him many months if I know anything. He will not resolve the differences between Beaufort and Gloucester in a trice.'

'How did the ceremony go today?' Alice was glad of a chance to turn the conversation in another direction.

'Well, everyone was glad to see Bedford, of course. But they made it clear they did not approve of Beaufort riding with him. Bedford did not like their behaviour and spoke mighty cold in reply to the speeches of welcome. He barely acknowledged the silver dishes they gave to him.'

'What has Beaufort done to make himself so unpopular? What sort of a man is he, father?'

'Beaufort has done nothing for which he should be blamed. The truth is Gloucester has always been popular with Londoners and in the past few months he has not scrupled to rouse the mobs in his own interests. He has even flooded London with notices urging labourers to rebel against recent wage regulations made by the mayor and aldermen. These irresponsible designs are aimed at discrediting Beaufort and they have led to violence on the streets so that shopkeepers have been forced to put up their shutters and honest citizens have feared to stir from their houses.' Thomas Chaucer became so angry as he spoke that his powerful hand crushed the delicate tracery forming the stem of his silver goblet.

79

'But why does Glocester hate his uncle so?'

'Because he thinks it is Beaufort who has prevented him from becoming Regent of England with full powers. Gloucester is not content to be Protector with a council to hold him in check.'

Alice told her father of the private conversation she had had with the young king and her suspicion that Beaufort was schooling him to dislike and mistrust his uncle Humphrey.

'Very likely he is,' Thomas Chaucer said shortly. 'Any man who has the interests of this country at heart must discourage Gloucester's influence in any part of its destiny.' He was silent for a long time. Alice was beginning to feel sleepy with the warmth of the fire and the soothing redolence of the spices rising from the mulling pot upon the hearth. But she had a feeling her father had something he wanted to say to her yet, so she did not stir.

Finally Thomas sighed and replenished their cups with wine.

'This one to help you on the road to pleasant dreams,' he said as he handed her the drink. 'And as you sup it you may listen to something I have to say. Mayhap I should have told you of it before, or again I may be wrong to tell it now . . . You know in what manner the Beauforts are kin to us?'

Alice did not trouble to answer. Her father was making an observation, not asking a question. How could she fail to remember a family tie that wove through the outrageous Katherine Swynford who had been John of Gaunt's mistress for years and bore him a whole family, the Beauforts, before he made her his third wife? Katherine had been strong, beautiful and passionate, a contrast to her gentle sister Philippa, who married Geoffrey Chaucer and was Alice's grandmother.

'You know, too, that we owe our advancement in the world to John of Gaunt. The ascendancy of his House of Lancaster, the coming of his son to the throne as Henry IV has brought us power, wealth and privilege. Our fortunes are inextricably linked with Lancaster. Never forget it. In working for the interests of the king and the good government of this country we labour to our own advantage. Therefore I am the king's man, though he is but a puling child, and I am Henry Beaufort's man – for he is a good statesman and worthy, despite an overliking for intrigue. But most of all I am my own man!'

As he spoke Thomas Chaucer's voice had sunk until it was only an intense whisper. His eyes held his daughter's willing her to accept and remember what he was saying through all time.

Alice felt the hairs tighten at the nape of her neck as if danger touched. She moved suddenly and walked to the window and back to dispel the feeling. But her father still did not seem ready to bid her good-night.

'I think you are sharp enough to keep your own counsel, so I will tell you something.' He continued to speak low and motioned Alice to the stool at his feet. 'John of Gaunt was a generous master to Geoffrey Chaucer and was well served in return. But the duke also extended his bounty to Philippa, my mother. She received direct allowances of money, gifts of fur robes and silver and so on. And you know of course that through him she was inducted into the Fellowship of Lincoln Cathedral, an exceptional honour . . . Do you follow the way that I am paving?' Thomas Chaucer broke off suddenly.

'I think so.' Mounting excitement caused Alice to twist the rings upon her fingers.

'Gaunt's kindness to my mother may be interpreted as a token of his great love for her sister Katherine . . . and that was a very great love indeed, for in the end he married her though all Europe laughed behind its hand. It is natural that he wished to advance her family, including Philippa and Philippa's children. My brother Lewis died alas and my sister Elizabeth entered the Abbey of Barking and took her vows. But you see what I am become through the favour of John of Gaunt . . . and his love for my mother's sister!' Thomas Chaucer broke off again. An ironic smile flickered about his mouth a moment and was gone.

'My mother, Philippa, was married to Geoffrey Chaucer while they were both employed in the royal household. What more natural than that in the course of time I should be born. It was later that my mother entered the service of John of Gaunt, when he brought his second wife, Constance of Castile, home from Spain to the Palace of Savoy. Katherine was in residence there of course, nominally responsible for the up-

6

bringing of his motherless children but openly recognised as his mistress. It cannot have been a very comfortable arrangement for Constance, I am bound to admit.'

Alice observed that her father could not refrain from the dryly delivered asides which were part of his manner of speaking, even when he had weighty things to say.

'John of Gaunt was the son of a king, the brother of a king and – though he did not live to know it – the father of a king. Such a man is above the reach of petty scandal you might think? But it is not so. If he had bedded two sisters and sired bastards on both of them do you think clacking tongues would have kept their peace? Well I never heard tell of any gossip about his relationship with my mother. But as I grew from boyhood into manhood I found that there were members of the royal family who believed I might be the son of John of Gaunt. The belief was implied rather than spoken. At first I was slow to understand but once I did, I realised that this might be a proud secret but it could also in certain circumstances be a dangerous one. I have often told you that I believe it is a man's own character which attracts his destiny. I have always been cautious and caution bade me receive such suggestions with a show of ignorance. The Chaucer origin may be in trade but that is no shame and my mother's blood, that of the Roet family, is good enough for me. And I believe it is because I neither encouraged nor denied the rumour that I have any blood tie with the royal family that certain favours have been shown me. I lay no claim to anything so I am given my share by those who cannot be sure about me but feel my silence deserves some reward . . .'

Unable to restrain herself any longer Alice burst out: 'But father, is it true? Never mind what you have let people believe – have we really the blood of John of Gaunt?'

'What if I say I do not know?'

'I cannot believe that. You must know. Your mother must have told you before she died . . . or something in Geoffrey Chaucer's manner towards you must have shown that you, the eldest of the three children, were not his child!'

Thomas Chaucer scowled thoughtfully into the fire and then draining off his wine set the cup down with finality.

'I think you will play your part better if you do not know the truth . . . No, do not storm at me . . . listen! I said earlier that I had raised you like a lad but you may still be weak in woman's ways. I cannot know how life may deal with you but if you keep silence as I have always done I think you will prosper. If you do not know the truth how can you tell it. Others may continue to wonder and their doubts may one day serve you.'

'But now I know something and nothing! How can that help me? Does my mother know?'

'She does not! And you will not mention the matter to her. As I have said, women are not to be trusted with this sort of information . . . But you are my heir and, who knows, one day you may be in a position where you can turn what I have told you to good account. Consider it a legacy like any other property and hold fast to it. Lock it away and never speak of it, even to your husband . . . And now you should go to bed. We will talk more tomorrow.'

*   *   *

During the weeks that followed Alice had little time to sit and brood on what her father had told her. The impulsive temperament of Anne of Burgundy did not encourage her attendants to lose themselves in thought. There was always a stir about her. She might be dancing, or listening to music, discussing books, or examining works of art brought from distant lands. And suddenly she would send a page running to order up their horses and they would ride, as if the devil himself pursued them, to hear mass sung, to take alms to the poor, to trail the little sisters who distributed food among the sick in the fever-ridden backwaters of the city. Sometimes it seemed to Alice that one had only to blink and in that instant the whole company might have disappeared.

But for a time her nights were broken by uneasy wakeful thoughts and dreams which menaced her unconscious spirit, until at last Alice assimilated the curious possibilities of her heritage and was able to push the knowledge to the back of her mind.

Owing to the unrest in London, Parliament met at Leicester that February. Members had been forbidden to carry arms, so many of them took stout staves and even, it was said, stones concealed beneath their garments. The atmosphere of the deliberations hardly encouraged inspired legislation and at the end of the first day the Commons sent a petition to the lords asking them to heal the breach in the country's leadership.

Bedford began to take a stronger line with the protagonists, and by mid-March he had prevailed upon them, backed by a carefully chosen commission who listened patiently to their grievances against each other, to make peace outwardly if not in their hearts.

Two days later Beaufort resigned the chancellorship to John Kemp, Bishop of London, and set out on a pilgrimage. He appeared to have withdrawn from the contest of power in his own country and to be turning his talents to ecclesiastical politics, for it was announced that he would shortly accept a cardinal's hat.

It was a time which encouraged speculation and every alehouse prophet found an audience to heed him. Foreign merchants, shrewd enough to guess that Gloucester in power would buy favour with the middle classes by imposing restrictions on their trade, met at the tables of bankers and alarmed each other behind fat, bejewelled hands. And in the court itself men watched Bedford and waited.

When Parliament rose at the beginning of June, Bedford took his wife to visit the shrine of Saint Alban, the first English martyr. They were to be the guests of scholarly John of Wheathamstead, head of the splendid Benedictine abbey a day's journey north of London. Alice was tempted to accept Anne's invitation to go with them, but she had seen so little of her mother since she returned to England that she begged leave to go home to Ewelme. There was no way of telling how soon Bedford might consider the country quiet enough for him to leave it with an easy mind. And it seemed unlikely that Salisbury would want her to remain in England when she could travel back to France with the court.

Anne, reluctant at first to let her go, had finally conceded

Alice's duty to her mother, overwhelmed her with gifts and speeded her on her way.

Her home-coming was a memorable day for Alice. As she came in sight of the village, riding between Cecily and her equerry, Richard de Nevy, she set such a pace for her household that they feared for their necks as the horses fought to keep a footing on the treacherously rutted, sun-baked road. Suddenly the sound of the church bell swung across the fields, struck an uncertain note at finding something more was required of it than a simple call to worship and finally summoned up an abandoned clamour of welcome.

Alice turned to say something to Cecily but her words were lost in the din and she shook her head, laughing and exhilarated. Ahead of them a tide of villagers were washed into the street by the noise; housewives swirled out of cottage doorways wiping wet arms on aprons and men, interrupted in the task of stalling beasts, came with straw in their leggings to bring a deeper note to the chorus of welcome.

Matt Bowman pushing through the crowd caught at Alice's bridle. 'My lady! My lady! What a joyous day this is.'

'The joy is mine in seeing you all again,' Alice cried. 'But how had you warning as we came?'

'The children have been watching from the rise, yonder, and signalled when they saw you,' shouted one.

'Father John himself waited at the church door to pass the message on to Luke Bellringer,' cried another.

'We looked for you to come yestere'en.'

'I stayed a day longer in London than I expected, but am among you now and right grateful for this show of your love. Now I must haste to my lady mother. I will ride this way tomorrow,' Alice promised as Matt led her horse through the press.

Matilda waited to greet her at the door of the manor and the servants knelt in the hall as she entered. Only one slight shadow touched the day, for Gundred was not there.

'Just after you were married she was taken with a sickness which caused her to fall down fainting,' Matilda told Alice sadly. 'She complained of terrible pain in her side. I nursed her right well and your father had a man of physic look at her. But it was to no avail and she died within a month. God give her peace.'

'I had no idea she was ailing,' Alice cried.

'Nor was she when you left. We did not tell you in a letter, not wishing to grieve you when you were far from home.'

'I wish I had shown her more kindness while she lived. Poor Gundred!'

'Well do not upset yourself. She had much of her own way in this house and was happy in her importance as your nurse. If you were not as affectionate towards her as you might have been, her own harshness of manner was to blame.'

As the weeks slipped by Alice confided in her mother about the difficulties she had encountered in her marriage. When they had met briefly in London two months earlier she had told Matilda only of the pleasures and advantages of her life in France. But she rightly guessed that her father would have told the rest and it was comforting to hear Matilda's view that she would find herself growing closer to Salisbury in time.

When she rode over to Adeliza's cottage she did not refer to her marriage. There was no need to. Adeliza peered at her with her remote eyes and seemed to sense a need for diversion. She did not ask questions but instead told Alice all the news of the village, rendering a lively and detailed account of the events which had kept the gossips busy. Only when she talked of Will Bylton did she cause Alice some unease.

'There is a change in that young man,' Adeliza said sadly. 'He has come to see me often while you have been away and I have been watching the laughter die out of him. You must have noticed the change in him yourself!'

Alice had. When she met Will the day after her return she found him quiet and reserved. His smile seemed a mechanical politeness, not at all like the frank and ready grin she remembered. But his eyes had been tender and he caressed the hand she extended to him while he asked the obvious, kindly questions of a close friend.

'I told him he should get himself a wife.' Adeliza spoke on through Alice's thoughts. 'They need a woman to look after them properly, the Bylton men. Agatha Lowell housekeeps for them well enough, but it's not the same.'

Unreasonably, Alice disliked the idea of Will being married and because she was accustomed to relax her guard with Adeliza it showed in her face.

'Ah! I knew you would not like to hear that,' Adeliza muttered. 'But you have nothing to do with Will. Let be, let be!'

'To the devil with you, you witch-woman.' Alice was forced to smile despite her irritation. 'Why must you be for ever jumping into my thoughts? It is not for you to tell me how I should go on. Besides I put no halter about Master Bylton's neck. He can do as he pleases.'

'You know that is not true. He sees you married but he does not see you a loving wife. He will never believe you entirely lost to him until he is convinced you have given your heart to another man.'

'What romantic nonsense is this talk of handing out hearts? I was lost to Will the day I was born and he knows it well. Anyway what would you have me do? I love my husband as is my duty. Do you want me to nail a proclamation on the church door?'

'Tush!' said Adeliza. 'The truth is you like to be adored by Master Will. You want to find him always waiting for you when you come to Ewelme. He is part of your property. I love you well, Alice Chaucer, but you are more ruthless than you know!'

'Silence!' Alice was suddenly angry. 'You presume too far. By the Mass I will have you turned out of Ewelme for such insolence.'

'Haughty countess though you be, you yet inspire no fear in me! I was told by one of the cottagers the other day that witches always talk in rhyme,' Adeliza said musing and unrepentant. 'I think I must teach myself to do it.'

'Oh Adeliza! You provoke me to rage and then make me laugh. You are a maddening creature. I have had enough of your company for a while.' Alice climbed into Minerva's saddle while she spoke, and as she smacked the palfrey's rump called back over her shoulder: 'Thomas Gascoigne has a fair niece in Oxford, I believe. Commend her to Will when next he visits you!'

*   *   *

There was business that needed attention at Donnington in Berkshire. This was one of the properties which had been settled on Alice at the time of her betrothal to John Phelip and she had a great liking for the manor-house with its crenellated walls and mellow gardens. Knowing this Matilda suggested they should make a short stay there while Ewelme was given a thorough cleansing before autumn closed in.

It seemed a happy plan and the household made an easy progress to their new quarters. But within a week of their arrival at Donnington a fever epidemic broke out and Alice was among the first of its victims.

Matilda watched through the first terrifying nights of sweating and moaning, when Alice knew no one and squandered her failing strength in the fruitless twisting, and arching of her fevered body. Her mother spent the long hours on her knees pleading that Alice might be spared. But when her prayers seemed to lack an answer, she prayed that at least her husband might be given the strength to bear the loss of his daughter, without bitterness.

'Holy Mother, you can understand so well the hopes and fears in my heart. Out of your infinite pity take me in place of Alice. You know my husband Thomas . . . he does not reverence you as he should, but he is a good man. Do not let him be punished . . . and . . . and do not let him blame me for bringing Alice to Donnington!'

Thomas Chaucer rode to Donnington and spoke no word to any man along the way. His captain watched him anxiously and ordered his men to keep silence too. In the crowded streets through which they must sometimes pass beggar children scrambled from the relentless hooves and looked with fear on the uncaring face of the man who nearly rode them down.

When he reached Donnington he paused only to grasp Matilda by the shoulders and look into her face for any sign of hopeful change and then pushed by her into Alice's chamber. He fell upon his knees beside the bed and, seeming unaware of Cecily's presence, watching in the darkened room, began to speak earnestly to his daughter.

'Alice, Alice my child. It is I, your father. Listen to me. You shall not slip away from life like this. You shall not leave me. In you *my life* continues. You know I have no other heir. Are all my dreams to founder and the well of my blood run dry because you will not fight?'

Thomas Chaucer spoke as if he were confident that he could reach Alice's wandering mind and compel her obedience. Cecily drew back into a corner feeling she had no right to witness the scene.

Suddenly there were urgent knockings at the door and Matilda entered with her confessor and a priest who was a stranger to the household.

'Thomas, oh Thomas! I dare delay no longer. I must beseech you to let Father Matthew prepare our child's soul to meet the Company of Heaven. He has with him a most holy man, Brother Martin, whom he discovered visiting the neighbourhood. I beg you let them approach.'

'No!' Thomas Chaucer had leaped to his feet and stood between the intruders and the bed. 'Alice is not going to die these many years! An end to your mumblings.' He rounded furiously upon the priests who had begun to chant. 'Why know you not that if she stood at the very gates of hell itself I would drag her back by the hair of her head?'

In that instance Alice uttered a strange cry and stirred as through she would lift herself. Cecily hurried to set an arm beneath her shoulders and Alice knew her.

'Cecily.' Her voice came surprisingly strong. 'Do I hear my father?'

'Yes! Peace lady, he is here. Soon you will be well.'

'Soon . . . well.' Alice breathed and fell back into a restful, easy sleep.

'Praise God,' cried Matilda, 'she will live! My prayers are answered.'

'My orders have been obeyed,' said Thomas Chaucer with a self-deriding smile.

But although it became obvious with the next twenty-four hours that Alice was out of danger her progress back to health was tediously slow. She was at first astonished and later fretful to find how weak the fever had left her. She had become desperately thin and the slightest exertion continued to weary her.

To please Matilda she supped possets, drank an incredible range of cordials and slept with a healing relic – the bone of some little-known saint – beneath her pillow. And in the shelter of the pleasaunce walls she read letters from her father and from Nicholas Bylton, who did their best to keep her in touch with events.

Her father wrote that Bedford and his wife would soon be leaving England. But it seemed that Bedford would be leaving behind a structure for the government of the country which did credit to his reputation as a statesman. Gloucester might have thought he would be stronger than ever with Beaufort gone to collect his cardinal's hat and Bedford called back to govern France. But he was headed for bitter disappointment. Bedford had foreseen this and guarded against it. He had increased the powers of the Council which governed in the king's name. By publicly swearing that he would himself be advised and ruled by the Council in all things he left his brother no choice but to make the same declaration.

The Chancellor, John Kemp, who was now Archbishop of York, would be in a strong position to curb Gloucester should he ever again try to manipulate the country's affairs for his own ends. Alice knew that the Council included some of the most responsible and able men in England. Her father was one of them. They shouldered the duties of their high office with pride and would not allow one of their number to shame the rest.

At least that was how things were at present. But suppose, thought Alice, suppose that a man came to join the Council who had Gloucester's ambition without his weaknesses; a single-purposed man minded to rule England as uncrowned king. He would need a persuasive eloquence, too, but it would be comparatively easy for such a man to gain ascendancy over his fellow councillors.

Alice was not much troubled by these musings, however. After so many months out of the mainstream of life, she felt her intellect growing lazy for want of exercise. She began to think it might be peaceful to spend her life as her mother did, in a succession of satisfying homely duties.

Unprotesting she made the journey home to Ewelme in a

litter, and Matilda, who knew how her daughter disliked this means of travel, watched her uneasily. They spent Christmas quietly. In no time it seemed the first snowdrops were thrusting up tentative green spears and with them came the news that Bedford was returning to France.

Anne of Burgundy sent a note to Alice telling her they would leave before the middle of March and enquiring in the kindest terms whether she was sufficiently recovered to go with them. Salisbury wrote, too, urging her make the journey as soon as she could.

Reading between the lines, Alice guessed that as the winter months discouraged campaigning, he had found time to miss her. She was grateful for the affectionate concern in his many letters throughout her illness. But she was in no frame of mind to tear herself away from Ewelme only to find when she reached Paris that her husband was about to set off with some new war objective.

Matilda strengthened her resolve to stay in England.

'You might get with child as soon as Salisbury sets eyes on you. It is often the way, my love, after a separation. And you are not yet well enough for that.'

So Alice wrote a pretty, dutiful letter, deploring 'the weakness which keeps me from my lord.' As soon as it was dispatched she began to feel better. And when the ship that carried it sailed for Calais, Alice and Cecily were putting their horses into a joyous canter across the downs.

*   *   *

At first Alice delighted in the extended freedom she had won. And now, with her married status, it was freedom such as she had never known before. Matilda set no restrictions on her. She might travel between her properties, making such decisions within her manors as she thought fit. She had a large personal income to indulge her tastes and the responsibilities that came with it to keep her occupied. It ought to have been enough.

But as the months went by and the impatient summons which she expected from her husband did not come, she grew uncertain. Had he forgotten he had a wife in England or did he perhaps think this was as good a way as any to make sure she stayed in the background? She felt piqued that he no longer even wrote that he missed her. His letters were all of the war, of the loss of men and the shortage of supplies and weapons. Things were not going well it seemed and she allowed that he had much to occupy him in the field. There had been reverses. The name of Montargis stood for a defeat and simultaneously disaster befell the English force under Sir John Fastolf at Ambrières in Maine.

Then, in the early summer of 1428, Salisbury sent word that he was coming to England on Bedford's orders to make a personal plea to the Council. Losses had been so heavy and morale had sunk so low that the army could not continue to hold what it had won unless the government would provide more men and more money.

Alice was in London to meet her husband and any doubts she had about his feelings for her were quickly dispelled.

'It is not only the Council he has come to woo,' Thomas Chaucer commented dryly, admiring the glory of an emerald collar worked by Byzantine craftsmen. It was one of several costly gifts Salisbury had brought her and his extravagance was the more surprising when he made it known to her that he himself intended to raise a large proportion of the money Bedford wanted.

'You must take back some of the jewels and borrow the money against them,' Alice suggested.

'I shall do no such thing,' Salisbury was roundly indignant. 'I am not so hard put that I am unable to give my wife a few trinkets. Never dare bring up such a matter again!'

'But Thomas, you will not secure against any of your property? If matters in France should still not prosper . . .'

'They will prosper, they must! And the rewards when the country is finally subdued will fall rich on those who have had a part in the conquest.'

'My father says you asked the Council for twenty-four thousand pounds. He says they are in no mood to spend such a sum in view of what the war has already cost.'

'As I am discovering to my cost. But I must raise at least

five hundred men-at-arms and better than two thousand archers, as well as bow-makers, carpenters, masons and miners. I will not return to France failed in the mission Bedford has entrusted to me. If the Council are too timid to take the long view I must encourage them with pledging more of my own fortune to the cause.'

'So be it then. My fortunes are yours.'

'And will be our children's.'

CHAPTER FIVE

ALICE AND Matilda were sorting skeins of wool, using the last of the pale light draining from a sharp November day. Fresh logs flared on the hearth, holding the dusk at bay a while longer. But when Cecily joined them, asking whether she should call the servants to prepare the supper table, Matilda sighed and dropped her hands in her lap.

'Aye and tell them to bring candles. I can no more in this gloom. See I am setting hanks of green by blue. My eyes are not young as once they were.'

'Why mother! I never thought to hear you admit such a thing! You are still so fair to look upon that age does not seem to have touched you.'

'Honey-tongue! My mirror tells me different – my eyes are not so dim as that . . . But listen, I hear horses. They are returned at last. I knew even your father must tire some time of putting that new hawk through its paces. Haste, Cecily, and take the wools away!'

'No, that is not my father and his friends. It is a solitary rider . . . and gathering up a weary horse by the sound of it!' Alice turned her head to listen to the erratic rhythm of the canter.

'Then let us see who comes.' Matilda led the way and two lads sprang to open the great oak door.

In the courtyard a man slipped easily from his saddle in the manner of one who spent the best part of his life there. Alice eyed his horse appreciatively. Even quivering with exhaustion and caked with mud it was a good mount.

'Look well to that mare,' she called suddenly to boys who swung their lanterns high, eager to see who the stranger was. 'Clean her down well with straw before you bed her.'

Alice turned back to the rider and nodded to him to enter. 'You have ridden hard but that beast must take some of the labour out of it,' she said over her shoulder as he followed her to the fire.

Matilda, hospitable with all who called at the manor, no matter what their degree, bustled forward with a cup of wine and a pie on a platter.

'Do you bring letters from my husband?'

'My news is for the lady Alice, Countess of Salisbury.'

'Then it is for me.' Alice was surprised. 'Have you come from France in such haste?'

'Yes lady.' The man took out a leather pouch which hung about his neck and drew from it a small package. 'I ride for my lord of Suffolk and on his orders this was passed to me at Calais. I was told that no time was to be lost on the way and scant rest taken,' he added meaningfully.

'Then take your ease now. You have earned it. Cecily see this good messenger is rewarded and tell John Edmondes he is to have a comfortable bed and all he needs.'

Matilda peered at the package in Alice's hands. 'It is from Thomas Montacute, sweeting? Why no, that is not his seal.'

'The leopards' heads are the arms of Suffolk.' Alice opened the letter and read what William de la Pole had to say:

My lady,

A heavy sorrow weights my hand as I struggle to make it do its task. It is loathe to give you pain but I compel it to its duty which is to tell you of the death of my revered commander and your honoured husband. I am the more bitter in my grief because the account I must give you is one of a most evil mischance.

It was during the action of the siege against Orleans which we are at present prosecuting. For sixty days the strife was unceasing with losses on both sides and the town's defence still appearing resolute despite all. My lord Salisbury, growing impatient of such delay, proposed a general assault and the better to consider what course to take, stood at the iron-barred window of one of the captured towers overlooking the city.

A great piece must have been levelled at the window and a shot struck the gratings which splintered, mortally wounding my lord about the head. Despite all that could be done by our surgeons he died two days later, that is yesternight, the third day of November. He was unable to speak clearly but when I watched with him in his last hours I made out the name 'Alice' murmured many times in the way of a man grieving to leave what is dearest to him on Earth, even for the privilege of meeting his God.

It shall be my tenderest care to carry out whatever instructions you send me regarding the conveyance of my lord's remains to their rest. No ceremony shall be overlooked which may do honour to this most honourable of men and I only regret that in succeeding to the command I am unable to escort his body back to England myself. Give your orders to the messenger who bears this letter and know they will be entirely fulfilled by one proud to serve you now and always.

Suffolk ..

Alice read the letter to its end before she spoke. Then she simply said: 'Salisbury is killed in action at Orleans.'

'God receive his soul!' Matilda made the sign of the cross and bowed her head in brief prayer. 'You will want to go to your prie-dieu, my love. I will send your father to you the minute he returns.' Matilda slipped her arm around her daughter's shoulders and turned her gently towards the stairs. 'Cecily, do you take her up and I will prepare a soothing cordial.'

When Thomas Chaucer entered Alice's bedchamber less than an hour later he found her dry-eyed and composed.

'So child, you must don the wimple! This is sad news – saddest of all for the army. Salisbury was one of the best generals England has ever had. He never suffered a single defeat in any engagement where he had overall command and men believed themselves invincible when they followed him.'

'Yes, I am proud to have been his wife,' Alice answered quietly. She knew her father would not expect any pretence that she was a broken-hearted widow but she added, clear-eyed in her honesty: 'And I am saddened because when we were together in the summer I came nearer to him than I had thought possible. I would have gone back with him to France in July if he had not wanted me to deal with some matters of business on his behalf, and God willing, I might have conceived a son for him. Now it is too late.'

'I know, I know. It is often too late for what we meant to do. But you must not blame yourself. Your marriage made an uneasy start but I saw how Salisbury appreciated having you at his side when he had politicians to deal with instead of soldiers. You would have fulfilled all your wifely duties in time, had he been spared.'

*   *   *

On the earliest day it could be deemed proper for Alice to receive a visit from a man outside the family, Will Bylton rode up to the manor early and found her writing letters in the winter parlour.

'Will! How good to see you again!' She rose to greet him, the folds of her dark velvet skirts scattering sheets of vellum as she swept past the table.

She allowed him to embrace her briefly and then stood back to look up at him, her eyes full of teasing laughter.

'What think you to the wimple then?' A slender finger traced the white lawn band which stretched beneath her chin from one side of the demure widowly coif to the other. 'I am not accustomed to it yet. I cannot imagine what it will be like in summer to wear so much covering about the head – stifling I should think!'

'It makes you look rather forbidding . . . But only because you are no longer the little girl I can put in her place, I suppose. Nay, to be truthful it becomes you. I have heard my father admire the way the chin-band makes a woman carry her head, high and proud. However, you always walked so . . . ' He appeared lost in thought for a moment and then added lightly: 'You can always shed it by marrying again, and this time why not try me for a husband?'

'Constant Will! Do you never change?'

'Not I! But let us talk of you. You are not sorrowing for Thomas Montacute it seems?'

'Then if it seems so it is *unseemly*! I act more suitable to widowhood with others, but not with my father or with you. I cannot bring myself to perform ritual expressions of grief all the time. Yet that is not to say I have not wept for Salisbury. His was a good life, cut short at the height of his ability and value to his country.'

'Aye, Bedford will miss him by all accounts. Suffolk has succeeded to the command I believe.'

'Yes. My father does not think it a good appointment. He feels Suffolk has other talents, other ambitions, and that his whole heart will not be in soldiering as Salisbury's was. He is seldom wrong in his judgement of men.'

'I saw Suffolk once. I was only a lad but I . . .'

'You saw him?' Alice failed to conceal the sudden interest which sharpened her tone. 'When was – oh, of course! That must have been when he came to Ewelme for the funeral of his brother, Michael, killed at Agincourt. I remember now. I was in Somerset visiting some connection of the Burghershs with my mother.'

'Strange that Michael de la Pole should decide he wanted to be buried here where he had no property. Was it really because of the way your father used to talk of the beauty of the countryside hereabouts when he happened to share an officers' watch with him?'

'So I have heard.'

'Where is Salisbury to be buried?'

'Oh, he has been most explicit in his directions. He wished a chantry to be built to house his tomb at Bisham Church in Berkshire. It is a triple tomb and he will lie in the centre with his first wife on the one hand leaving a vacant place for me to join him in God's good time on the other. In accordance with his orders his own position will be slightly elevated above his womenfolk.' She savoured the last remark as if enjoying a wry, private joke, but added without bitterness: 'However, I shall not make my last bed in Bisham but here in Ewelme were my father and mother will also lie – God keep the time afar off!'

'That is well for I shall bide here, too,' said Will simply.

'Why, what a gloomy turn we take – though it is not surprising for I have had so much to do with the trappings of death these last weeks. Even now I am arranging for the giving of meat, bread and drink to three poor people daily in his name. Also a thousand masses are to be said for his soul and I must provide for payment. He left orders that I should be present to hear the masses and serve the poor folk food with my own hands! What do you think to that?'

'I think he mistook his woman!' Will laughed. 'But are you not afraid to disobey the last wishes of the dead?'

'What a curious question to come from you, Will. I have heard you doubt the teaching of Holy Church often enough.'

'Nay, softly. Not all of it.'

'Well, I am not irreverent. I make a good confession, attend Mass regularly, give alms generously . . . what would you? But I did not fear Salisbury alive and I do not fear him dead. God alone judges me if anyone does and He knows my point of view as well as Thomas Montacute's.'

*   *   *

Affairs which had to be cleared up following Salisbury's death continued to occupy Alice over the ensuing months but at last there came a day when she was able to say: 'It is done. Now let him rest. My duties as Thomas Montacute's wife are surely over.'

Her father had been helping her to dispatch some last business. They were alone in the quaint lozenge-shaped gallery room at their London home and, as she watched him handling the documents which she had just signed under his direction, it occurred to her that his movements were unusually deliberate. Meticulously he rolled the sheets of heavy parchment for all the world like some hired clerk making importance about little tasks – and he normally brisk and decisive. She had watched him times uncounted when he shuffled state papers into deft bundles, signing and sealing them as casually as if they be his wife's housekeeping accounts.

'Oh, I know you so well, Thomas Chaucer,' she thought fondly. 'You are not arranging my papers, you are choosing your words.' She waited.

'Aye, well! You have blunted many a quill on this work. You had best get yourself a reliable secretary,' he said at last. 'You cannot be always borrowing one of mine and the correspondence relating to your property alone is full-time employment for an industrious man . . . You have enough to do with your personal letters . . . On that subject may I observe that you and William de la Pole appear to have a great deal to say to one another . . .'

Ah, there it was at last. Alice smiled inwardly at the oblique approach.

'My lord Suffolk has been most helpful, most attentive', she replied in an indifferent tone.

'The correspondence between you seems somewhat protracted. He dispatched Salisbury's bones last November and it is now nearly June. I confess I am curious to know what you can still find to say.'

This was surrender indeed! Thomas Chaucer frankly owning to curiosity.

'He has written me of his problems in command and I have answered as befits me, telling how the building of the chantry went forward and describing the design of Salisbury's tomb, its brasses and such-like.

'As a soldier he will find that very cheerful no doubt.'

Alice ignored the challenge and her father went on: 'You might be interested to know that Suffolk's command has been something less than successful up to now. The latest news I have is that he has been forced to raise the siege of Orleans and retire to Jargeau. This chit they have started to call the Maid of Orleans is giving a deal of trouble. The last dispatch said she was heading her troops towards Jargeau itself!'

'You have always said England could not hope to rule France beyond the span of a few years . . . Could this be the turning point you predicted, father?'

'Pah! England has never ruled France but only occupied

a portion of it. Titles, treaties – these are tokens and may be set aside. Given a resurgence of French national feeling the Treaty of Troyes will not deter the dauphin from reclaiming his inheritance, while the Duke of Burgundy is too shifty an ally for my liking . . . And now there is this tiresome wench putting ideas into Charles of Valois' doddering head and the fear of God into our army, it appears.' For the moment both had forgotten Suffolk.

'But surely this peasant girl, this Maid of Orleans who has set herself at the head of the dauphin's army, can be of no account!'

'She is a visionary and that is always dangerous. Our own King Hal believed he had God on his side and it was the inspiration of his command. If the French – and our own army too – believe that God has changed his loyalty . . . '

They regarded each other in thoughtful silence until Thomas Chaucer recalled his interest in de la Pole.

'I have seen little of Suffolk since he succeeded to the title. He was among the first to be stricken with the flux at Harfleur and when his father himself fell ill he had William conveyed back to England. It was a wise precaution as it turned out. The old earl died shortly afterwards and his eldest son, Michael, fell at Agincourt, as you know, leaving no sons. How has William de la Pole filled out to manhood? He was a slender handsome boy as I remember.'

Alice felt sure her father must have met Suffolk on some occasion in recent years and understood that this was merely his way of eliciting an opinion from her.

She answered frankly with a laugh: 'There is nothing of the slender boy about him now. He is strongly built and very much a man. Handsome as you say and graceful in his manners.' She hesitated conjuring up a face in her mind, a face not well enough known to be sharp in every detail but haunting none the less. A squarish face with a determined close-bearded jaw and a strong brow overshadowing dark brooding eyes.

'Pah! You answer and you do not answer! An end to this tourney of words, daughter, and tell me plainly if you think to wed the man!'

101

'He has not asked me yet!'

'But you know that he will, eh? And you will have him . . . aye, I see it in your face. Well, well, it is reasonable you should make your own choice of a mate this time. Suffolk is a wealthy man and your joint property could make you both a power in this realm. Mark you, I have sometimes thought the de la Poles a reckless breed. You should consider, too, what is to become of your William if peace is made with France and he comes home to civil life.'

'You would like the match, though?'

'I would like to see you happily settled and raising my grandchildren! No use to go on amassing riches and honours if there is none of our blood to inherit. If you want de la Pole for husband it is well with me.' Thomas Chaucer broke off passing a hand wearily across his forehead.

Alice was puzzled to find her father hesitant and unsure where such a vital family matter was in question.

He straightened suddenly and to her relief said more in his usual way: 'In truth it is an alliance we may take pride in and I scarcely know what arouses these misgivings in me . . . Ah, it is nothing but a folly! I grow old and like any chimney-corner-granny feel a premonition in every change of the wind.'

*   *   *

William had been defeated and captured. His desperate ten-day defence of Jargeau was finally unavailing and he was a prisoner in the hands of Joan of Arc.

'I am now doing what I can to arrange my ransom and release, also that of my brother John, who was taken with me. God send the matter does not take long. We are not shown such courtesy here as would make us disposed to stay long,' he wrote to Alice irritably.

The months went by and Alice was surprised to find that she had grown close to Suffolk, even while their separation lengthened. It amused her to think that she could be wooed by the excellence of a man's prose style, but there was no doubt that his ability to write in a way which made her identify herself with his problems and his dreams had tipped the balance, if anything were needed to decide her in the choice of a third husband.

So in time she found herself betrothed – just as she had been courted – by letter. Nothing would have induced her to admit impatience for his coming but the days passed slowly until at last he sent word that he was free. His brother, John, must remain a hostage until he could complete payment of the twenty thousand pounds ransom. But this might be more speedily accomplished once he reached England.

He came for her in the early summer of 1430. Alice had thankfully cast aside her widow's clothes and was waiting in the shade of the pink blossoming chestnut tree, which dappled the modest courtyard of her father's London house, making the sunlight play upon the cobbles and shimmer over the ornamental fountain brought from Italy and the well-stocked fish-pond where Friday's supper sought obscurity.

She heard when Suffolk and his men arrived at the front of the house but she did not stir. Her father appeared briefly, and indicating where she sat, left William de la Pole regarding her from the doorway.

For some seconds he continued to look at her until she found the scrutiny unnerving and rose, her hands fluttering in agitation amid the folds of her gown.

When he came towards her she was aware of a quality in the way he moved which made her think of an animal in its hunting prime, unconsciously graceful, wasting no energy, covering the ground in his own good time.

'So, my Alice. We are together at last!' He did not touch her but his eyes were so intense that it was like a physical contact. 'You are incomparably beautiful. I desired you even when I looked on you as Salisbury's wife. I do not have to learn you to love you. I know how to encompass you with love, as instinct tells me how to draw breath.'

She recoiled, her mind groping for the protection of formal phrases and was surprised to hear herself saying: 'I recognise you, too, William de la Pole. You are the man I have known in my heart.'

'Your hand in mine, then . . .'

'My hand in yours!' said Alice surrendering both of them. She was instantly snatched into the sort of embrace which presumed the courtyard to be a private place. Behind discreet stone tracery ornamenting the upper storey of the house, Matilda gasped and stepped heavily upon her husband's foot.

*   *   *

Alice drew her furred cloak closer about her and wondered, not for the first time in the space of half-an-hour, why William had to be taking part in a tournament on such a bitter November day. They had been married for two years and this was the first opportunity she had had to see his skill in arms. Unthinkable that she should have missed it, but truly it was hard to find enjoyment while freezing almost to insensibility.

One did not expect men to relish full plate armour and the oppressive weight of a jousting helm in mid-summer. Yet out of consideration for their womenfolk, who must sit inactive for some hours on an ill-sheltered dais, they might at least confine the contest to spring or early autumn, she thought.

She turned to bid Cecily fetch her a cup of warmed wine. 'Merciful Heaven, girl, I only pray I do not look as you. You look like a plucked fowl!'

Cecily stretched a stiff smile. 'I wish my lord might take his turn so that we could at least cheer and stamp to warm ourselves.'

'We will do no such thing! This is a royal tournament not a ram-wrestling on one of our manors.' It was a private game they sometimes permitted themselves. Cecily would pretend she was about to forget the graceful manners Alice had taught her and the prospect of how she might outrage the company if she did, amused them. The masquerade of Cecily as a well-born lady had been so successful that even William accepted her status unquestioning and the young king addressed her almost timidly. Stature and dignity of bearing gave her a formidable presence and few guessed that her chilly reserve was an armour against questions about family and background which might prove embarrassing to answer.

It pleased Alice very much to see Cecily treated with respect, for the elegant composure of this gaunt young woman was her own achievement. But she considered herself amply repaid by the companionship of a personality for which she took no credit. Cecily had a logical mind and a placid nature, invaluable qualities in a waiting-woman. Furthermore she was incorruptibly loyal.

'With Cecily you have no need of a bodyguard. I'd as lief try to shoe a swan as get by her to do you harm,' William had said.

Looking along the stand Alice saw that a brazier of warm coals was being set close to the boy on the carved wooden throne. He looked glad to see it, holding out his childish hands to the glow. Had he wanted to come to Greenwich to watch the tournament? They said it was in his honour, but it was held for the amusement and pleasure of those who governed him and his kingdom. Some eleven-year-old boys might have delighted in the exhilaration of the charge, the skill of men and horses weaving in close combat, the atmosphere of dedicated ferocity in which contestants went through the ritual of killing in order to learn better how to live. Not Henry, thought Alice. He would have preferred to hear a well-sung mass or a learned sermon.

Poor Henry! What a lad to follow his father. He had had two coronations but it took more than blessed oil to make a king, and neither ceremony had augured well for his reign. The first coronation, in England, had been hastily performed in order that he might go to France and be ready when his Uncle Bedford considered the moment auspicious for a second crowning. And although Bedford had done all in his power to make the coronation in Paris a success, that had been an ill-managed affair, too, by all accounts.

A sudden stir among the women along the royal stand brought Alice's attention back to the tournament ground. She saw that at last William's turn had come and he was riding to claim her scarf upon the tip of his lance. He was indeed a sight to arouse the interest of the women, she noted with satisfaction. His armour, worked by Milanese craftsmen, was uncluttered with ornament and its sheer, gleaming lines were skilfully moulded over his powerful body. While the squire waited at

105

his master's stirrup with the plumed helm in his hands, William smiled down upon her from his courser, lips drawn back to show strong white teeth in a smile of fierce exhilaration.

'He looks as though just to be alive were inspiration of the most noble kind,' she thought, and her heart beat faster making her forget how cold she was. She rose, drawing from under her fur cloak the scarf of gold gauze and speared it on the lance-point while courtiers applauded.

'I ride for you, my lady.' He saluted her and taking up his helm cantered back to the end of the barrier from which he would make his charge.

He was followed by six of his men in livery and Alice watched as his armourer stepped forward to ensure that the guiders securing his breastplate were in position. More of their men waited in the background. It was a formidable show of strength. Alice sat forward in sudden awareness. None of the other combatants representing the king that day had such an impressive company on the field. Her eyes took in the leopards' heads on the banners on William's shield, on the trapper covering his horse. Such display might well give offence, she thought uneasily. It was a fault of William's that, being so much accustomed to a lavish style of living, he was unaware of its effect on others.

The young stranger knight who had come to challenge him was simply accoutred. But he bore himself well and was clearly a favourite among the comers or else he would not have been facing her husband in the sixth and final contest.

The trumpets sounded for the encounter and the two coursers thundered to meet one another in the middle of the field.

'As well they now use a barrier betwixt the riders,' Cecily commented.

'Aye, there used to be horrible injuries when they crashed by all accounts and these events are not always without ugly mishaps even under today's rules . . . Ah, they have both missed their aim! How well Suffolk handles the courser – only see how short he makes it swerve!'

'He is far more skilled than his opponent, of course.'

'But the young man rides debonair enough,' Alice was prepared to be generous. 'He may well take the prize for the best of the stranger knights.'

'That is to be a fine falcon, I believe. What does my lord stand to win?'

'Ah, there is a rare diamond at stake! I shall have it set in a pendant necklet if it is judged to be ours.'

As the contestants rode against one another yet again there was a sudden unrelated sound. William's opponent appeared to be arrested in full charge and his courser was forced back on its haunches, hooves flailing. Then it swung away from the barrier and galloped across the field.

The crowd could not at first grasp what had happened. They saw that the rider was lying still on the ground, his arms and legs asprawl. Yet he had not been thrown from his horse. He seemed to have been dragged backwards from the saddle.

Alice saw that William, who was not within a lance-length of his opponent when he disappeared, was peering in a bewildered way over the barrier.

'Why, whatever . . . Oh, see the barrier is rent! That sound was the wood tearing. His lance caught in it and he was jerked from the saddle before the shaft splintered. Is he hurt or just stunned?' Alice viewed the still figure on the ground with anxiety.

'They are going to look at him. There is the king's own surgeon. Would you like me to send one of the pages to ask what ails him?'

'Yes, Cecily, do so . . . No stay! Look, I see the men shaking their heads. Dear God, he cannot be dead of such a mischance!'

'Here is my lord. Indeed he looks grave.'

'Alice, my love.' William stood below the dais looking up at her with all the vitality gone out of him. 'This is an unhappy affair. De Mordrey is dead. His neck is broken, the surgeon says. I can scarce believe it.'

'Oh, rest his soul!' Alice was aware of the moans and gasps of the women sitting around her as they overheard the news. She leaned down to William laying the palm of her hand against his cheek and caring nothing for those who looked on.

'Do not blame yourself, dear heart. You had naught to do with the accident.'

'But such a thing to happen in a day's sport! He was his old father's only son, given to him late in life. Who can break such news? Had he gone into battle it . . . Ah well, I must go speak with the king. Wait here for me.'

There was already a crowd about the king and Alice watched William make his way through them. Henry listened to what he had to say and passed a hand across his eyes in a tired gesture at odds with his years. Then she saw that he was showing William a roll of parchment. Cardinal Beaufort stood beside him shaking his head and fingering the great jewelled crucifix upon his breast.

'Cecily, what are they saying I wonder. I feel that something has happened more than we know. The king has a letter it seems. And are those not Bedford's riders standing behind the king?'

She saw William beckon forward the heralds. Their trumpets called that the king would speak and when they died away there was Henry's clear young voice telling of the death of Anne, Duchess of Bedford. The news took everyone by surprise and the murmur as it was relayed to those at the back of the crowding spectators, overwhelmed the king's added regrets about de Mordrey.

'This is an ill-omened day!' said Alice. 'I shall be thankful to be gone from this place, lest worse befall. We see one tragedy and in the instant news of another reaches us. Anne of Bedford gone! It seems impossible, she who was so alive!'

'Some sickness must have overtaken her,' Cecily replied. 'My lord returns and he will tell us more.'

Alice went to meet him. 'William, what a sad thing this is!'

'Yes, you attended Anne closely and she held you a good friend, I know. Ah, Bedford will feel this deeply.' He took her hand and patted it soothingly, but she could see that his thoughts were not with her. 'You know Anne's death has political implications too. She often managed to smooth over misunderstandings between her husband and Philip of Burgundy. But come, the king wants to speak with you.'

108

As they approached the royal party, Henry stepped forward staying Alice from the low curtsy she would have made.

'Lady Alice, we know that you were some time with our aunt, Anne of Bedford. You will remember with us that Christmas we spent together and how she was always laughing. We shall think of her whenever we are at Eltham.'

'Sire, may I ask how the duchess came to her death?'

'Through her good-heartedness, through her compassion for the poor! There has been widespread infection in Paris this autumn and this dispatch from Uncle Bedford relates that she insisted upon visiting the poor in hospital, the Hôtel Dieu. She took the fever herself and despite all that could be done, weakened and died. It was the death of a truly pious woman. God will receive her soul joyously.'

He spoke with such fervour that Alice was startled. Surely she must be mistaken in thinking he told the tale with relish?

He continued speaking rapidly, his eyes bright with zeal for every detail. 'There was a mass celebrated in Notre Dame and the relics of Saint Genevieve were taken to the cathedral, while prayers were said for her recovery. Our Uncle of Bedford made a pilgrimage, walking round the churches of Paris, too, so you see nothing that could be done to save her was overlooked. We will mourn with my Uncle . . . but we will rejoice for Anne.'

Alice sought William's eyes. She was thankful that he understood and at once excused himself from the king's presence. When they reached their apartments she found herself unable to control a violent shivering. Not the cheerful blaze of logs upon the hearth, not the warm colour of the wine of Burgundy, not even the comforting clasp of William's arms about her could shut out the chill sensation of death.

'I am surprised, sweeting, that you take Anne's death so hard . . . It is after all in the nature of things that we must lose many if we ourselves be spared.'

'But it is not grief for Anne that robs me of my ease!'

'Why, what then?'

'I scarce know. She was but twenty-nine, about the same age as I, and that prompts the thought that I am not immortal.

Nor are you, as the accident to de Mordrey warns. Moreover I am anxious over the way Henry is developing!'

'The king!' William threw himself back in his chair with a roar of laughter. 'Oh I am blessed with such a wife! So you mislike the way Henry is being reared do you? Alack for Beaufort and Gloucester, they will tremble at your displeasure!'

Alice smiled despite herself, but answered firmly: 'Mock if you will, but that boy is becoming too preoccupied with spiritual matters. It is not usual in a young lad. In fact, to be plain I believe it denotes an unhealthy mind!'

'Alice! Never say such a thing. Never even think it unless we are safe on one of our own manors! Merciful God you speak treason . . . Besides you are wrong. Henry is an intelligent boy and takes his duties very seriously. If he is unworldly, his ministers can more than compensate for the deficiency.'

She noticed then that although William had sounded shocked he was inwardly pleased. Their eyes held and she understood what was in his mind.

'I intend to serve the House of Lancaster right ardently,' he said softly. 'And the House of de la Pole likewise.'

'Aye,' Alice nodded. Then on a sudden thought: 'What the House of de la Pole needs most just now is an heir.'

'Agreed! Well that is a matter we can attend to without delay.'

CHAPTER SIX

IN BUSTLING townships and proud cities, in ale-houses and counting houses, wherever Englishmen met together in the spring months of 1433, they deplored the uneasy state of the country and said times had never been so bad. Those who had journeyed on lonely roads curdled the blood with tales of marauding robber bands, ambushing travellers with impunity, while the haute lords who might have brought them to justice were either engaged in France or preoccupied with political conspiracy and no longer cared if the law was broken upon their property.

Furthermore, these same lords now had such vast numbers of retainers under arms that when they approached a town the burgesses must look hard lest it be an invasion force, so great was the clamour of their coming and so menacing the show of weapons.

Old men shook their heads and said the younger generation no longer gave their loyalty where an unquestioning sense of duty once directed, but bartered it for advancement or protection. There was a mood of factions and talk of this champion rather than that champion – Gloucester against Beaufort. It boded no good to anyone.

This was tavern gossip and the chatter of good wives across market stalls. But for those who were more closely involved with the government of the country, the focus of dissatisfaction was sharper. It resolved itself upon the three men who were steering England through the years of the king's minority, Gloucester and Beaufort at home and Bedford in France.

111

It had become apparent that Gloucester would be content with nothing short of absolute power in England. He had challenged Beaufort's right to a seat on the governing council, 'throwing his cardinal's hat in his face', so it was said, claiming that His Eminence would put the interests of Rome above those of his own country. Deviously the duke worked his own supporters into the Council. The treasurer, Sir Walter Hungerford, was forced to make way for Lord Scrope of Masham. Lord Cromwell was dismissed from the office of Chamberlain and the Great Seal given to John Stafford.

Gloucester might not be strong enough to control both the Council and Parliament yet. But who could halt the thrust of his ambition?

Bedford had curbed him in the past, but he was in France and, moreover, public feeling had turned suddenly and viciously against him. His conduct of affairs in the territory which had been won had failed to enrich the economy at home, while England continued to be drained of manpower in order to hold these unprofitable boundaries. Nor did this personal attack overlook the Regent's marriage to Jacquetta of Luxembourg only four months after the death of his first wife, Anne.

An ageing man's fancy had turned to a pretty young maid not eighteen summers, people said, and he had married her. He knew Philip of Burgundy well, knew he would regard the short mourning period as an insult to a beloved sister's memory. Marrying Jacquetta without Philip's permission – for he was her overlord – would be another blow to the crumbling Anglo-Burgundian alliance.

But he had wed her despite all.

'Some say Bedford is as besotted with this wife as he was with Anne and that she has made him forget statecraft.' William related to Alice what he had heard at Westminster.

'Then they do him much wrong! An alliance with Luxembourg must strengthen his position in Paris, while Burgundy serves his own interests in any event and has never been a reliable ally.'

'Peace, my heart's companion! Do not round on me so fiercely. You know I am for Bedford.'

'Those memories are short which do not prize his past ser-

112

vice to this country. He has been fighting a war on two fronts this long while . . . not only the enemy but the Council here at home who have kept him short of men, money and supplies.'

'Aye, you speak truth. I fear that in the end his life's work in France will have gone for nothing. It seems to me that the only solution must ultimately be to make a peace. It is a pity England has been deprived of his wise government at home all these years.'

Doubt flickered in Alice's eyes for a moment. If Bedford had held the place he deserved in the government of England it would surely have hampered designs which she believed were taking shape in her husband's mind. But she was not so foolish as to let him read that thought.

With womanly irrelevance she said: 'Bedford deserves some comfort in his private life. He must be a lonely man without his Anne.'

In mid-summer Bedford came home to England, bringing his bride with him. At the end of July he appeared before Parliament to defend himself against charges of negligence and maladministration, which had been made known to him in France. Chancellor John Stafford played the part of peace-maker assuring Bedford that neither the king, nor the Duke of Gloucester, nor any member of the Council, believed ill of him and that the king declared him his 'dearest uncle'.

An outbreak of plague caused Parliament to be prorogued in August and by the time it re-assembled at the end of November the stabilising influence of Bedford's presence in the country was already being felt.

This time he was received by the members with every honour. The Speaker, Roger Hunt, paid tribute to his sense of duty and his valour in the field, entreating him, for England's sake, not to risk his life in battle again. It was a testimony of genuine affection. Men might speak ill of Bedford in his absence, but when he was among them his ability and his honesty shamed their injustice.

Having regained his good standing at home Bedford used it to curb his brother's influence on the Council. He contrived to replace Lord Scrope as treasurer, by Lord Cromwell and

William was appointed Steward of the royal household, succeeding Sir Robert Babthorpe.

Alice looked forward to telling her father of the appointment. The news would cheer him. He had not been in the best of health for some months, suffering sudden pains in the chest which made him gasp and reel, though he hastened to conceal the fact.

Matilda had begged him to allow their physician to make an examination but he stalwartly refused. When she urged him to rest he rode all the more ardently after hounds and sat longer with his friends over many a cask of choice wine.

Her mother's letters being full of concern, Alice was thankful to have an excuse for going home.

*   *   *

At first she thought her mother had been unduly alarmed. Thomas Chaucer was as vital a figure as ever, welcoming her at the door of the manor. But she soon observed that he looked fatigued by the excitement of her arrival and later, when they talked across the remnants of a lavish supper, she saw his hand grope beneath the folds of his robe at his breast.

Her own heart turned faint within her. She wanted to cry out 'Oh my father, do not leave me. We have so much to do yet to make you proud. I have not set my child upon your knee, nor added my honour to yours.' But there had never been such words between them.

Aloud, she said roundly: 'I declare I am come home for some good sport. I have brought a gerfalcon with me, my father, who will fly to a partridge or a hare so that you have but to blink your eyes and will not see him strike.'

'Ho! And have I not a bird out of Norway who can better him? Say, my Mald,' he appealed to his wife, 'what wager will you put on my Kersten against all comers?'

They rode out the following day with their champion birds on their wrists. Behind them rode their falconers and Alice had to wait until her father left off praising his new man – who had views on luring, diet and handling when in mew which clearly inspired his master's respect – before she could fit in an account of William's appointment.

'Ah, that is good to hear. It will be but the first step on a climb to much higher office if I am not mistaken. I believe your husband desires a hand upon this country's reins above everything. But you must tell him from me that the strong are not always popular, the best leaders must not fear the clamour of a mob nor bow to it.'

'Why do you bid me tell him that? Do you think William has need of such a warning? He has a strong stomach for a fight.'

'He will need guile, too, and a cool head,' Thomas Chaucer answered indirectly.

Alice felt herself drawn to Ewelme many times during the following months. The country seemed better ordered – at least on the surface – and even after Bedford had returned to France, the feeling of confidence which he had restored in established authority was maintained. So whenever William would spare her, she slipped away from court to be with her father and they enjoyed again the companionship of earlier days.

Realising that his strength was failing, she discouraged him from the chase when she could and coaxed him instead to their collection of books. Often they spent a day re-appraising their favourite passages from Geoffrey Chaucer's writings, and Nicholas Bylton would ride over to join them at this pastime with much relish. Sometimes, when he could tear himself away from his troublesome tenants, Will came too, though he seldom stayed long, seeming always restless in Alice's company.

Yet Alice was at Windsor, as ill-chance would have it, when her father collapsed after entertaining a number of his friends to supper on a late autumn day in 1434. Matilda sent a messenger in haste. But before the man had put ten miles between himself and the manor-house Thomas Chaucer died in his wife's arms.

'Do not weep for me, Mald, and do not be spending great sums on Masses for my soul. Rather pray that you come to the same destination as I, one day, for I shall never be quite

115

comfortable without you to look after me.' His wife saw that he was slipping into unconsciousness when with a final effort, his voice slow but strong, he said: 'Tell Alice I got nothing in this life I loved better than my daughter . . . And bid her . . . get with child!'

*   *   *

By the following year it had become apparent to many men of reason that there must be peace with France. The Earl of Arundel, a cool-headed and imaginative general, on whom Bedford had relied heavily, died of battle-wounds, and Bedford himself was in Rouen, too weak and ill to travel.

A peace conference was called in Arras and William was named among the British ambassadors.

'We intend to make a good showing,' he told Alice. 'I shall take some of our best gold and silver plate with me and do you look what jewelled chains and clasps will be richest for my apparel, my love. I will be guided by your choice!'

'So you are away to France in great state and will leave me to my embroidery,' she teased. 'Who else goes?'

'Huntingdon is with me and Hungerford. Lyndwood goes too, of course.'

'Oh, they go with *you*, do they? Are you leading the party, then?'

'Peace to your bantering tongue, you know I do not.' William's sudden scowl was a dangerous sign to those who stood in awe of him. But to Alice it made him seem like a sulky boy. He recognised the expression in her eyes and smiled wryly. 'Beaufort is nominally head of the embassy, but he will not be there part of the time and the Archbishop of York, John Kemp, leads us . . . They will hear my voice just the same. It is well known that I favour peace. I have been at some pains to make it so.'

'Aye, but what price will buy a peace at this time? It seems to me England chooses a foul day to go to market!'

'You are right. I fear we shall be asked much. Yet whatever the cost it will have to be met in the end.'

'Well, I shall spend some time in Ewelme. My mother has

a great need of me just now. She writes that she will not survive my father long and her mind is taken up with the brass like-nesses on the tomb in which they will both lie.'

'Ah yes, the tomb! To be sure, you showed me the draughts. It is a modest memorial for such a great man as your father.'

Alice saw his slight, disparaging frown and said coolly: 'It is as he directed. My father had no love of display for its own sake.'

'No, by the Host, he had solid worth!' William answered quick and hearty. 'Why, when I only think of the offices he held – Constable of Wallingford Castle, aye and Taunton, Steward of the Chiltern Hundreds, Chief Butler to the king in three reigns, Speaker of the Commons are but the first that come to mind . . . Tell me, I have often wondered, yet never asked, why with so many honours and such great wealth he was not knighted?'

Alice smiled slowly. 'He paid a sum in the right quarter to buy himself free of a knighthood.'

William was astonished. 'But why? Surely it cannot be true!'

'Of a certainty it is. As you well know the government places heavier financial burdens on those who wish to flaunt titles than those who style themselves simply. And it suited him in politics to be just Thomas Chaucer, a man of the people.'

'By heaven, I should never have thought of such a thing!'

'No, my husband. You are a very different man from my father. But you will have power in your way as he gained it in his.'

*　　　*　　　*

The delegation had gone to Arras prepared to acknowledge Charles of Valois as ruler of the territory currently under his control. But it was demanded they should recognise him as Charles VII thus yielding Henry's claim to the crown of France. It was a condition that could not possibly be met and the English quit the conference room in anger.

Philip of Burgundy at last saw an opportunity to break

117

his alliance, and with an easy conscience. He blamed England for the breakdown of talks and immediately opened his own negotiations with the French. Territorially he was allowed to retain Mâcon, Auxerre and Ponthieu, Boulogne and a number of Somme towns of strategic value. In addition he was freed from the payment of homage for all his fiefs while Charles lived. He was well pleased.

But for Bedford, the news which his messengers rode relay to bring him from Arras, worked like a slow poison. Lying sick and helpless at Rouen he knew that his efforts to hold France for his brother's son would end in failure. He was forty-six years old and he died with a defeated heart.

'I was with him in his last moments on this earth,' William wrote to Alice. 'I knew not how to comfort him for he clearly foresaw what will come of events at Arras. He entrusted to my keeping the Great Seal of silver which his brother, our late king, gave him to authenticate his acts as Regent. I shall bear it home with me. You may look for my coming before the end of the year.'

*　　　*　　　*

Four months after his return to England, in March of 1436, William went into Norfolk on business for the king. He was appointed commissioner to suppress riots which had broken out in Norwich.

'Give the leaders a patient hearing, my lord,' Alice urged earnestly. 'My father was always used to say let a man speak out his anger and you disarm him.'

'Thomas Chaucer is not dealing with this affray – I am! What might be good advice for the conduct of the Commons does not answer a show of violence,' William growled.

'I think only of your good and just name. You are sometimes hasty in your temper and if a wife may not warn you against it, who may?' Alice was placating but persistent.

'Very well. I will mind me of your counsel. Get you to see your mother and take my blessing and loving duty to her.'

Alice knew the dismissal was her punishment for presuming to advise William, unasked. But she was glad to accept it. Nicholas Bylton had written to her of Matilda's growing infirmity.

'It seems rather a failure of the spirit than the flesh,' he had said. 'You alone could bring her into better cheer.'

Alice set out for Ewelme without delay, and once there fell vigorously to the task of bracing Matilda. Her efforts to halt her mother's decline, however, met with small success. Not by any persuasion could Matilda be induced to take proper nourishment or rest. At meals she waved aside the tempting dishes she had ordered to please her daughter, and pecked meagrely at a wafer of bread and a morsel of cold game. She filled her days with meticulous attention to every task about the household, flitting from the still-room to the laundry, the kitchens to the dairy. Before her fled the maids who shook the hangings and beat the tapestries, who churned the butter and brewed the ale, who scrubbed and polished and washed, sewed – and sighed to find their tasks never done while Matilda's eyes searched restlessly about the manor. Her nights she filled with prayers and with vigils at the window of her chamber, as though she watched for a tardy traveller.

Alice pleaded, coaxed and reasoned by turns, trying to get her mother to take better care of herself. When all failed she considered frightening her with the consequences of sinful self-destruction. But she could not find the heart to be so cruel. A pious woman all her life, Matilda was advancing with a simple, eager faith towards a benign Father who would reunite her with her Thomas. And in the end Alice let her go.

It was April when Matilda died. In the same month terrible news reached England. Paris fell to the French.

'I thank God my Uncle Matt did not live to hear this news,' Cecily said when Alice told her. 'He had such proud memories of leading the Ewelme archers behind your father at Agincourt, and talked of the rich land they helped to win for England. We are seeing much change in our time, are we not?'

'Aye, and will see more.'

'What will my lord, your husband, say to these tidings?'

'As to that, I learn he will go into Normandy with York.

119

They will be looking for a peaceful means to safeguard what we still hold in France. William has advocated peace this long while as you know.'

'Yes and this will strengthen support for him, and weaken the position of the Duke of Gloucester leading the war party, will it not?'

Alice wheeled round from the packets of letters before her on the table and regarded Cecily keenly, watching the swift decisive strokes of her needle and her head bent diligently over her work.

'You are very sharp, mistress,' she replied at last and Cecily could hear by the tone that she was smiling.

'I have been well-tutored, madam,' was the deceptively meek answer.

CHAPTER SEVEN

It was little more than a half-hour after eight and already the freshness had faded from the day leaving it prematurely full-blown. The air in the little church was stale and Alice buried her nose in a spice-scented kerchief. She really must insist that John Seynesbury called the villagers to Mass earlier when she was spending the summer months at Ewelme.

Of course they liked to be out at first light in the fields, getting a few hours work done before the heat of day. Father John was a tolerant man and turned a blind eye to this Sunday labour. But she could not abide in this rank heat again.

Then looking through the carved chancel screen she became ashamed of her petulance. The sight of the kneeling people – some honest and hard-working, some shiftless and ne'er-do-well, but all her people – aroused feelings of maternal responsibility in her, never previously acknowledged. They knelt gingerly on the broken, ill-kept floor, afraid for their brave little show of finery hoarded away for Sundays and fair-days. It was not their fault if the church was poor and dark and airless, Alice thought, it was hers.

John Seynesbury did not set great store by long sermons. He got better results from short, highly-coloured exhortations. But this was the first opportunity he had had to preach before the lady Alice and her lord since they entered fully, in practice as well as title, to the holding of the manor. So he chose to preach against slothfulness, as a subject likely to have some meaning to all his listeners. The distinguished audience inspired him. He had never been in better voice. He raised his clenched fist high above his head and, grasping texts out of the air, juggled with them a while, finally hurling them like thunderbolts upon his flock. William listened attentively and nodded his approval. Alice continued to watch through the chancel screen.

She saw how the villagers pointed towards her, chattered among themselves, and nodded and smiled. Then they would turn to look at William's men, who stood with folded arms at the back of the church, watchful and suspicious even in the presence of the word of God.

If the parade of strength was out of place, it gratified the villagers, as Alice had guessed it would when she encouraged William to pick the tallest and best of his men to attend them at Mass. Their banners and the liveries of their heralds were bright with the new achievement of arms. William had quartered his gold leopards' faces with the gold fork-tailed lion of Burghersh for Chaucer and these were enriched by the silver field and red chief of her own quartering and the azure field of de la Pole.

Shifting and whispering among the congregation gradually died away. The sermon was coming to a close and now the moment of the Mass itself was at hand. Solemnly the bell relayed the message to empty fields and deserted cottages. There was the heavy murmur of prayer, slight metallic sounds as the holy vessels were handled, movement unexpectedly graceful from long practice, the Paternoster spoken loudly and clearly by all because it was the part of the service they knew best.

Outside the church Alice and William spoke to tenants. They encountered Nicholas Bylton and, discovering that Will was gone off to Leicester to look into a small property he had unexpectedly fallen heir to, congratulated him and insisted he return to the manor with them rather than dine alone.

Then William must laud the sentiments of John Seynesbury's address and bid him to supper the following day and Alice must find Cecily being led about by a proud brother.

'Good-day to you Stephen. There is no cause to be dragging poor Cecily about so. We are here for some time and you will have many opportunities to meet!'

'Madame, I can never serve you well enough to repay your kindness to my sister. She has told me of the position she has with you and how you guard her dignity as if she were a lady born.'

'Hush! All my household believe she *is* of gentle birth. Indeed, I think I must wheedle you from your forge and give you some position more suitable to one claiming kinship with her . . .'

'But we were just come to tell you,' Cecily broke in eagerly. 'Stephen is to be married at last and a good property comes with his bride if he can match her dower satisfactorily.'

'Why, this is good news! It is more than time you closed a marriage bargain, Stephen. Every maid in the village has been moping and hoping this long while. What is her name then?'

'Margery Walcote, my lady, the daughter of Robert Walcote who farms t'other side of Swyncombe.'

'Have you the money? If not you shall have it from me and gladly.'

'Our good Uncle Matt left me the sum he had under the will of your father, my lady. Then there is whatever the forge will fetch. I think it will serve, for Robert Walcote has no son and will be glad of my help. It would not be right that I should ask more of you when you have been so generous already.'

Alice was pleased to see that the dignity and honest goodness which had impressed her when they first met were even stronger characteristics in the man he had become.

'My father was loyally served by your Uncle Matt and it is my pleasure to have a care for you. I will ride over one day and see Robert Walcote. In the meantime you may tell him that whatever sum you raise I will double it as my marriage gift.'

As she rode back to the manor with William, Alice's mind was much occupied with the interests of the villagers. One thing was certain, she must have her husband's co-operation. And it would be preferable if he believed her plans had been his own idea.

'You are very thoughtful, my dear one. You have said

scarcely a word to me this day! Are you not happy to be in Ewelme? By my oath it is a lovely piece of England. I often used to wonder why, with all your properties, you and your father and mother clung to this place and called it home. Now I understand.'

Alice looked at him keenly. He seemed more good-humoured and contented than she had ever known him. Perhaps now was as good a time as any.

'Truth to tell I was overcome by the heat in church. I was thinking shame upon my father that he never sought to improve the building.'

She watched William's face. He frowned thoughtfully. It was the first time she had ever criticised her father and she felt a twinge of disloyalty. Would William take the bait?

'Aye, it is an old church and the village has outgrown it. Now you speak of it I was in some discomfort myself. Of course it is close weather – see how the horses are sweating even at this walk.'

He did not refer to the matter again that day. But on the next afternoon when they were sitting companionably in the pleasaunce, she saw that he was busy with some calculations upon a piece of vellum. Plying her needle even more languidly she waited impatiently for the outcome.

At last William turned to her abruptly and said: 'How would it please you if I rebuilt the church and founded an alms-house in Ewelme?'

Alice looked astonished, and then after a suitable pause dropped her embroidery and sank on her knees beside her husband. 'Oh William! Would you really do such a thing? What a marvellous gift that would be – a church and an alms-house!'

William savoured his moment of glory, and then went on: 'I could bring in skilled builders from my manor of Wingfield. I have a master of works there who has such a sense of proportion and lighting as you cannot imagine. He designed and supervised the re-building of Wingfield Church – indeed I believe I presented him to you when you came last with me into Suffolk.'

'Oh yes! I remember – Master Henry!'

'Well it is my belief that the present tower of the church could be maintained and the remainder of the church demolished and entirely rebuilt on its present site. On the south side a chapel could be incorporated for the use of the almsmen.'

Alice's surprise was no longer assumed as she listened to her husband's plans.

'Why, William, how can you produce such a scheme straight out of your head? I never knew you had a knowledge of architecture.'

'As to that I am remembering something similar that I have seen in some other part of the country. Master Henry will do the real planning. I think we will have the alms-house built in brick and part of the exterior of the church might be decorated with the squared stones and flints after the style of many Suffolk churches.'

'It will be a costly business,' Alice suggested tentatively.

'We do not lack money, my love, and it is well spent to the glory of God. After the cost of the building is met, we should need to endow the alms-house with perhaps a hundred marks a year, not more I think. Besides it will please our young king when I ask him to grant a licence in such a cause. And I shall do that without delay.'

That evening at supper William had the pleasure of revealing his plans to a larger company. The reaction was gratifying and John Seynesbury was speechless with delight.

'God will indeed be moved by this wondrous gift. Only to think a fine new church *and* an alms-house . . . '

Alice leaned against her husband and softly whispered in his ear. He scowled briefly and then, well pleased with his role of benefactor to the community, slapped the table heartily, crying: 'Aye, and to please my sweet wife – a school! We will make this so contented and well cared for a village that all England will clamour to live in it.'

This was too much for Father John, however, and it became necessary to revive him with several glasses of wine before his tongue could be loosed sufficiently to say what was in his heart.

*   *   *

The licence for the foundation of the alms-house was granted in July of that year. It was 1437, the year when the minority ended and Henry VI, at fifteen years of age, took his rightful place on the governing council.

He was a pleasant-mannered young man, studious and deeply religious, yet not entirely lacking in spirit or a will of his own, so William told Alice. For once she was at a loss to know whether this discovery pleased or troubled him. There was no doubt, however, that the young king trusted her husband and she guessed that there was some affection between them, stemming from the time when William had attended Henry in Paris for his coronation – such a lonely ordeal for a little boy to face.

Alice sometimes wondered how far William's ambition would carry him and then she would feel an inexplicable sensation of dread, as if she were reading a tale in which the combination of characters was sinister and must inevitably lead to tragedy. But these were only fleeting thoughts and, as she had no one in whom to confide them, were soon driven away by pressures of day-to-day living.

In November William was nominated by the king as one of the nineteen members of the Privy Council. Cardinal Beaufort had regained ascendancy and his peace policies were so clearly favoured by the young king that the balance of power on the Council was weighted against Gloucester as it had never been before.

Suffolk stood directly behind Beaufort and closely grouped about them were Archbishop Kemp of York, Bishop Moleyns and the earls of Huntingdon, Stafford and Northumberland. Gloucester and his supporters, aware that power was slipping from their grasp, did everything they could to obstruct measures recommended by the opposing army.

While state matters took up most of William's time, Alice had to look after his private affairs as well as her own. There were days when she seemed to do little else save dictate letters to her secretaries, until she became hoarse of voice and her head ached from the strain of taking decisions, often with only secondhand knowledge upon which to base them.

Even when William did tear himself away from the Council

she found him unhelpful. He was preoccupied and fretful and seemed incapable of enjoying any of his old pursuits.

Alice did her best to understand. When he had learned all there was to know about the ordering of the country's economic and social systems, then their life together would resume the pleasant pattern of earlier days, she promised herself.

There was another matter which sometimes came between them in their hearts at this time. Only once did they turn it loose in hard words, however, for it was not a thing to be lightly spoken. They were alone in the luxurious apartments allotted to them on a visit to Windsor. The king had invited a small hunting party, composed only of those he liked best to have about him, and formality was relaxed, permitting the guests to spend their time as they chose.

Alice and William were looking at plans for the almshouse, which had now been finalised. The site was already prepared and work on the foundations had begun. Alice was so engrossed in following the detailed report from Master Henry that she could not at first understand her husband's meaning when he suddenly pushed back the parchments and said abruptly: 'Well now, Madame, is there nothing you wish to tell me, as we have this time to ourselves?' She met his scowl with wide, puzzled eyes. Then as the significance of the question penetrated her mind, there was a flicker of anger before she looked away.

'I have nothing to tell you.'

'In that case, it is a matter for some concern,' William went on relentlessly. 'You are thirty-four years old and I am minded that you were Salisbury's wife before you were mine and got no child by him either. You must consult this man Tessonelli. They say he is the finest physician in Europe, much skilled in overcoming barrenness in women.'

Alice stood up, clutching the edge of the table. She was shivering with anger and dread. Had she not consulted a score of such wise men during the past five years and had they not all advised her that there was no apparent reason why she should not conceive?

'So,' she cried, 'and how does this fine physician work his art? Does he bed with the women who consult him?'

William began to look uneasy and said soothingly: 'Of course not, of course not. Only send for him and ask him to give you a draught of his concocting and we will have faith in Our Lord to do his work.'

Alice dare not say that the Lord of Heaven might find it impossible to work through the lord of Suffolk, but she could not help resenting the presumption that it was always the woman who must be at fault. Ardent lover though William might be, it did not prove his ability as a sire. Many lusty men got no heirs, even though they strove by more than one wife.

She said coldly: 'I have already taken the advice of learned physicians and all remarked that my health was exceptionally good and my body sound. Moreover, though I mislike your reference to Salisbury, I will answer it. There was not that sympathy between us which must needs go to make a child and we had scant time together in the four years of our marriage to foster a better relationship.'

'Enough, then! I do not choose to wrangle with you on this matter. I hope you are not suggesting there is a want of sympathy between *us*.'

'Of course not. And I do not wrangle, I only say I do not believe I am barren.'

William toyed irritably with the heavy gold chain about his neck. 'But your mother bore only one child, is it not possible you share some womanly contrariness that makes it exceptional for you to conceive? After all, you will scarcely say I have been inattentive!'

'No, oh no!' Alice felt defensive, vulnerable. Tears filled her eyes but she would not let them fall. 'But I carry my years lightly. There must still be time for me to get with child.'

At once William was tender, clasping her warmly in his arms, telling her that he loved her above everything in life.

'I make no reproach to you, Alice, my heart's true love. It is only that I long to see continuance in our House, to know that I am striving for a future beyond our span. But if this cannot be, I am well content to have you and none other. And by my faith when you said you carried years light you spoke truth. You look not a day past twenty-five!' He stroked her cheek teasingly. 'No wonder you inspire every troubadour who entertains the court!'

*   *   *

Leaving the house of a certain merchant prince, where they had been admiring jewel-embroidered Italian silks of a much sought-after quality, Alice and Cecily were astounded to find the streets about Westminster thronged with angry people. William always insisted that as well as her squire, Philip Lammerac and two pages, she must never ride out in London with fewer than ten men as escort. She had thought this excessive in the past but in the presence of such a mob, every man was needed to force a way for her.

'What has happened – what do they say?' Alice shouted at Cecily as she fought with her discomforted mare and strove to avoid the ragged urchins, who scrambled between the legs of bystanders hoping to find a purse dropped in the crush.

'Ho! Stand back there if you know what's good for you! Make a passage for the Countess of Suffolk, friend of our king!'

Cecily struggled alongside Alice. 'They are saying the Duchess of Gloucester has practised witchcraft against the king!'

William came to their London house late that evening and Alice hurried to meet him.

'My love, at last you are here! What is this wild rumour that Eleanor Cobham is a witch? The people are mad with it in the streets. However has such a rumour been spread about?'

'It is no rumour. She has conspired with others in evil arts to waste away the king. Roger Bolingbroke, the astronomer, is involved and so, Heaven forgive him, is Master Thomas Southwell, canon of St. Stephen's Chapel! There are others have been used – Eleanor Cobham's chaplain for one.'

'I can scarce credit what you say. Is there proof of this . . . this witchcraft?'

William settled himself comfortably in a chair and stretched out his legs upon a footstool. Alice noticed that although his voice sounded angry, his expression was confident rather than concerned.

'It seems they employed Margery Jourdemayne . . . You must have heard of her, they call her the Witch of Eye. She fashioned a wax image of the king and they have been wasting it away with a slow fire. They will all be indicted for treason in the Guildhall.'

'Who will judge them?'

'I will,' William answered slowly, 'with Stafford and Huntingdon and judges of both benches. They shall have a just hearing.'

'But the king is in good health, praise be! Never say they will burn Eleanor Cobham?'

'No, her accomplices may be put to death, but it will be enough if the duchess is found guilty. Gloucester,' he added smoothly, 'has cause to rue the day he made such a mistress his wife!'

His last words made Alice very thoughtful. Had Eleanor Cobham really been guilty? Could it be coincidence that such a powerful weapon had fallen into the grasp of those who most wanted to see Gloucester disgraced? On the other hand Gloucester was heir to the throne and it was conceivable that, with or without his knowledge, his wife had tried to put him there. The duchess, for all she was handsome, had a certain slyness in her manner which Alice had never liked.

As evidence was unfolded at the trial it became apparent that the Duchess of Gloucester had made more enemies at court than friends. Even the men whose fortunes were linked with those of her husband cried out against her.

The verdict was guilty, and a terrible punishment was devised for the duchess. On three successive days she must walk barefoot, and dressed like a penitent, through the London streets. For her accomplices there was only death.

Watching the grim procession and hearing the roar of anger from citizens thronging the route to see Dame Eleanor humbled, Alice thought death preferable to such humiliation. And when public penance was done the duchess must look ahead into years emptied of meaning by the prison walls which would encompass her all the days of her life.

Overshadowed by his wife's disgrace, Gloucester began to drop into the background of public life. His attendance at meetings of the Council became infrequent and William felt able at last to take a rest from court duties with an easy mind. To Alice's joy he suggested they should spend Christmas of 1441 at Ewelme, and fill the house with cheerful company.

* * *

The alms-house was now virtually completed, and the church taking shape before the eyes of an admiring countryside. Alice and William were well pleased with both projects, full of praises for Master Henry and his workmen, eager with suggestions.

Thirteen poor men and two chaplains had settled in the alms-house and John Seynesbury proudly took up office as its first Master in the new year. After some consideration William decided that the future of their charitable work would be better safeguarded if they put it in possession of the incomes from three manors – Marsh in Buckinghamshire, Connock in Wiltshire, and Ramridge, Southampton – rather than allotting a fixed annual sum.

It was a happy time. Alice delighted in the affectionate greetings of the villagers, even more than she did in the pleasant reception neighbouring gentlefolk gave them wherever they went. She saw that William felt at home, too.

Once, as they were leaving the site of the school, which would soon receive its first scholars, he stopped to look about him, exclaiming: 'How I have come to love this place. Do I love it for your sake, my dearest wife? Or is it really as fair in every season as it strikes my eye?'

'I am thankful if you love it for my sake,' Alice answered softly. 'But truly it is fair country and loyal friends live here.'

'We will improve the house next, William said happily.

In the third week of February it was necessary for him to return to London, but Alice did not travel with him. There were many reasons why she wished to delay her return to London. The workmen who were now busy about the house needed her personal direction and then there were the new tapestries. They would arrive any day and she would see them hung.

There was yet another reason. She wanted to talk to Adeliza, and William would never have approved her visiting one said to have supernatural powers while tongues still wagged over Gloucester's scandal. It must be done without his knowledge.

When Alice and Cecily rode out to see Adeliza they found the cottage deserted. But a cheerful twig fire burned on the neatly swept hearth-stone and they set themselves down beside it to wait. After a while the door burst open and a huge, grey hound slipped into the room. Cecily started violently and watched with apprehension as the great beast circled her in a close inspection of her sweeping skirts. It barely glanced at Alice and suddenly left the cottage.

'Was . . . was that Adeliza, do you suppose?' Cecily whispered nervously.

Alice hooted a throaty laugh. 'Oh dear, oh dear me! How Adeliza will enjoy that idea! Was that Adeliza indeed! Did it look like her? Really Cecily, I have told you times-a-number Adeliza has no magic powers. She cannot change herself into a lion or disappear in a pale green mist. Such arts are for romancers to tell. No. Adeliza has a singular wisdom, and perhaps some power to see a little ahead into time – though I can scarce understand how it can be and have laughed at her visions before now . . . '

'Aye, you have laughed!' said a soft voice.

Alice and Cecily both jumped this time and found Adeliza regarding them from the doorway, with her hound at her side.

'Why, Adeliza.' Alice stretched out her hand in greeting. 'You are not changed at all and it is years since I have seen you.'

'Not changed into a dog certainly,' said Adeliza with a slight smile for Cecily's stiffening back. 'But you are changed. You are older, more womanly – softer in some ways, harder in others. Beautiful you are, prouder than ever . . . and you are with child.'

Cecily gasped but Alice became still and silent as though her spirit had left her. There was no sound in the little room save the shifting of the fire and the heavy breathing of the dog.

132

At last Alice lowered herself slowly and carefully on to a stool and, keeping her eyes on Adeliza, asked intensely: 'What makes you say that I am with child?'

'Pouff! I can tell by your face. It is there for all to see. Many who are to be mothers come to my door, hoping or regretting. One learns to know the look: Mistress Thatcher, who has delivered every babe in the village the past twenty years, will tell you the same.'

'And are you sure? There . . . there can be no mistake?'

'I think not. When I heard you had not left Ewelme with your husband I thought you might come to see me. You have been married more than ten years and naturally you have been watching for an heir this long while. So it was the first thing I looked for in your face.'

'Oh Adeliza, you have made me so joyful. I came to you because I thought certain signs might mean it was already too late.'

'What? At eight-and-thirty years? No, you misread the signs.'

'Cecily, pray you step outside awhile.' She waited until her maid, almost as radiant as Alice was herself, had closed the door and said: 'Adeliza, you used to say that you could sometimes read the future. Can you read it now for me, for my child . . . and . . . and my husband?'

'Why do you ask? Are you afraid?'

'Afraid?' Alice was surprised. She weighed the word in her mind. 'Yes, perhaps I am. There is feeling in this land, as though a pot simmered upon a fire. Men have lost an old faith. What will replace it? What will become of my House in my time?'

Adeliza's still beautiful face was expressionless. In latter years she had subdued her wild mane of hair into two thick braids and for a few minutes she was silent, twisting one of them about her fingers.

'I can tell you nothing. Life will deal with you as it does with many of your station. It has given you much and if one day you have to pay the price I believe you will think it a fair bargain.'

Alice could get no other answer and in the end ceased plaguing her. While Cecily untethered the horses, Alice remarked that the cottage was in much better repair than it had once been.

'Aye, Will Bylton came with two of his men and mended it. It keeeps the weather out wondrously now.'

'Does Will visit you often?'

'Well, he has been away to Leicestershire many times these past years, but he does not forget me and he tells me news of you when he comes.'

'You will get your tidings at first-hand now for I shall surely bear my child at Ewelme.'

*   *   *

The whole village was waiting. The whole county was waiting. In the manor-house everyone from its lord – up long before dawn since Alice had wakened him in triumph and thrust him from their bed – to the meanest potboy, were worn sick with waiting.

The brilliant young surgeon, who had learned all he knew from a man who learned all *he* knew from the famous John of Arderne, was beginning to regret that his reputation had reached the ears of the puissant lord of Suffolk. For three months he had scarcely left Alice's side, so anxious was her husband for the welfare of his wife and this precious burden she carried. Since her labour began he had tried everything he knew from herbs to pressure on the abdomen. He had made Alice walk up and down. He had made her sit on the parturition chair. It was to no avail. His patient was slender-boned and weakening in the prolonged struggle. The baby was large.

Reluctantly he picked up an apertorium and advanced towards the bed.

'Merciful Mother of Heaven, what is it you have there?' cried Cecily in alarm.

Alice's eyes flew open and she saw the sharp-clawed instrument in his hand.

'Come no nearer me with that!' The exclamation was sharp and full of vigour. 'I know what it is. My mother told me it was used on her. You will injure me for ever and the babe too, mayhap! Keep away from me, I say.' She was like an animal standing off its attacker with a final ferocity. She saw him quail and relaxed, waving him away. 'Be gone! You know at once too much and too little. I will contrive this matter myself. I was but resting. Now to work.'

Within the hour a son was born to her, a lusty, well-formed child whose cry brought William racing up the stairs, three-at-a-time.

'Ouch! William, pray leave off! You are crushing the breath out of me.' Alice was forced to protest from the depth of an exuberant hug.

William gathered up a handful of her pale hair and kissed it before turning to look at the pink-faced, linen bundle which Cecily held out to him.

'So! What a fine lad we have got! We will call him John. Lord John, you shall have a silver bell to play with as I had from my godfather, William Wingfield. And it shall be scribed with your name and your birth-date, the twenty-seventh day of September . . . When you are older you shall have the finest horse in the land to ride upon . . . Ah, but you will see what a splendid thing it is to be heir to the House of de la Pole!'

CHAPTER EIGHT

WHEN THE king reached twenty-three years of age, his ministers agreed that it was time he had a wife. All very well if he busied himself with projects such as his colleges at Eton and Cambridge. Men would honour him for these endeavours. But it was not learning they prized in kings so much as fruitfulness. Only let the right consort be found and she would draw him away from his books, focus his interest on this world rather than the next, and by giving him an heir, strengthen the House of Lancaster and the policies of its adherents. Not unnaturally the Lancastrian peace faction saw the king's marriage as a French alliance.

The Duke of Gloucester, however, continued to favour a more vigorous war. Since his wife's imprisonment he had been living in semi-retirement, collecting books and manuscripts for the library of Oxford University. He no longer commanded enough support to be effective on the Council, yet he continued to wield considerable influence in the country and forced those who opposed him to employ devious methods to pursue their ultimate goal of peace.

In this strained atmosphere William was appointed to lead an embassy to France with the object of negotiating a truce. It was an assignment he strove to avoid. Inevitably the French would demand return of hard-won territory and he foresaw that the man who signed it away might be hated in England.

Only when the Council persisted did he finally undertake the commission, with the king's assurance that he would not personally be blamed if negotiations were unsatisfactory.

Travelling conditions were bad that February of 1444, as William set about ordering preparations for his journey. Alice was at Ewelme and reports of drifting snow upon the Oxfordshire road made him reluctant to ask if she would come to London and help him. But he had no need to ask. When his letter telling of the mission to France reached her, she looked its bearer up and down and said shortly: 'If this stripling lad could press his horse through the snow then so can I.'

Leaving John, now a cheerful, crowing infant of sixteen months, to the watchful care of his nurse, Sibilla Berney, she set out upon the road. With her went Cecily, Philip Lammerac and ten of her men and Alice extracted much merriment from their floundering progress and made such a charming appearance in her hooded cloak of gay blue velvet and sable, with snowflakes glinting in her hair, that all swore they would not have missed the journey for a purse of gold.

William greeted her arrival with relief and while she wrote out crisp instructions for the considerable number of his household who would accompany him and dealt efficiently with the important matter of his wardrobe, he talked to her about his mission.

'I like it not. The Council has given me orders worded with cunning so that no man can readily perceive what they may mean. I am told to bring about a peaceful agreement and to look upon Margaret, the daughter of René of Anjou, as a bride for our king. This marriage will not be popular and the Council knows it . . . Why, I had much labour to get in writing any reference to it.'

'But why would they not want to have their instructions writ? People must know of the marriage in good time.'

'Yes, but then the contract would be signed. And it might be expedient to blame me for having exceeded the authority I was given.'

Alice said anxiously: 'Could you not feign a sickness so that another must go.'

'No, because given success, great gain could come of it and I must take the risk.'

'I cannot understand why the Council should be so deep with you. I thought you were strong enough to have your way.'

137

'Beaufort is still my leader and he is a cautious man. When he is gone he knows I must succeed him. But he intends to stay the course in office. Who can blame him?' William shrugged his powerful shoulders with curious Gallic grace.

Alice noticed it and was reminded of the far-off, unreal days they had all spent with Bedford's court in France. 'Will it be remembered to your disfavour that you lived some years in France and are intimate with many of their nobility?'

'Those are the very reasons I gave the Council when I told them I did not want to serve on the embassy. But they would have none of them. In truth I have heard there is already some public clamour that I am a friend of the French and will betray England's interests. I had not intended to tell you of that, but now it is out. By God's wrath,' his voice grew thunderous, 'I should like to answer those who say it with my sword!'

*   *   *

On the twenty-eighth of May, William and his embassy concluded a truce between England and France which was to continue until the end of March 1446. At the same time terms were agreed upon for the marriage between Henry and Margaret of Anjou, and the embassy returned to England to ratify them.

William had been deeply impressed by the girl he had gone to inspect, and described her to the young king with such enthusiasm that Henry grew to look upon the match with as much favour as his ministers could wish.

Margaret was beautiful, witty, intelligent and strong-minded beyond her fifteen years. Her father was a cousin of Charles VII of France and his favourite counsellor. He was also King of Jerusalem and Sicily. But these titles meant little since Jerusalem was in the hands of the Turks and he owned no land in Sicily. Moreover half his inheritance in Maine and Anjou was in England's hands. So his daughter must come without a dower.

Alice and William were appointed to bring Margaret of Anjou to England. But first there must be a proxy marriage

138

in France, when William would play the part of the bridegroom and make his vows in the name of his king.

In September they joined the court at Eltham to finalise arrangements for the bride's escort. Among the leading members of the nobility, who had been carefully chosen for the splendour of the display their personal fortunes might be expected to provide, was Alice's stepdaughter, the Countess of Salisbury. The two women exchanged greetings with pleasure, for though circumstances had afforded them little time in each other's company over the intervening years, they had always recognised a mutual liking, and planned to ride together on much of the journey, preferring good mounts to the rigours of the travelling coach.

The king received Alice with loving courtesy and many kind enquiries about her son. Soon after her arrival he drew her aside and asked, with close interest, about the progress that had been made on the new buildings at Ewelme.

'We take delight in this benevolence towards our humblest subjects, and give thanks for every poor man you shelter in your house of alms and the children you teach within your school. Let us see you as often at our court as your good works will spare you. We like well to have about us those lords and their ladies, whose deeds speak sweetly to us.'

He stopped suddenly and stared, frowning into space as though he had forgotten her presence.

But just as Alice concluded she was dismissed and prepared to leave him, he turned and took her hand.

'Dear Lady Alice, there are many at our court whose way of life we cannot approve. Their pleasures seem vicious to us and their conversation unwholesome. Kings, you see, may not always choose their company. We pray you have a care for our young queen, stand her friend and shield her from evil influence.'

'Sire, I will readily do as you ask. But . . . if you will not think it presumptuous in me . . .'

'Nay, nay, I value your counsel . . . speak!'

'The lady Margaret has been some time at the French court and was in early years schooled by her grandmother, Queen Yolande of Aragon. I believe she will know how to recognise and shun those influences you dread. Take ease that she was raised to play a consort's part.'

Henry's face relaxed into a smile. 'Aye, what you say sets us at rest. Now here approaches our Uncle Beaufort, come to give you greeting.'

By the time Alice and William left the court, to put their domestic affairs in order before setting out for France, their rank had been advanced to that of Marquis and Marchioness of Suffolk and they were the richer for a grant of two good Suffolk manors, Neddyng and Kettelberston. At future coronations William would carry the golden sceptre surmounted by a dove as service for the manors.

'And that will be no hardship,' Alice observed when William told her of the condition. 'You will make a fine figure at the crowning of our young queen.'

'Since I am in my fiftieth year I shall, with God's grace, see no other coronation in my time.'

*   *   *

With the greatest reluctance Alice decided to leave Cecily at Ewelme while she was in France. John was accustomed to accept her discipline in his mother's absence and it would be reassuring to know he was surrounded by those to whom his welfare would be always a first concern.

'Sibilla Berney might fall sick while we are away and I cannot find another I would trust to care for him so well as you, in the short time before we go,' she explained to Cecily. 'I have written to Will Bylton and he will visit you often. You may refer my bailiffs to him and if there is need he can write to me on your behalf.'

'But how will you do without me to wait on you?' Cecily asked, concerned.

'Any number of the ladies of the court go with us and I may have Constance Courtenay, who is kin by marriage to the Beauforts, as mistress of my wardrobe . . . But never think I would not rather have you!'

On the twenty-eighth day of October, William received a warrant from the king . . . 'to his dearest cousin, William,

Marquis and Earl of Suffolk, High Steward of our household, greeting. Whereas, by the propitious blessing of God you have lately contracted a marriage for us and in our name with Margaret, the Excellent Noble and Illustrious daughter of the most Serene King of Sicily, and by the law of matrimony have agreed in our name to take the same to wife and with the words of matrimony reciprocally spoken have received and accepted her consent given unto us by herself in person; and furthermore have made a treaty as to the place where unto she ought to be conveyed at the expense of her parents. We, earnestly desiring our same spouse should be brought to our presence, have given unto you powers to pass into parts beyond the sea, with those persons who may chance to set out with you . . . and have given you authority to command, rule and govern all such persons on this occasion . . . '

Alice was entranced. 'Why, what a wondrous document this is. Henry sends you forth like a king, and the wording is almost poetic!'

'Well, I am going to marry a queen am I not,' replied William, with a teasing smile.

'By proxy, yes. But you will not overlook your lawful wife, a mere marchioness in your royal train?' She made him a sweeping curtsy.

He caught hold of her round the waist in his exuberance. 'Nay, I am married to a queen already,' he said, and kissed her soundly for good measure.

'Then you are knocking her crown awry,' Alice protested, fearing for the fragile confection upon her head.

*   *   *

The marriage by proxy took place at Nancy the following February in the presence of Charles VII and his court. It was made the occasion for much magnificence and on the eight successive fête days no courtier was so ill-equipped as to appear twice in the same robes or with the same jewels.

In the banqueting hall each evening the opulence was almost oppressive. So many piquant dishes and so much good wine exhausted the palate with repeated provocation. Jewels blazed

141

and dazzled in the light of hundreds of candles. The air was heavy with exotic fragrances – spices from the food, musk and crushed roses from the women. And when talk and jest failed, there were dancers and acrobats to entertain or music of rebec, fiddle, flute and gittern.

When at last the festivities were at an end, the cavalcade set out for England. But with such a number of coaches, horse-litters and baggage wagons, their advance was slower than had been anticipated and William grew impatient.

'We appear to make the least progress possible, short of going backwards,' he exploded to his wife when they were alone. 'I keep sending couriers ahead saying we have reached such-and-such a point and three days later I am telling them we are five miles farther on!'

'I do not understand why you are in such a fret. We are conducting a royal bride not fleeing the country!' Alice looked quizzically at her husband. She suspected that he had some private reason for wanting the journey completed in the time he had allowed. But she knew better than to question him. He would tell her of his own accord or not at all.

Came their last night in France. The next day, given fair weather, they would board ship. The young queen was in a whirl of excitement and Alice had been hard put to get her settled down comfortably for the night. So it was at a late hour that she thankfully turned her attention to her own bed, and just then William entered their chamber purposefully.

'Ah, there you are, my lord!' Alice forced herself exhaustedly out of a chair to greet him. 'As you see, my women are having some difficulty with the canopy. I fear it has taken some damage along the road, but our bed will soon be ready. Let me pour you a cup of wine.'

'No, no wine.' He was looking in dismay at her furred night-robe and the silken curtain of hair she had been brushing through her hands when he arrived. 'I had not thought you would be ready to retire yet . . . I wanted you to come with me and meet . . . someone.'

'Meet someone? At this hour! But who?'

'A young woman . . . to whose family I owe some obligation.

It would be mighty pleasing to me if . . . To speak truth I had hoped you . . . '

'Would take her under my protection?'

'Precisely. Come and see her, anyway. She is waiting in the next room. You are women both and it is no matter that you have put off your clothes.'

Alice, made thoroughly curious, followed him along the low-roofed gallery until they reached a small door.

'Before we go in will you not tell me a little more about this woman, who she is and how she comes into our charge?'

'Her name is Jeanne. Her mother is dead these many years since and she has been living in a convent in Normandy,' he said in an impatient whisper.

'Jeanne who? What is her family name?' Alice hissed back.

'Does it matter at this moment? I cannot be whispering her entire history to you in this place. We shall appear ridiculous if we are seen. Let us go in.'

Alice followed him into the room. At first it appeared to hold nothing save a truckle bed, and a chair set before a wretched fire. Then a figure stepped out of the shadows and stood beneath the light of a single torch which was set in an iron bracket upon the wall.

The girl before them was simply yet elegantly dressed in a gown of murrey, furred with miniver. Alice swept an approving glance over this attire but it was the face which riveted her attention.

William said: 'Alice, my love, permit me to present Jeanne to you and commend her to your good opinion.'

Jeanne curtsied deeply. She was struggling to appear composed and succeeded so largely that only fluttering eyelids and a slight trembling betrayed her.

'So you are Jeanne . . . Is this the best shelter my lord could find for you? I only hope you may be able to sleep on that bed. I will send a woman to attend you and bring some quilts for your easier rest. Tomorrow you shall join my women.'

Jeanne took the hand Alice held out to her and knelt to kiss it.

'Most gracious lady! I shall strive to be worthy of your interest and protection.'

'Prettily spoken. Good repose, child!'

William said nothing, only nodded and smiled at the girl and escorted his wife back to their chamber.

Later, when the curtains about the bed were drawn and she was alone with William, Alice asked: 'How old is Jeanne.'

'Twenty.'

'She seems gently born and reared. What of her mother's family?'

'They were old in Normandy when a Saxon king ruled England! Reverse of fortune has reduced them to miserable poverty, however. Now only an aged grandmother survives, and an uncle who struggles to keep their crumbling chateau weather-sound. But why do you not ask about her father?'

Alice heard the suggestion of a smile in her husband's voice.

'No one who looks at Jeanne de la Pole will doubt who sired her,' Alice said crisply.

'Hah! I knew there would be no need to tell you anything once you saw the girl! Well, it is all long in the past you know. I was unwed and in need of company. I placed Jeanne's mother in care of a kindly abbess when her time came. She died giving birth and since then I have supported the child. I will dower her well, you understand.'

'And you want me to find her a husband? That should present no difficulty.'

'Alice you are a wonderful woman! Have I told you that before?'

'Perhaps. I forget.'

'And, you know, had you then been my wife instead of Salisbury's, there would have been no Jeanne.'

'So you say, my lord, so you say! But thank you for not bringing this daughter to England before John was born. It would have grieved me to know you had a child when I had not borne you an heir.'

William groped for her hand in the darkness and drew it across his mouth.

*   *   *

On a fresh April day they sailed at last into Porchester where a great welcome awaited the young queen. But the crossing had been stormy, leaving Margaret weak and sickly. A short rest and she must needs take ship again for Southampton to meet the king.

The next morning there were tidings to dismay them all. Going early to the chamber where the queen lay, Alice was horrified to find her face disfigured by unsightly pimples.

'Heaven defend us! Whatever ails you, Madame?'

Margaret struggled to raise herself, frightened by Alice's expression.

'Why, what is it . . . I . . . oh, I feel so hot and there is a sickness in my stomach . . . ' Her voice trailed away as she patted her cheeks with a distracted hand. Then she screamed: 'A mirror! Get me a mirror!'

For the next hour Alice found herself quelling hysteria among Margaret's women, with many resounding slaps in all directions. At last she was able to soothe the bride with a sleeping-draught and go in search of William.

He had already been told of the queen's disorder and was white-faced with concern.

'Can it be the plague, Alice? By the Mass we are all in danger if it is. And I . . . Why, I carried her ashore!'

'What of me, then? I have been attending to her this last hour!' Alice was half amused, half impatient. 'But I do not believe it is an infectious complaint at all. She is not ill enough to have taken the plague. More likely the rough crossing upset her – or the shellfish she ate last night at supper. I am on my way to instruct our physician to concoct a purge.'

'God grant what you say is true then. But I must send a message to delay the king from riding to meet her. We shall have to stay here until we see if she improves.'

'Yes. And do you not look so grim. Even if it *were* the plague, we should still have to stay with her. What use to put those around us in a flurry.'

It was two weeks before Margaret regained her strength and her good looks. Everyone concluded that it had indeed been shellfish and in an atmosphere of happy relief went about the preparations for the royal wedding.

The marriage took place at the Abbey of St. Mary Titchfield, on the twenty-second day of April. When it was over

Alice and William were able to slip away to Ewelme for a brief reunion with their son before the queen's formal entry into London and her coronation, which was to be held on the last Sunday in May, at Westminster Abbey.

Immediately after these ceremonies William would have important business to conduct with the Commons, however, and Alice saw that even while he dandled John upon his knee he could not keep his thoughts off it.

'I shall use every persuasion I can on those members whose ears are inclined towards me,' he had told her. 'I want it recorded that all my actions in securing the truce and bringing the queen to England have their heartiest approval.'

'But it seems plain that they approve. Why must you be striving after further acknowledgment? Alice was puzzled by his obsession with written authorisation. She applied her mind to a better understanding of her husband's motives and finally a troubling suspicion revealed its shape. When they were next alone she took the opportunity to ask him about it.

'William, my love, you know you may trust me unto the grave and beyond, tell me are there some terms of the truce which are not yet known?'

He cast her a troubled look but did not answer at once.

At last he said with great deliberation: 'In return for Margaret of Anjou we are ceding Maine to the French. I agreed to pay the price because it was the only one they would take. Margaret's father is very close to Charles of Valois and this match stands as a plea for peace between our two countries.'

'What! You have given away a whole province! Mother of Heaven! They will never forgive you.'

'They? They? Who are *they* to give or withhold forgiveness? Were *they* at the conference? The king knows of the cession and so do others of the Council. Bishop Moleyns sat at my right hand throughout the negotiations. It was on his advice that I finally took my decision.'

Alice understood that he was angry at having to justify himself to a woman but she persisted steadily. 'You know I mean the people. Why, before you went to France you told me you feared this embassy and that men were saying you were too much a friend of France. Only think what they will say when it is known that Maine is gone.'

'The clause is a close-kept secret. For the present no one must know of it.'

'But when the French take possession of Maine they will know.'

'By then Margaret will have produced an heir to the throne and gained England's love. The people will not think the cost high.'

'God grant that you are right! In these untrustful times no man who has a hand in our country's affairs can be beyond the reach of slander. Only remember what they said of Bedford, worthy man.'

'Aye, but never fear. We shall prosper. I shall build our House on such a foundation that none shall challenge it.'

*   *   *

William had his way with the Commons, even Gloucester supporting the tributes that were paid to his good service, both in negotiating the truce and arranging the royal marriage.

In mid-July the king gave an audience to ambassadors from France. It was felt by all to be an occasion of great significance, marking the newly-forged friendship between the two countries, and the English court put on its bravest display to receive the guests. Alice, waiting apart with the queen and their women until the formalities should be at an end, looked with appreciation at the scene taking place beyond an arched doorway.

The king made a splendid appearance, his robe of vermilion cloth of gold sweeping a wide area of the floor behind him as he entered the hall and made his way to the high chair of state, draped with a magnificent blue tapestry. Gloucester and William walked beside him, matching their pace exactly to his. The sombre setting of the hall of Westminster Palace was a perfect foil for such majesty of colour, Alice thought.

When the ambassadors advanced and presented their credentials with a flourish, the king raised his hat to salute them and said in his gracious, gentle manner that he did not hold them strangers at his court. The ambassadors spoke in return of the love and goodwill borne him by the King of France.

Hearing them, Alice sighed. How curious that men had evolved such rules by which to play the game. Yesterday's enemy was today's ally and threats gave way to courtesy. But who knew tomorrow?

The formalities came to an end and the queen moved slowly out into the hall to receive the obeisances of the French embassy. Alice walked beside her and behind them the wives, mothers, daughters and sisters of the English nobility formed a stately procession.

Later when there was feasting and music, William drew his wife aside. 'I want to tell you, my dearest, that you are looking incomparably beautiful this day.'

'Flattery indeed, after fifteen years of marriage!' Alice smiled.

'I watched you as you made your approach down the great hall beside the queen, and I could see no one else in all that parade of beauty.'

'Oh come, you are not serious. Why, the queen is exquisite and I am nearly forty years of age!'

'You do not look more than thirty! Anyway, the Frenchmen remarked you. I overheard them praising your elegance and saying how clever it was of you to wear only silver tissue and diamonds to set off your pale beauty.' He kissed his fingers and flourished his sleeve in fair imitation of the ambassadors.

'They are mistaken. I wore silver to set off my Order of the Garter.'

'Ah yes.' He glanced at the decoration about her left arm.

'It was the first honour I was able to procure for you after our marriage. The king was pleased to show you some favour and it was Beaufort's happy suggestion that the Garter be given you because your grandmother's sister, Katherine Swynford, had also received it in her time.'

'You never told me before that it was Beaufort's idea,' Alice said with sudden interest.

'Did I not? Well it hardly seemed important. The honour came from the king and you received it because you married me. But I must go now and wait upon the queen. I cannot be

148

seen to dally any longer with my own wife for very shame.'
He kissed her hand and left her.

Alice's squire, Philip Lammerac, never far away, came forward immediately to take her husband's place beside her.

'You look very thoughtful, my lady. Does my company intrude or may I serve you in some way?'

Alice turned to the fair, honest-faced youth and smiled gently at his eagerness.

'It is nothing. A chance remark from my lord brought an old riddle to mind and I am plagued for the answer.'

'Do you tell it me and I will not sleep until I have the answer for you!'

'Nay, you would have a long vigil, for only my father had the key to it and he is dead.'

* * *

That year of 1445 continued to be a successful and happy one for William and Alice. At court they were the constant close companions of the king and queen, treated as second only to them, deferred to, honoured, flattered – and envied. In Oxfordshire they found domestic happiness and content and watched their child grow into a strong-limbed, fearless boy of quick understanding and pleasant temper.

Sometimes they travelled to Donnington. Alice favoured this property next after Ewelme and William, finding to his surprise that he could be happiest wherever Alice's taste and enterprise had set its mark, seldom visited his own property in Suffolk any more. Only on occasions when he had cause to question the judgment of his bailiffs, or thought it necessary to back up their authority by a personal appearance among his tenants, would he tear himself away from his wife's home.

His interests in Oxfordshire were further increased when he was granted the office of Constable of Wallingford Castle.

'Take heed, my love, that you as my wife and John, our son, are named conjointly in this appointment,' he told Alice. 'That means that in the event of my death you will hold the office until John is of age. It will of course be necessary for us to employ a deputy constable and pay him out of our salary. I have also secured for us joint Stewardship of the honours of Wallingford and Saint Vallery, another office your father held during his lifetime. I thought we should lay claim to it.'

'I wish you will not talk of dying before John is grown to manhood.'

'Calm yourself, woman, I do not mean to die before my time, but I must protect you and our son by every means I can.' He laughed suddenly, without humour. 'Besides, we de la Poles are ill-fated stock. There was my grand-sire, Chancellor of England and nearest to Richard II until the king was challenged in his right to rule. Though he had loved my grandfather and ennobled him, Richard could not save him. Exiled to France, he died among strangers. My father went at Harfleur, my brother fell at Agincourt. I wonder if any of our line will die peaceful in old age.'

* * *

Alice was kneeling at her prie-dieu in the withdrawing room set aside for her personal day-time use within the Palace of Westminster. It was a pleasant room, benefiting from a southwest aspect and although it was not large she had chosen it in preference to the echoing grandeur of the rest of their apartments.

A book of devotions lay open before her and her attitude, head resting on one elegant hand, was meditative. But Alice was not praying or studying, she was thinking.

In the very public life at court, she had discovered that only her prie-dieu afforded a refuge from continuous company and it was necessary to her temperament to have some time of privacy each day. The deception might not succeed with William, who would interrupt her even in the middle of her bath if he wanted to speak to her and devil take her shocked, protesting women! But the king gave strict orders with every summons he sent that 'our dear lady Alice should not be troubled to receive it if she were at prayer', and his pages would scuff their shoes outside her door until she pleased to call them in.

The queen, however, was another matter, Alice thought

bitterly. Nothing stood between Margaret of Anjou and the instant gratification of her will at all times. She was a little like William in that respect. Perhaps that was why they got on so well. They were always together these days, heads bent over state papers, he explaining and she an apt pupil saying: 'Oui, oui, je comprends' in her decisive way.

Ah, but little Margaret was not the consort they had all expected, not content merely to keep the king amused. And as for providing an heir to the throne . . . well there was no sign of that yet. No, Margaret wanted power. The more Henry was prepared to leave matters in the hands of his ministers, the faster his wife gathered up those threads he dropped and wove them into a web of intrigue about herself.

'And she is weaving William into the web too,' Alice thought resentfully. 'She encourages him to take decisions without consulting the Council and he will no longer listen to me when I warn him that by so doing he forges new weapons for his enemies.'

The sound of hurrying footsteps brought her back to the present moment and she heard Constance Courtenay putting up a spirited defence in the ante-room.

'My lady is at her devotions and the king himself has said . . .'

'I come from the queen and she would receive the lady of Suffolk at once!'

Just so, Alice rose, smoothing her amber-coloured gown. When Constance tapped nervously for admittance she was already on her way to the door.

She looked at the messenger and he was an unhappy man, driven by one imperious mistress and now confronting another. 'I heard your clamour. Go back to the queen and tell her I am coming. When aught else brings you here, see you match your voice to your company. *My* women are not accustomed to loud manners.'

The man bowed himself backwards from her presence. Alice saw Constance smiling and her own expression warmed in response. She had grown to like this Devon-bred cousin who, despite a rather ponderous mind, was doggedly thorough in her duties and possessed a frank and pleasant nature. But she missed Cecily.

'Well come, girl! We must not keep the queen waiting. Call my heralds!'

Constance's mouth gaped in astonishment. Alice did not usually have her two heralds accompany her on informal visits to the royal presence.

'Go along then!' said Alice impatiently. 'And those four lazy pages may follow us.'

'Yes, at once!' Constance understood. They would show the queen who came.

The young heralds, pleased to be active, surged ahead along busy corridors, calling: 'Stand aside, comes my lady of Suffolk!' Alice glided after them with her cousin and the four pages trotted behind. At last they came to the queen's reception room, the heralds threw open the door and Alice swept past them.

'Enfin! Come in my dear Lady Alice. I have been waiting. Tell me, where is your husband? No one can find him for me!'

The queen's reception room was vast but Margaret filled it with her presence, pacing the floor with a restless stride, starting a flock of echoes with her vigorous voice.

'My lord has business with some members of the Commons. He will return directly I do not doubt.' Alice deliberately held herself aloof from the aura of excitement that greeted her. She wondered with slight irritation if Margaret had summoned her simply to enquire William's whereabouts.

It seemed this was not so, however, for Margaret appeared to take a decision in the space of two quick turns before the window and said abruptly: 'No matter. I will speak to Suffolk later. First I have something to say to you.'

Alice inclined her head.

'Come, we will sit here.' Margaret led the way to a long, low seat within the window embrasure. 'Now we cannot be overheard you will forgive me if I speak plainly. We are friends, are we not?'

'Madame you do me great honour in saying so. It is my pleasure to serve you howsoever I can.'

'Oh, I know you do not always understand my ways, you are so cool, so full of the English restraint, while I . . . I must live hot for every moment. But for all that, we have something of the same woman in us.'

She stood up and began to pace the room again. Then she said: 'Gloucester is a great trouble to us all.'

Alice was astonished at this turn of the conversation and made no reply.

'He is dangerous to us. He has always been your husband's enemy has he not, therefore he is also yours. I know that he sought to control this country by gaining a hold upon my lord, the king, when he was but a child. Now he seeks to work his mischief through me!'

'Madame, I do not think you perfectly understand the situation. Gloucester is not my husband's enemy but a political opponent . . .'

'Words, words . . . what do they mean? He seeks to destroy me by spreading scandalous rumours that I am . . . I am a woman careless with her chastity and prepared to barter it for power. Surely that is enough to make him our foe?'

Alice was shocked, not more by the thought than the expression of it. She said slowly: 'Where heard you this slander? I cannot believe Gloucester would have said such a thing. For the sake of his nephew, the king, and his honour he would not use these means to attack you.'

'Nevertheless, he said it. It has been reported to me.'

'Sometimes those who spy find nothing, yet still they bear a tale if it will serve their own ends. Have you thought of that?'

'Yes, but it would be like Gloucester to speak ill of me. He wanted war with France not an alliance through marriage. He has always been against me and sees a way to bring me to disgrace. We must move against him at once before he does us any further harm.'

It alarmed Alice to think William might be impelled to rash action and she said urgently: 'Madame, Gloucester is the brother of our late and well-loved king. He has ever been a loyal supporter of his House. I do not deny that he has troubled this realm with his ambitions and rivalry against the king's great-uncle, my lord the cardinal. But Gloucester is an ageing man now and not in good health. He lives retired. If, in angry spite born of many disappointments, he spoke some folly, he would mean no real harm by it and could do none. I beg you disregard it.'

'Parbleu! I thought as a woman you would understand. I do not know how you can plead for him. However, I promise you for my own part I will take no action without the approval of those who are our valued counsellors.'

'Have I your leave to withdraw?' Alice asked.

Margaret smiled her enchanting curved smile. 'Of course. Perhaps it was wrong of me to burden you with this matter. I value your friendship, you see, and wanted you to know this evil rumour from me. I see you give the lie to it utterly and am glad.'

When she had regained her own room Alice found her head was aching violently. She took off her elaborate butterfly-winged head-dress to relieve the strain and unbound her hair so that it fell about her shoulders. From the low west window she looked out across green lawns and fruit trees to the river, finding little comfort in the fair prospect. Could there be any grounds for the rumour that had come to the queen's ears? Margaret had seemed innocent in her indignation but she had a quality of boldness about her, a kind of flagrant feminity.

It might mean something, it might mean nothing. And if she was suspected of having a paramour who did they say the man was? Better not to guess, better not to know. If it were true, God pity Henry who had come to adore his wife and God defend William – for he had made her queen.

When William came in an hour later he found Alice sitting before the window, her hands folded in her lap.

'You look like a sun goddess in this light,' he said drawing up a chair beside her.

'The sun is setting. I have been watching it fall this last hour.'

William leaned forward and took hold of her hands. It was a gesture he often made when he was uncertain of her mood or his ability to reach her in it.

154

'I have just come from the queen. She said she had spoken with you . . . This is a detestable rumour that has come to her ears. It is more than time Gloucester was called to account for some of the mischief he has stirred up in this kingdom.'

'He was ever a man of hasty tongue but I should be surprised to hear he had dishonoured the king through a base slander on his consort.'

'To be plain so would I. His opposition to us encourages this sort of irresponsible attack to be made by the war-bent fanatics in his following. He has become a focus of malcontents.'

'Even so one does not remove a royal duke without arousing comment,' Alice said dryly.

'No. But it is my task to defend the king and queen from those who threaten their secure reign . . . The queen knows, of course, that Gloucester favoured the daughter of the Count of Armagnac when a wife was being sought for the king and that Beaufort and I were her champions. Naturally she looks to us now for protection.'

An emotion such as jealousy was alien to Alice's nature yet she understood that William might be beguiled from caution by a beautiful young woman, in whose reckless confidence he glimpsed his own youth. Margaret of Anjou would know how to play upon his vanity and his chivalry. Alice could resent that although she did not know how to fight it.

CHAPTER NINE

'WHY, COUSIN! "Thou lookest as thou woudst find an hare,
For ever up-on the ground I see thee stare".'

Alice glanced up quickly. She had indeed been lost to the
world, pacing her thoughts about a small lawn before the
house at St. Edmondsbury in Suffolk, where William had
lodged her.

'My lord Somerset. I had no idea you knew the writings
of Geoffrey Chaucer well enough to quote from them so blithe.'

She gave him a slight, graceful bow precisely suited to one
who, though of ducal rank, could equal neither her personal
fortune nor her husband's power. Moreover, there was kinship
between them through their paternal grandmothers, the Roet
sisters, and even this was somehow acknowledged in the rallying tone she used to greet him.

Edmund Beaufort smiled his admiration. He appreciated
subtlety in a woman, liked her to be proud but not haughty,
clever without ostentation, beautiful in a way which roused
the imagination before the senses. Alice seemed to him to
have all these qualities and he took pleasure in her company.

'Suffolk asked me to come to you. He thought you might
be in some unsettlement of mind and bade me tell you that
the enterprise you know of has prospered.'

'My husband was mistaken if he thought I would be anxious.
I knew we must succeed.' Alice believed Somerset was trying
to draw a confidence from her. It would be unlike William
to reveal to anyone that she had been uneasy about the plan
to arrest the Duke of Gloucester.

'We cannot be overheard here, I think, so I may tell you more plainly that Gloucester rode into the town unsuspecting. He was arrested on charges of malpractice during his protectorate and is even now in close keeping.'

'There was no blood spilled?'

'No.' Edmund Beaufort considered for an instant and then challenged Alice directly. 'You do not like this day's work? Speak freely to me. You fear it will not look well that Gloucester was taken while attending a parliament called in your husband's own countryside.'

'My husband is not a man to act rashly, if that is what you are asking me to say, cousin. I stand with him and for him in all his endeavours to protect the good order of this realm and the sanctity of our king's majesty . . . as I am sure do you.' She had allowed only the slightest preceding pause to weight her last words.

'By the Holy Cross, it is as my uncle says. You are your father's daughter, Alice Chaucer.'

'My lord, you presume much on the ties of blood between us,' Alice said with mock severity. But she could not resist her kinsman's infectious smile. 'And I am astonished you should seek out the opinion of a woman, even were she indiscreet enough to hazard one. What mean you by it?'

'Why, as to that your father was renowned for his intuitive judgment of the people's mood. Got you no legacy of it?'

'A woman's business is to govern her own house not public policy.'

Edmund Beaufort gave a short laugh. 'Margaret of Anjou would not agree with you . . . But come, make no pretence. It is widely held that the lady Alice is a woman who can keep her own counsel. She watches and she learns. For once I want to know what she thinks!'

He spoke lightly but Alice saw that he was serious.

'When you know my husband's thoughts, you know mine also,' she answered slowly. Somerset accepted the finality of her tone, gave a gesture of feigned despair, and, after saluting her warmly, took his leave.

So it was done, Alice thought. Gloucester was brought down, but at what cost? If she had, as Edmund Beaufort believed, some inherited awareness of popular opinion, then it warned her William would rue this day. By luring Gloucester into his own county of Suffolk in order to take him, she sensed he had broken some unwritten code and that this breach would not be overlooked.

William himself had not been without misgivings when he agreed to move decisively against Gloucester. But the queen and Buckingham had argued strongly. The king would travel with them to St. Edmondsbury and it would be seen that what they did was in his name. Even waverers like Edmund Beaufort were tempted by the appearance of ease about the plot. All had gone as smoothly as the optimists in the party prophesied.

Within five days, however, an unpredictable event occurred. Gloucester died. The final disaster of his arrest, following years of frustrated ambition and a lifetime of excess, which had already bankrupted his health, caused him to suffer a seizure. No worse calamity could have befallen his enemies in their moment of triumph.

From this time Alice could mark a change in her husband. His manner became withdrawn and watchful. When he answered criticism of his policies, his words were persuasively chosen as ever, but they were delivered with menace.

She had no need to ask him why. Gossip had it that Gloucester had been murdered on William's instructions. The public display of the body, so that all might see there was no mark upon it, had done nothing to quell the ugly rumour. There were ways, people said, that the deed might be accomplished and keep its own secret. Dark ways.

'They believe what they want to believe,' William had answered Alice almost with indifference on the only occasion she summoned courage to mention what she heard. 'I have done courting the people. They would rather have a bragging warmonger like Gloucester to lead them to ruin and death, than a man who wants peace and prosperity for his country. Because I do not brandish my sword and shout "to horse, to horse and ride over the bodies of our enemies", but prefer instead to make skilful parley for a truce, they call me traitor.

Well, God witnesses it as a base slander. Yet I will have a livelode for my labour, if no thanks. You shall see.'

'Why, what mean you? The king has rewarded us generously. Is this the time to be striving after more?' Alice spoke irritably out of her anxiety.

'Of course now is the time. If I am brought down from office it will be too late . . . And I will have a dukedom ere I quit.' He smiled suddenly in his old way, seeking to carry her with him in good heart. 'Come, are you not panting to be my duchess . . . does the thought of ducal rank for John's inheritance leave you unmoved?'

Alice was thoughtful. She said slowly: 'It might be that if the king bestowed a dukedom on you at this time it would quench the spark in many of your opponents. It will also inflame those enemies who stand most near to you in rank.'

'Hah! You weigh a dukedom as if it were a quantity of butter! Well, I have calculated even as you do, and am resolved upon my course. First I will get a hearing at Westminster to justify the action I took against Gloucester and give the lie to those who cry murder . . . have no fear, I shall find the words to persuade them of my innocence . . . Afterwards I will move the king to bestow on us the dukedom of Suffolk.'

'Is there anything you would have me do?'

'Yes . . . yes! It would be helpful if you arranged to be with me at court throughout this time. You might go to the city and call upon those worthy merchants who were your father's friends. Some of them may be encouraged to speak in my favour on your account.'

'I will do as you say.'

'There is one other task you might accept.' William hesitated.

'Tell me then and it is done.'

'Call in rents wherever you can do so without causing remark. I want a goodly sum banked in France. But not with a French banker.'

Alice understood that he was already preparing against possible exile. She said: 'It is a wise thought. There is an

Italian house my father used. I know one Girolamo Torlanini, who will manage the matter with discretion.'

Three months after Gloucester's death William had his hearing at the Palace of Westminster. If there were those who muttered that the judges were chosen principally from among his friends, many more who heard him were won over by his eloquence and did not wait for the judgment of other men to find him innocent of murder.

Another factor helped to sway them. Within the space of a few weeks Cardinal Beaufort followed his old adversary, Gloucester, to the grave. Suffolk was now the undisputed power in England, if he could but ride out the storm raised by his enemies. Those who from motives of envy, resentment, and personal ambition longed to drag him down from office, were afraid to risk the catastrophic consequences of failure. They held their peace.

By the end of the year, William's position appeared unassailable. Cardinal Beaufort and Humphrey, Duke of Gloucester, had fought each other for supreme power the better part of their lives. Their struggle had left its scars upon the country but the contest had prevented either from total authority. Now William de la Pole, Chamberlain of England, succeeded to the eminence they had coveted, without challenge. He had the experience of government, he had the strength and the wealth to support the position. Above all he had the love of the king and queen.

Then, in February 1448, the French repossessed Maine, according to the agreement William had negotiated with them. When news of the formal surrender became known at home, it blew through the country like a hot wind, fusing individual opinions and emotions. With one voice it seemed, Englishmen were crying: 'We are betrayed by those who lead us.'

In living memory there had not been such hatred of authority throughout the land. Only the king was exempt from blame – a good man, a saintly man, the people said, but too simple to see that crafty ministers were lining their own pockets from the sale of his inheritance.

They hated the queen, who had cost England so dear. Was she not a Frenchwoman, serving the interests of her own country? Aye, and this meddling vixen conspired to bring Gloucester to his death, let it be remembered. They hated the Council, for were not all its members the tools of Suffolk? And they hated Suffolk most of all.

Yet still his fortunes advanced. In little more than a year he had added to his already formidable list of offices, the posts of Constable of Dover Castle and Warden of the Cinque Ports, Admiral of England, and Governor of Calais. In addition, Gloucester's earldom of Pembroke, together with the castles and lordships of Pembroke, Llanstephan, Tenby and Kilgarren and the wardenship of the New Forest had reverted to him. Finally, at the beginning of July, he was created Duke of Suffolk.

But if the title brought William a sense of achievement, it appeared to give him little pleasure. He was becoming accustomed to live with grandeur and dread and Alice was saddened by the change in him. He no longer looked like the same man she had married. In latter years he had allowed a moustache to grow, which gave his countenance a new ferocity. He seldom smiled and the expression of his eyes was bleak.

He would propitiate no one, rode his fellow members of the council hard and sometimes even took a bullying tone to the king. Not that Henry showed himself offended by it. Alice thought. He seemed to think that William could never be wrong and strove to earn his approval with an almost child-like eagerness.

As the queen involved herself more and more in the affairs of the country, it happened that Alice was often left to bear Henry company while his wife was with his ministers. He did not appear to feel any humiliation in this circumstance, but rather to enjoy the quiet talks he shared with Alice at one end of the royal apartments, leaving William and Margaret to argue across a table laden with state papers.

'Dear cousin,' he said to her on one such occasion, observing her attention had been caught by Margaret's voice raised in anger, 'are we not blessed in such a wife, who devotes her energy to the good of our realm . . . Not that we wish you to think we are idle, letting the burden fall only on her shoulders.

We rise long before dawn betimes, and pray, without a kneeling cushion, for God's intervention in the deliberations of our ministers. We all serve as we are best fitted, do we not? Sometimes' – he leaned towards her confidingly – 'sometimes we do feel – if it is not a presumption – that we have the ear of God, and therefore who better to plead for England's good?'

But if Henry exasperated Alice by an approach to his responsibilities which seemed to her inane, at other moments his affectionate and trusting nature disarmed her.

And he could surprise her too. 'Lady Alice, do you think Richard of York wants our throne?'

'Sire! Why should you think such a thing?'

'Great-uncle Beaufort used to say Uncle Gloucester wanted to take it from us. Now he is dead the Duke of York is our heir.'

'It will not always be so. You will perpetuate the House of Lancaster. And although I trust my lord of York is loyal, be assured, Sire, while my husband lives none can plot against you and succeed.'

'Aye, good Suffolk had ever a tender care of us, this we know.'

'And the people, Sire. They love you and would accept no usurper.' But even as she spoke Alice was remembering what she had learned from her father, how the people had turned against Richard Plantagenet and stood by while the Earl of Derby, founder of the House of Lancaster, was proclaimed Henry IV.

*   *   *

As the months went by, no small part of Alice's anxiety for William were his unrestful nights. She would often awaken to find he had left their bed and was striding about the room. Or again when she watched over his troubled sleep, would hear him muttering, until he started up out of a fearful dream.

One night, after the watch had cried three-of-the-clock and she still lay sleepless herself, with William turning fitfully beside her, his murmured words suddenly took shape.

'The Tower . . . beware the Tower . . . must beware . . .

Master Stacy tell me . . . What of . . . my wife and son? . . . What of them? . . . The Tower! . . . The Tower!'

'William! William! Wake up, for the love of Heaven! You are dreaming.' Alice shook him by the shoulder. 'Why do you call out to beware the Tower and who is Master Stacy?'

William's eyes focused on her reluctantly. 'Mercy, Alice! A man cannot remember what nonsense has crossed his mind in sleep.'

'But Master Stacy did not sound like nonsense to me. Why, I almost recall having heard the name but the connection escapes me . . . No, wait! I have it now. Master Stacy has some repute as a scholar, an astronomer if I mistake not?'

'Aye, well he is known to me. I may have spoken his name but –'

'You have consulted him! William, you must tell me the truth. Did he predict that you would be confined in the Tower?'

'No – that is not precisely. I do not want to discuss it with you. I know you learned from your father to make light of those powers which are outside charted experience. It is an oddity for which I do not call you to account. But we cannot talk of this.'

And he remained unmoved by Alice's humble entreaty to tell her more.

While this incident added to her own unease, she did at least contrive to turn it to good account on William's behalf. She persuaded him that his abilities would soon be impaired by nights that were either sleepless or bedevilled by dreams and at last prevailed on him to seek some rest at Ewelme.

* * *

'Upon my oath, this is a house of children! John, John, no need to come hallooing down the stairs like that – see now you have set all the dogs barking. Silence! No John, I know you did not speak, I am trying to quiet this great beast.'

'If you please, father, Sage only understands French Doucement, doucement Sage. Va-t'en! There now father you have quiet to finish your letters.'

'What is this talk of letters?' Alice emerged from the still-

163

room and crossed the hall to peer over her husband's shoulder. 'You promised me you would forget state matters while you were at Ewelme.'

'Well I have writ little enough this morning. There is John making noise for ten lads.' He leaned forward and ruffled his son's hair fondly. 'And as for young Anne, she has been crying ever since she awoke. What is the matter with her?'

Alice sighed. The nine-year-old Countess Anne of Warwick was a frail and fretful child. Since the recent death of her father, Henry, Duke of Warwick, she had been staying at Ewelme. William intended her to be John's wife when they were both of age, for the girl was heiress to a significant property. But it was questionable whether she would survive childhood.

'Cecily had gone on an errand for me and Anne was wanting her to tell stories, I believe,' Alice explained.

'Well, you must not indulge such behaviour. The child needs discipline.'

'No really, William, that she does not! Her health is far from good, as you have seen for yourself. She needs just the understanding treatment Cecily gives her – blithe tales to raise her spirits and good nourishment.'

'Well, well. You know more of such matters than I,' William growled.

Alice saw that John was following their conversation closely and, thinking it unsuitable for him to overhear his father criticising one who might be his future bride, she said: 'Go walk the hounds, my son. Why are you inside the house on such a fine, fresh day?'

'Aye, take the hounds by all means,' William urged, 'especially this brute which knows no English. It will do my loyal reputation no good to be seen in its company.'

'What, you have taken a mislike to Sage, have you?' Alice laughed. 'You have no need to fear, however, she was pupped by the queen's favourite bitch and though of French parentage was born and bred in Westminster!'

When John had ushered out the dogs and reluctantly closed the door behind him, William would have returned to his writing. But Alice claimed his attention by settling herself deliberately in a chair beside him.

'Now what are you about, my lady?'

'I want you to bind up those documents and rest, as you promised me you would.'

'I will when I have dispatched these matters. Go away and jangle your household keys like any other dutiful wife . . . Go and look to that tiresome child. I can still hear her wailing.'

Alice listened. 'No you cannot. You are saying that to be rid of me. I have a duty here, however, and it is to care for your weal.'

William smiled at her absently.

'You are not heeding me, are you?' Alice asked. 'Where have your thoughts gone now?'

'I was wishing Anne of Warwick was more like young Margaret Beaufort.'

The king had granted William wardship of Margaret after the death of her father, John, Duke of Somerset, three years earlier.

'Aye, she has a lively spirit, more like a lad than a maid. She has persuaded Sibilla Berney to take her down to the stables, and I make no doubt is even now coaxing one of the grooms to take her up on the pommel.'

'Like as not!' William slapped his thigh in approval 'Why, when I asked her what she would have as a gift to mark her fifth fête-day, the answer was a goshawk if you please!'

'Mercy! You will not give it to her, I hope.'

'Yes I will. And one of the best men I can find to train it withal. He shall teach her the skills of falconry and see she comes to no harm with the bird.' He added musingly: 'By my oath, though, she has the makings of a good wife, such a one as would bear John brave sons.'

'But you have always maintained that there would be no advantage in reasserting our union with the Beauforts. Anne of Warwick would strengthen John's future position, with new alliances.'

'I know. And I still believe in the advantages of the match we planned. It is merely that I have been beguiled by the lady Margaret! Now away with you, woman, for I must have this writ before noon. Thomas Gascoigne is sending a man to London this day and he has undertaken to carry it for me.'

Alice left him at last and went thoughtfully in search of little Anne. As she climbed the sweep of the wide staircase to the gallery she reflected that Ewelme had indeed become a house of children as William said. In bygone years how many hopeful young feet had hurried up and down, wearing the slight curve in each stone step? How many more would follow?

It was good to have the girls here with John. His games were perhaps a little lonely without brothers and sisters and there was no child of suitable age in the neighbourhood, as there had once been Will Bylton to give her companionship. John was not yet old enough to join in the sports of her pages. She must look out for a suitable boy of good family to join the household.

Anne of Warwick was not in the room she shared with Margaret Beaufort, but along the gallery Alice could hear the gentle rise and fall of Cecily's voice. She must have returned then and come in by the outside stairs. Alice hesitated and then decided to join them in the parlour.

'So Anne,' she greeted the child who rose and curtsied at her entrance, 'that was a dismal to-do you were making earlier. I sent Kate to tell you a story. Would she not do as well as Cecily?' She smoothed the untidy braids back from a woeful, little face turned up to her.

'No one but Cecily can make me really listen to a tale so that I forget everything else,' was the revealing answer.

'And are you so unhappy here that you must forget everything?' Alice wondered in affectionate concern.

'I am not unhappy because I am at Ewelme, ma'am. Oh no! You are all kind to me but . . .'

'But you loved your father dearly and cannot help remembering him?'

'Yes I d-do miss him.' Tears began to flow again.

'Now Anne, dear child, I lost a beloved father too. It is harder for you to understand, because you are very young, but these things must be bravely borne. He would want you, above all things, to live your life fully, adding to his honour with your own endeavour. You must not weep the hours away.

Try to be braver.' She slipped her arm about the fragile shoulders and gave them a squeeze. Looking over the child's head her eyes met Cecily's and they both shook their heads sadly.

Peaceful days filled with the laughter and tears of children could only be an interlude for William and Alice. Soon a royal messenger clattered into the courtyard bringing affectionate greetings from the king and an urgent summons from the queen.

Before they returned to court, however, there was time to entertain at one last banquet, those good Oxfordshire families who stood their friends. The Gascoignes came, the Broughtons and the Dormers. Will Bylton was there, grown more serious of aspect than ever since his father died. Alice had found him an industrious widow to keep his house, and his clothes bore evidence that he was being better cared for than at any time in the past ten years. But he had the inward-turned look of a lonely man, and she saw with concern that although his grizzled hair and lean face gave him a close resemblance to Nicholas Bylton, he lacked his father's enjoyment of good fellowship and company. He was highly respected in the county as a responsible landlord and a modest scholar, yet she knew he had few close friends, for men found him difficult to jest with and had long since given up hope that he would espouse any of their female relatives.

The Stonor family, by long custom, held a notable position at the table. Alice's father had been a close friend of the late Thomas Stonor. They had a common experience of the war in France and parliamentary service. The present Thomas Stonor, born in 1424, had been left to the guardianship of Thomas Chaucer when his father died seven years later, and Alice inherited the responsibility for the young Stonor heir along with the rest of her father's fortune and obligations.

It had been her happy thought to offer him Jeanne de la Pole as a bride. William had dowered his natural daughter lavishly and the young couple had appeared from the first to find each other wholly enchanting.

Looking along her supper-table Alice smiled complacently upon the match she had made. There had been intermarriage between the two families before in the time of her mother's mother. She was very fond of Thomas and delighted to treat him as a son-in-law.

William saw his wife's smile and, following its direction, said: 'You continue to congratulate yourself on that piece of work, my love. Aye but they do make a good pairing.'

'Better than you know, my lord! When I greeted Jeanne she whispered to me with many blushes that you will be a grandfather before long.'

CHAPTER TEN

THE KING'S highway of Thames Street was an unshifting mass of people, wagons and horses. A few minutes earlier, when her heralds entered the thoroughfare, there had been a slowly continuing progress of traffic in both directions. Now, with her entire company halted Alice saw the crowd closing in behind them.

She was instantly and intensely alive to their danger. While her men were still questioning those ahead why they did not move, she had already recognised the unnatural stillness of the people, the sullen faces turned towards her.

They had seen the de la Pole crest and colours, symbols become hateful to them and this day – she thought – this particular day, without any conspiracy, they would snarl and even bite, in a pack.

Then Alice heard a holloa and saw the crowd make way for a newcomer. 'There is always a leader for any hunt at any time in any place', she seemed to hear her father's voice saying: and again 'one should always let an opponent have his say, for then you have the advantage of him – you know what is in his mind but he does not know what is in yours'.

'The Duchess of Suffolk wants a way through here, my good people! What do you say to her? Shall we throw ourselves down in the mire so that her company may ride over us?'

The leader had climbed upon a pedlar's hand-cart, a little ahead of her to the right. A gross man whose greasy apron proclaimed the cook-shop. He stood with huge hairy fists, driven hard against his bulging thighs, elbows jutting.

'See the proud lady, my friends. She sets there mighty cool. We do not exist for her, you know.' His raucous voice adopted a conversational form and his face twisted in an exaggerated sneer, 'We are muck to my lady – not flesh and blood, just so much muck. They do not have folks like us about the palaces where she moves.'

The mob listened, waited. They were so still that a child's cough drew all eyes for an instant. Alice saw that Lammerac had unsheathed his dagger and would have leapt from his horse upon the man.

She snapped at him: 'Do nothing as you stand in peril of me!' and leaning across to Castellet, captain of her body-guard, who was passing orders among his immobilised men in a desperate attempt to launch a charge, she added: 'Neither will you make any move until I tell you.'

The speaker went on: 'Of course it is a very right and proper thing that Alice of Suffolk should walk in palaces. We know her husband seeks to be king.' He mocked her with a bow. 'Your husband's subjects attend you. Speak to them. Tell them why William de la Pole is a traitor to his country? Why, not content with giving the French the land we bled for at Agincourt, he wants to give them England too.'

Other voices joined in. 'Aye, why has he recalled York from the command in France and made him Lieutenant of Ireland?' . . . 'Why has Edmund Beaufort been sent to lead the army in France?'

'I will answer that,' roared the cook. 'York is heir to the throne and my lord of Suffolk is not so schitel-witted as to leave him empowered of the army in France.' The crowd growled angrily and he raised his hand for silence. 'It was a right decision Suffolk made an' all. Beaufort is better fitted to lead the army in France! No, hear me good people! I say he is better fitted to lead them to disaster, and that is what Suffolk wants!'

Now he had roused them and Alice heard another voice from somewhere in the crowd shout: 'Pull down the wife of Jackanapes.' And another: 'Death to the House of de la Pole! Death to all traitors and those who serve them! Death to Jackanapes!'

170

Jackanapes! So that was the name they had dared to mint for *her* husband, William, Duke of Suffolk. It was a reference to his badge, of course, a clog attached to a chain like that worn by tame apes kept for amusement. The nickname was not intended to amuse however. The implication was that William worked mischief in the realm. She looked at the people pressing about her and anger drove away fear. But she must not allow it to rob her of guile.

It was time she spoke. She could sense that the crowd was waiting for her to answer the challenge, growing impatient to hear her plead for mercy.

'Master cook!' Her voice rang clear over the hushed crowd. 'I find your words persuasive and vow I could listen to them all day. But I am concerned for your roasts! Pray go and baste them before they char. We will all wait here until you return.'

There was a startled gasp and then good-humoured laughter rippled among the people. Impatient horses stamped and shook their harness; women eased their baskets on another arm; men's hands left the hilts of their knives and groped to ensure the safety of their purses.

The cook, not wanting to lose grip upon his audience, shouted threateningly: 'Never you mind the meat in my shop. You watch that your own pot does not boil over and put out your fire, my lady.'

'I promise you I will have a care of it. Indeed, my father, Thomas Chaucer, who was some time known to you all,' she stressed the name lightly turning with an easy smile to include everyone about her, 'advised me in the same wise. "Look to your kitchen," he said, "for a well-fed husband smiles upon his wife".'

'Aye, and I wager you have kept him happy in other ways too," a hearty voice sang out.

Alice raised her hand in affable protest and frowned down on her squire, whose outraged chivalry seemed likely to undo them all.

Now the people talked among themselves and one cried: 'Let the lady Alice Chaucer go her ways. She comes of no traitor brood. God bless her for a true Englishwoman!'

171

'Aye,' said another. 'She is Salisbury's widow remember. We used to cry the name of Thomas Montacute as we let our arrows fly against the French!'

They used to cry William's name, too, Alice thought bitterly, but they have forgotten that.

Abruptly it was over. The way was cleared for her heralds. A wagoner whipped up his horses and moved aside to let her party pass without losing its formation. There were even scattered cheers as they rode forwards. The last sight she had of the cook he was spluttering curses at a horde of beggar-boys who danced around him in irrational joy at his defeat.

As Philip Lammerac lifted her down from her palfrey in Westminster Palace yard Alice said: 'Do not look so forlorn. I know you would have died at the hands of that mob rather than countenance such words as were spoken to me. But your death would not have served me, you know.'

He nodded miserably.

'Go and tell Castellet not to dismiss the men. I want to speak to them.' She gave him her hand to kiss but as he knelt he seized the hem of her gown and pressed that to his lips instead.

'I am not worthy, I am not worthy,' he muttered.

'What nonsense! The shame of this day was mine, not yours.'

Castellet and his company stood, each man at his horse's head, watching her approach across the cobbles.

Alice stopped a little way in front of them. 'I would like to commend you all on the restraint you showed in the face of our unlucky encounter. It would have grieved me beyond measure if Englishmen had shed the blood of Englishmen because I had a whim to ride along Thames Street. Now go take your ease.'

She turned to Castellet and added with a sigh: 'I must find my lord and tell him of this day's work.' But she did not leave at once. Her captain was scowling thoughtfully at her and she knew his value well enough to attend when he looked in that way.

'My lady, I do not believe you will need to tell him anything. He would know even before we returned. Flint Hawthorne was in Thames Street.'

'Who is Flint Hawthorne and why should he tell my husband?'

'You do not know him?' Castellet was surprised. 'He was a scout for m'lord when we fought against the French, and has served him ever since.'

'I am sure I have never seen him, nor heard his name before.'

'Well that is curious. He stalks us wherever we go. His special duty is to guard you . . . when . . . when he does not have special business for m'lord! I thought you must know.' Castellet rasped a thoughtful finger against his close-bearded chin. 'Aye, but I was glad to see him suddenly appear at a window above the crowd. He has a foreign skill with a knife . . . can bring a man down with it as surely as an arrow would and almost at the same range it seems! I knew the first man who had durst lay a hand upon you was already dead.'

'Mother of God! He sounds formidable, this man. We should be thankful he is on our side,' Alice said wryly, gathering her cloak about her with an expressive shiver.

'Hist! Here he comes! It looks as if he is sent to fetch me.' Castellet laid a warning hand on her arm. 'Say nothing of what I have told you. Some things better not be known, my lady.'

Alice had her back to the approaching man but after what she had just learned of him she thought she could feel the stealthy advance of his shadow across the ground towards her.

She looked round sharply and although she had heard no footfall he was so close he could have touched her.

He said: 'Castellet, Suffolk wants to hear from you.' But his pale eyes were fixed on Alice and he did not look at the captain, who hesitated not liking to leave his mistress unescorted in the courtyard.

'My lady, Lammerac does not seem to be here. Let me lead you to your apartments as I do my errand to m'lord.'

'No Castellet. Do you haste along. I am not alone after all. If this gentleman is of our service he will bear me company.'

The captain left them with many uneasy backward glances. But neither saw him go. Alice appraised Hawthorne steadily.

173

A man with a predatory face, she thought, but not ill-looking. The sun had darkened his skin and made the curious light blue of his eyes more startling by contrast. Otherwise there was no feature about him that would be recalled. He was neither tall nor short, not heavily built nor yet thin. His dress was unobtrusive, and his hair somewhere between flax and grey.

'You will know me again, my lady.' The voice was soft like a whisper at a keyhole and Hawthorne's mouth twitched at the corners.

Alice imagined it was the closest he ever came to smiling. 'I like to recognise those who are in my lord's pay and I was thinking you must stand high in his regard that you felt free to call him Suffolk when you spoke to Castellet just now.'

'We have known each other many years, your husband and I. He pays me for my labour, and I make a gift of loyalty. He does not ask me to mouth courtesies.' There was an indifference about the answer.

Alice was not often addressed with so little grace. But she understood conventional custom could not apply to a man like Flint Hawthorne.

Apparently interpreting the thought, he said: 'You must pardon me. My manners are not such as to find favour with a lady. Allow me to summon your squire, or may I see you to your apartments?'

'You will do very well. And as we go you must tell me the nature of your services to our household. I cannot understand why I have never encountered you before.'

'I think Castellet must already have told you about me.' Again there was the twitching of the mouth that might be a smile.

Alice quickened her pace up the long flight of shallow stone steps which led to the first floor of the palace.

'No he has never spoken of you so far as I remember,' she said firmly.

'Well it is not fitting for me to speak of my own worth so perhaps you had best ask your husband what use I serve'

They had reached the gallery in which her rooms were situated. Hawthorne bowed briefly and left her defeated by his mockery.

174

Later, when she had the opportunity to ask William about him, she did not take it.

*   *   *

'Dear Will! What brings you to London? Holy Cross, but I am glad to see you!'

'I thought you might welcome the face of an old friend at this time and I had some business to put through in the city. Thomas Stonor came up with me and will call upon you later.' Will Bylton let the cloak slip from his shoulders and tossed it to a waiting page. His face was unsmiling, full of tender concern. He crossed the room and ignoring Alice's extended hands drew her into a protective embrace.

Over Will's shoulder, Alice could see the astonishment on the faces of her attendants. She hastened to disengage herself and led Will to the comparative privacy of her own withdrawing room in the Westminster Palace apartments, beckoning only Constance Courtenay and Maud Whaleborough to follow.

When the two waiting women had engaged themselves with a piece of tapestry at a discreet distance, Will leaned close to Alice and said determinedly: 'I am here to talk to you with a brother's privilege, my dear one, and you shall not silence me!' He caught her protesting hand and held it. 'You must return to Ewelme and keep close there. All Oxfordshire can be raised to guard you and John, if needs be. You must leave London at once.'

'But Will I am in no danger. True there is some . . some unrest now . . . '

'There is more than unrest, by God! There is a mighty upheaval on its way. Do not be trying to deceive me or yourself. I cannot imagine what Suffolk was at, ever to become involved with a scoundrel like Tailboys. That they should plot to murder Lord Cromwell! Why England rings with it.'

'But William swears to me that he had nothing to do with the incident of which you speak. Tailboys attacked Cromwell because of a personal quarrel. It is only because everyone knows he is under my lord's protection that evilmongers are saying William put him up to it.'

'Surely you do not believe that. It is well known that Cromwell is your husband's chief adversary on the Council these days. Besides in his position Tailboys was not likely to have a quarrel of his own with someone of Cromwell's stature. He must have been acting on the orders of another. Can you not see that?'

Alice did not want to see it. She had been shocked when she heard that Tailboys had tried to stab Cromwell as he entered the Star Chamber at Westminster. The man denied it of course, pretending that he only jostled him in anger. But his knife had been unsheathed and Cromwell's supporters maintained that Tailboys had intended to kill him under the clumsy disguise of accident.

She argued as bravely as she could. 'I am certain you have mistook the matter. Tailboys is no churl but an honest Lincolnshire squire, heir to the Kyme estates, and a loyal Lancastrian.'

'Alice, his name has been linked with more than one slaying. He is a man who will spare none in the path of his ambition and will serve whoever pays him the most.'

'The queen thinks highly of him.' It was only a token persistence. Alice had disliked Tailboys' bullying manner when she first encountered him in her husband's company and she found herself all too readily convinced by Will's words.

'The queen is a dangerous woman to the House of Lancaster and this whole kingdom,' Will said slowly and deliberately. 'Many men, loyal and true to the king, can see this. We can discount her opinion.'

Alice said dully: 'Tailboys is in the Tower but William is going to get him freed upon a fine of three thousand livres. Nothing I say will make him change his mind. He no longer listens to me.' She glanced at her women to make sure they were not overhearing and added: 'You know of course that he is losing his ministers? Marmaduke Lumley resigned the Treasury in September and now Adam Moleyns has given up the Privy Seal.'

'Aye, and believe me others will follow. One may get a mistaken feeling of safety within the walls of a royal palace.

Your husband has become the most hated man in England. Does he know it?'

'Oh Will, what do these words mean? Hated by whom? Not by me, not by you, not by anyone who knows him intimately. Not by his sovereign nor his queen. Not by those lesser men who have been glad to cast in the fortunes of their political careers with him.'

'No to be sure,' Will agreed earnestly. 'But what of those who have grown lean watching him push the boundaries of his properties to swallow up lands they claimed. And the humble folk who can get no protection of themselves or their rights from the law because Suffolk has bent and twisted it to suit himself so that it no longer functions for those who cannot buy its interest!'

'Enough!' Alice kept her voice low, but Will could see by the chiselled expression of her face that he had gone too far and she was angry. 'For the sake of the old understanding that is between us we will not quarrel, only speak no more to me of my lord.'

*   *   *

That Christmas of 1449 seemed to Alice the most wretched she could ever know. Smiling, so that none would guess her anxiety, she applauded the courtly verses which William had written for the queen; listened patiently to ornamented compliments on her own grace and beauty; and talked to the king of new books that were being copied for her library.

But the merry-making seemed like a desperate pretence for many of those taking part. They were dancing out a calamitous year. Abroad an impetuous young captain had reopened hostilities in France by taking Fougères in a surprise attack. Vigorous French retaliation led to a series of English losses culminating in the fall of Rouen. At home effective government was crumbling and the authority of the throne itself was being questioned.

Alice, feeling more alone than she had ever been in her life, unable any longer to confide in her husband and knowing estrangement lay between them even when he still sought her bed, began to devote all her concentration towards one object – the strengthening of her personal friendship with the king.

Meanwhile she watched William fix his hopes of political survival on the young queen's self-interested protection, underlining at every opportunity the fact that her power was non-existent unless he governed for her. 'They have come to believe each is a talisman for the other,' Alice thought, 'but I . . . I will trust only in myself.'

In the second week of January her confidence in her own judgment was confirmed in dramatic circumstances. She had been showing the king a prayer which young John had translated into English, when messengers bringing urgent news were announced. He left her to receive their reports and on his return, she saw that his usually benign face was overcast.

'We have the gravest news. Adam Moleyns is dead, murdered.'

'Sire! How has this terrible deed been done?'

'You do not ask by whom, lady. Is that significant we wonder?'

The note of chill enquiry surprised Alice. She said: 'No, Sire. There was no significance.'

Henry regarded her intently and she had never seen him look so much a king, so awesome. Then his eyes softened.

'Very well. We asked because there is a strange aspect to this evil mischance. As you must know the good Bishop Moleyns had gone to Portsmouth to pay our Navy.'

Yes, thought Alice, and it was short pay they were to get, too.

'The unrest which is such a sad sickness in our land at this time has had an effect even upon our loyal Fleet,' Henry continued. 'It appears that rioting broke out among the men – not only sailors were involved, but also our troops who were about to embark as reinforcements for Somerset in France. Indeed it distresses us to tell it, but they cried out upon Moleyns as a traitor, saying he had ruined his country by selling our conquests in France. Taking no heed that he was a man of Holy Church they fell upon him. Alas the savagery! God forgive them, they are like destructive children, who rage without reason.'

Alice said: 'Sire, does my lord know of this? Shall I send word to him?'

'Ah, does he know of it?' the king repeated and his voice again held the forbidding note that had startled Alice a few minutes earlier. 'We desire above everything – except our hope of salvation – to learn whether he knows of it, lady! Though mortally wounded, Moleyns cried out against Suffolk before he died. Why did he do that? He accused your lord of misconduct in regard to the ceding of Maine to the French. We do not know the rights or wrongs of this, having always been content to be advised by those older and wiser in the ways of governaunce than we are. But why, lady, did Moleyns, who was with your lord on embassy to France, make that accusation? Did he believe Suffolk had reached out through the long arm of his influence and struck him down? Was it his way of identifying one who might have reason to silence him for ever?'

Alice's heart shrank within her. She had no need to assume an expression of horror and Henry could not know that it was more for the danger in which William stood than outrage at the suggestion he had made.

'Sire,' she said intently, 'I know my lord had no part in this murder. Moleyns was his close confidant. Surely the bishop cried out because he was afraid. He did not know he was dying and thought his attackers would spare him if he blamed another.'

She saw that Henry was listening to her closely, wanting to believe.

She dropped on her knees before him. 'On the immortality of my soul, I swear that William cannot be guilty. A woman does not live with a man as his wife and not know if he is capable of such a thing. He fears God, loves and serves you honourably. If he has any fault, he is too true a man to speak honeyed words that might win friends out of enemies.'

Henry was moved. He raised her up saying: 'No more, Lady Alice, no more. You are a good woman, true daughter of your honest father who served my father and the father of my father. Your oath upon your soul persuades me Suffolk must be innocent.'

179

Alice kissed his ring fervently and still clung to Henry's hand. 'Your majesty, you will protect my lord from the wrath of his enemies, for the sake of the love he bears you, for the sake of our sweet child?'

The king braced his drooping shoulders and said in a determined manner: 'Be assured I will stand your friend.'

CHAPTER ELEVEN

WHEN PARLIAMENT reassembled a week later it was at once apparent that members would be content with nothing short of Suffolk's downfall. Opinion had unified that this was the first vital step towards the restoration of peace and ordered rule throughout the country.

Quick to perceive he must win or lose all on this session, he asked to be heard by the lords, so that he might answer the accusation of the dying Moleyns.

A bleak January day was appointed and within the Palace of Westminster the question in men's minds seemed as visible as their breathing upon the frozen air.

Hearing that the lords and the Commons were dividing after their preliminary meeting in the painted Chamber, Alice caught the ear of a hurrying page and shook him by it in her anxiety. 'Where will the king and his lords sit to hear my lord Suffolk speak? Say! Say!'

'In the White Chamber, may it please, gracious lady' The lad shrank before the expression on her face. Fearful of not giving satisfaction he added: 'The knights and burgesses of the Commons are expected to go to the Chapter House.'

Alice released the ear. 'You look like a bright boy and I dare swear know every hiding place about these parts. If you can keep your tongue from wagging, and show me a way I might hear without being seen in the White Chamber, I will fatten your purse by five gold pieces.'

The eyes of the little page shone at the prospect. 'Aye, my lady, there is such a place.'

181

'Take me there!'

She waved aside the protests raised by Lammerac who, standing close beside had heard all and, dismissing him curtly, set off down a maze of passages behind her eager guide.

At last, when it seemed they had travelled a great distance in the wrong direction, the boy stopped at a curved stone wall and pointed to a narrow staircase, partially concealed behind it.

'Up there, my lady. You come into a small room carved out of a hollow pillar. There is a lion's head in the White Chamber and you will find yourself looking out of its eyes. You may hear quite clearly what is said.'

'God-a-mercy!' said Alice surprised. 'How comes it that this spy-hole is not guarded. Who else knows of it?' She had drawn a purse from under her cloak and counted out the gold into the boy's hand as she spoke.

'When the lords meet, the Watcher is always up there, my lady. Now may I go, for the lady Margaret Roos is my mistress and I shall not lack a whipping if she looks for me in vain.'

He knelt briefly and was gone out of sight in the gloom before Alice could ask about the mysterious Watcher.

She hesitated, trying to guess who awaited her in the secret chamber. Ah well, no use to come thus far without achieving her object. Holding her skirts and cloak close about her, she struggled up the steeply twisting steps and stood at last upon the level.

Light shining through the eyes and mouth of the lion drew her startled attention at once. She had a fleeting impression that this was the Watcher but it was quickly dispelled when she felt her wrist taken in a close grip and a voice spoke close to her ear.

'So, lady Alice, you have discovered this place have you? I think my lord did not tell you of it. Nor would he want you to be here.'

It was Flint Hawthorne. She knew the flat, expressionless tone and, as her eyes began to see in the dim light, recognised his lean outline.

'No he would not want me to be here. But you will not tell him,' Alice said firmly.

'Peraunter.' He returned the impertinent answer with a shrug.

Striving to muffle her anger, she asked: 'Why do you watch from here?'

He indicated a narrow slit of about an ell's length in the wall to the right of the lion's head. 'For this reason. And this!' Then she saw the bow leaning against the wall.

'Almighty God! What is this? Never say you are here to do murder!'

'Nay, lady, calm yourself. I am here to guard your husband, no more. My task is to bring down any man who draws his knife in anger.'

'You have stood guard here before, I understand. The page who showed me this place spoke of the Watcher.'

'Aye, they see me come and go. But I take care to pull my hood low over my eyes and as I choose to wear my leathers cut in the style of one of the royal archers I am thought to be here on the king's business. No one knows I have any connection with Suffolk.'

'That I can believe,' Alice said dryly.

She walked to the lion's head and found herself looking down over the throne at the faces of her husband's judges. It was a commanding view and she was just in time for the lords were all assembled. Lord Saye and Sele, who had succeeded Marmaduke Lumley as Treasurer, was leaning forward in his chair and talking behind his hand to John, Lord Beaumont, Constable of England, who did not appear gratified by the communication. Richard of York seemed to be holding himself aloof from his fellow peers, choosing to sit between two vacant chairs. William was standing at the farthest end of the chamber and had his back turned to her. Henry of Buckingham was talking to him earnestly, and appeared dissatisfied with the responses he received.

Then there was a call for the Lord of Suffolk to approach the throne and William turned and strode, proud and purposeful, to stand directly below the royal dais.

'How magnificent he looks,' Alice murmured aloud, forgetting that she was not alone. He stood with one foot resting easily upon the first step to the throne, his lavishly furred cloak swept back by one negligent hand. William had always an impeccable sense of occasion, she reflected, and his bearing was confident. But as he directed his gaze towards the king there was reverence, too.

'Our greatest, most high and dread sovereign lord. I must suppose that it be come to your ears – to my great heaviness and sorrow, God knows – that odious slanders against me run through your land, almost in every commoner's mouth. It is said they arise from a certain accusation made by the keeper of your Privy Seal at his death. As the Lord seeth and knoweth I am full unguilty of the wrongs, sounding to my highest charge.' He paused and directed a long, deliberate look at the men who sat as still as figures in a tapestry frieze to hear him.

When he began to speak again William reminded the king of the tradition of royal service in the family of de la Pole . . . 'My father served the king of noble memory, your grandsire, in all the voyages of his days both by sea and land . . . And after, in the days of the most victorious prince, your father, in whose service he died at Harfleur.'

His voice, warm and deep, welled up to Alice and its familiarity brought back a forgotten sweetness. For a few moments she ceased to take in the words drinking only the sound. Then an involuntary movement of her hands caused her to graze her knuckles against the stone wall and brought her back to reality.

William was talking of his brothers, who had died in the French war, of his own imprisonment and the ransom of twenty thousand pounds he had paid for his freedom. He recalled that he had borne arms in the service of the House of Lancaster for thirty-four years and had belonged to the fellowship of the Garter for thirty of them.

'If the Lord wills that I die otherwise than in my bed, may I die in a quarrel with one that says I am not true to you and England!'

'Gallantly said.' Flint Hawthorne spoke softly beside her. 'From the look of some of them, he has hit the mark.'

'Pray God you may be right,' said Alice fervently.

*　　　*　　　*

Three days later William saw that his public acknowledgment of the outcry against him had been a mistake. The Commons petitioned that in view of the unrest in the country, which he himself admitted, he should be placed in the safe custody of the Tower.

At first the lords declined to commit him, saying there were no grounds. Still the Commons persisted. At last they accused him of having plotted a French invasion of England and alleged he had armed the castle of Wallingford to provide a headquarters for the enemy.

In his capacity as Constable of England, Lord Beaumont formally conducted William to an apartment in the Tower of London.

Alice was permitted to visit him, but the concession brought little comfort to either of them. William seemed displeased that she had come at all, and urged her to leave London for Oxfordshire without delay.

'You can do nothing for me. It has come to pass even as it was foretold to me, that I should meet a shameful death and must beware the Tower. I am here now and the end cannot be far away. Your task is to protect our son.'

'No, I will not leave London. John is safe at Ewelme. Will Bylton, Thomas Stonor, my good, loyal Cecily – they will guard him with their lives. There is work for me here, where I may sue to the king every hour of every day if needs be.'

As she left the Tower, Alice was recognised by passers-by and soon a crowd had gathered behind her company, chanting a sinister little verse.

'Now is the fox drevin to hole, hoo to him, hoo! hoo!
... Wherefore Beaumont, that gentille rache,
Hath brought Jackanapes in an evil cache.'

So they likened Beaumont to a hound did they? Well there could never have been one more reluctant to face its quarry, Alice thought wryly, urging her palfrey forward through the press.

But even while she looked with cold contempt upon the distorted faces with their gaping mouths, she felt no hatred for

185

the people who hounded her and knew they did not hate her.

'I understand them,' she thought. 'They are a mindless rabble here in the streets, yet in their own homes one would find them capable of reason, love, hope, responsibility. I know this and they see that I know it.'

And so she rode through them without fear and none laid hands upon her.

On the seventh day of February the Commons presented a petition to the king indicting Suffolk in eight articles. They accused him not only of helping to plan a French invasion but of intending to depose the king and set his son John on the throne. He had intended to achieve this design, they said, by marrying John to his ward, Margaret Beaufort, 'presuming and pretending' her to be the next in succession to the crown through her descent from John of Gaunt.

Alice found the suggestion alarming. Poor, frail Anne of Warwick had died some months earlier and they had indeed contracted a match between Margaret and John. This would seem to give some substance to the accusation and sway the simple-minded to believe the whole outrageous proposition.

Other accusations such as the disclosure of secrets of the king's Council to the French, betraying the strength of English forces to the enemy, and treacherously delaying the shipment of arms could surely be disproved with ease, she thought. But the delivery of Maine and Anjou to the French would be as hard to argue as it had always been, harder now that Moleyns and Cardinal Beaufort were no longer alive to answer for their part.

Although she had been so stout in her denials to the king, Alice had still some doubts about Moleyns' death. Had William any part in it? She could not forget that he had asked the bishop to make that ill-fated journey to Portsmouth when a lesser man might well have carried the money. Or that Moleyns had denounced him as he lay dying. But she must banish these troubling thoughts. She might never know the truth and it was better to believe William innocent, if her plea for him was to be convincing.

A month later Suffolk was brought from the Tower to Westminster to answer the indictment. He asked the king to grant him time to prepare his defence and Henry at last made a decisive move to show his friendship. Not only did he grant time but insisted that William should be confined within the Palace of Westminster rather than the Tower, showing every consideration for his comfort under these conditions.

This new arrangement brought William and Alice fresh hope and, reunited by common danger, they spent hours together acting out the parts of advocate and defendant, seeking to penetrate the minds of the judges.

'I shall throw more responsibility for the cession of Anjou and Maine on to Moleyns – although God knows all the Council had a part in it, and even to this day I believe we were right. If we had not surrendered the territory it would have been taken from us by force.'

But in the end they were bound to admit to each other that there could be no hope for a complete acquittal. In the face of national feeling William could not continue in office.

'My love,' William greeted Alice after a night's thoughtful vigil. 'I have resolved how the best may be brought out of this evil misfortune. I will elect to have my case judged and punishment decided by the king alone and we must persuade him to send me into exile for a short space. While I am absent you may look after our interests and, when the people have had time to soften their opinion towards me, I can return in safety.'

'But will the king be able to do this? What if the Commons are not satisfied with his judgment?'

'He can do it if he will stand firm and overrule those who object, as it is his right to do.'

'He must then,' said Alice determinedly. 'I will seek an audience with him.'

'The queen will intercede on my behalf. Appeal to her. She can get anything she wants from Henry.'

'From any man!' Alice agreed coolly. 'But I do not lack influence with Henry myself and believe I can go about it with greater discretion than Margaret of Anjou knows how to employ. At the moment she is protesting your innocence in such a heated fashion that she makes more people suspicious of you than ever were before.'

But the Commons had not been idle during this time and,

early in March, presented an additional list of accusations. These were of a more domestic nature alleging embezzlement of public money, misappropriation of taxes, and the corrupt sale of offices either for money or in return for unquestioning obedience to Suffolk's personal commands.

Two of them related to William's association with Tailboys. Alice read the complaint that her husband had persuaded the Sheriff of Lincolnshire not to serve writs of exigas against Tailboys, when he was being sued by a number of women for the death of their husbands. Worse still it was recorded that William had asked the king to grant a pardon to the sheriff for not carrying out his duty in this respect.

'Never say you did all this for Tailboys! How could you compromise yourself so rashly on his account?' Alice cried out impatiently at her husband.

'Like all women your attitude to government is unrealistic. I am disappointed for I would have thought you had wit enough to know such doings are inseparable from power.'

Alice dare not pursue the matter further. She knew, however, that on this occasion her judgment was sounder than William's and that commerce with one of Tailboy's reputation must turn men's minds against him, although they would have blinked an eye at the bribery charges.

Convinced that only the king's intervention could save William she asked for a private audience. Henry received her as readily as ever and saluted her on the cheek.

'Lady Alice, we greet you in sad condition. But for the love we bear you, are made happy by your coming. You sent word you were in need. Sit here beside us and say how we may serve you.'

'Sire, you told me once that you would always stand my friend. So now I make bold to ask for your intercession on my lord's behalf. Those who through envy and malice, have brought false charges against him, will not shrink from producing false witnesses to give evidence. There can be no hope of justice for him, unless you in your bountiful wisdom see fit to administer it yourself.'

Henry heard her with an expression at once harried and resigned. When she had finished speaking he sat silent, twisting the great rings, heavy and loose, upon his emaciated fingers. He had begun to appear much older than his twenty-eight years, Alice reflected while she waited for his answer. Overmuch fasting had accentuated the hollows about his mild eyes and worn away the soft oval curve of his cheeks to a bony prominence. The drab clothes he favoured in his pious humility – and to the offence of his courtiers' nostrils seldom changed – did nothing to alleviate his wasted look.

Yet, when he was arrayed in gold-encrusted robes of state, and cloaked in ermine, his hair brushed and burnished as bright as its encircling crown, such a radiance would transform his face that none doubted his God-given right to kingly inheritance.

Henry still said nothing. She restrained her impatience, knowing he could not be hurried, knowing that the step she had asked him to take was a momentous one. Dare he outface his lords, force them to his will to save the man they wanted to cut down. It was no small boon to ask.

'We will make a fair answer to this entreaty,' he said at last as if speaking to himself. 'Suffolk has a right to our protection. We must seek guidance from Our Blessed Lord to know how it may best be given.'

*   *   *

True to his promise Henry laid his plans carefully. On the seventeenth day of March, without warning, he sent for those lords who were in the vicinity of Westminster. It might seem a random summons, but Henry had chosen his hour. Some of Suffolk's worst enemies had left town, anticipating that the king would give his minister as long a period to prepare his defence as they themselves would allow.

The lords who assembled at the appointed time were ushered into the king's innermost chamber. He received them from the throne and all were amazed by his unusually testy greeting.

Suffolk was brought under guard from his apartments. He came in sombre robes without ornament, only the massive seal ring gleaming upon his left hand. Yet he seemed not so much

189

captive, as leader of the soldiers who marched behind him.

Henry desired that the charges against his chief minister be read out and when they were concluded asked Suffolk what he had to say in answer to them. William denied his guilt as he had previously done. But not at such length, for the king directed his Chancellor to hasten the proceedings.

A murmur of discontent stirred the meeting as the lords became aware of their passive role. One or two attempted to direct questions to the Chancellor, but the king refused to recognise them when they rose to their feet and even the boldest would not defy convention and speak without Henry's nod of assent.

Then with an abruptness that left them too astonished to speak, the Chancellor announced that the king had decided to judge Suffolk's case himself without benefit of further consultation. On the treason charges he had found his minister not guilty; but in relation to the misdemeanours listed in the second bill he banished Suffolk, for five years, from any country under his dominion.

The sentence was greeted by a general outcry, only those lords who adhered most closely to the queen's faction holding their peace.

'Silence!' Henry's voice, no longer mild and placating but invested with a new authority, roared above the outrage of his nobles. It was the first time he had attempted to force his will upon them, and they lapsed into a wary stillness, trying to sound the strength of his determination.

'What is the meaning of this disorder?' Henry asked. And his bleak tone discouraged an answer. 'It is our desire, with God's grace, to give justice to all our subjects – the great and the proud,' he regarded them deliberately, ' – as also the humble and the meek. Before one among you seeks to deny our right to give judgment, let him consider that even he may one day stand in need of our mercy.'

The warning was not without effect. Who could be confident in such uncertain times? Moreover, they were reluctant to challenge the royal authority openly and bring themselves into disrepute with an older generation still holding the throne in chivalrous regard.

Returning under guard to the apartments where he had been quartered during his open arrest, William found Alice waiting for him.

'My beloved, he did it! Henry did it!' William was as jubilant for his king's personal triumph as he was for the clement sentence he had received. 'Holy Mass! I wish you could have seen him, heard him speak! They did not like it, you know. Bayed like a pack of hounds that have lost the scent when he gave judgment.'

'Yes, yes! Tell me all that later. Whe *was* the judgment, for the love of Heaven?'

'I am exiled for five years.' He shrugged. 'It can be borne, I suppose. And I make no doubt that I shall be pardoned before that time.'

'Where will you go?'

'That is yet to be decided. I cannot go to the king's territory in France and if I go to any other part it will be said I have gone to make further plots with the enemy. Italy perhaps or the Lowlands.'

'Oh William, how shall I contrive without you?' Sudden panic robbed Alice of her self-control and drove her trembling into his arms.

'You must contrive! Come, gather your spirits and do not weep. It will be your task to hold our property intact and let no man make use of my absence to set a claim against it.' His voice was gentle but resolute. 'Our property in Suffolk and Norfolk will be hardest to hold. As soon as I have escorted you to Ewelme and taken my leave of John, I will go to Wingfield to make matters as secure as possible. My most reliable men of business shall be left behind to administer from there. But you must watch them closely.'

Alice, drying her eyes, said huskily: 'You will sail from Ipswich then? Shall I send word to your captain to ready the ships?'

'Aye, do so. I will leave the *Fair Katherine* lest you have need of her and take the two other ships and the little spinner.'

*   *   *

So they continued to lay their plans, unaware that enemies were at work among the townspeople. Only on the morning set for their departure did they fully understand the diligence of the forces ranged against them. Outside the main gates of the palace a crowd waited. But it was not a crowd that jostled, joked and argued, waiting to jeer and enjoy its own shouted abuse. The people waited orderly and quiet, as though drilled and held in check. Taking stock of them from a window above the gate-house, William grew suspicious and sent Flint Hawthorne to see what was afoot.

Alice encountering him as he returned from his mission demanded to know what he had seen.

'Some faces that are known to me. They belong to men whose weapons are hired in stealth.'

'Hired? But by whom?' Alice gasped.

'How should I know that? They do not wear livery you may be sure.'

'We cannot allow my lord to risk leaving by the main gateway. Though we have our company with us anyone might come at him in that press.'

'Aye, you speak the truth. But I have a plan that may serve. Suffolk's chestnut with the one white foot is well known, and his silver-mounted saddle also. If I were to wear our colours – ill-concealed under a cloak perhaps – and stood with his horse and mine own in the porch of the little used north gate, the people might be brought to think he would leave secretly that way.'

'Yes, I believe you have hit upon it. I will leave with the company by the main gate and my lord shall slip out later on foot when the crowd is misled by you. Lammerac can wait with a spare horse at some distance from the palace . . . '

'And Suffolk can mount and ride after you. You will be safe once you are beyond the city walls, for there your men have space to fight if needs be.'

Well pleased with their plan, Alice and Hawthorne pressed William to agree to it and, much as he disliked having to leave the palace under such indignity, he accepted their arguments.

The deception was successful and in less than two hours

Alice and William were riding side by side, well along the road towards Ewelme.

Three days after their safe arrival in Oxfordshire, Flint Hawthorne rode into the courtyard, leading the chestnut stallion. Alice and William were visiting the alms-house when he arrived and learned of his coming from John who ran ahead of Cecily to meet them on their return.

'Mother, Father! A man called Hawthorne is here. He was stabbed in the leg and the arm and his face cut and the people even cut and slashed your horse, father! Poor Badin, they have wounded him sorely. How could they do such a thing to a horse?'

From Hawthorne himself they learned that the angry Londoners, discovering how they had been duped, attacked him with such ferocity that it had seemed his last hour was come.

'I heard as I left town that there were upwards of two thousand gathered in that mob. I could do little to save myself against those odds,' he told William with his thin smile. 'But happily, as they pressed upon me, rumour started that you were still close at hand and they all hurried away to search about St. Giles. I contrived to get myself to a Cheapside tavern and the host sheltered me.'

'And here you are, God be praised.' William laid his hand gently on his man's shoulder. 'I should not have liked to set forth on my travels without your company, Flint Hawthorne.'

As the hour of William's departure for Wingfield drew nearer, Alice begged him to let her travel to the coast and see him safely out of the country.

'I dread that there may be another attempt upon your life and shall know no rest while I wait here to learn you have sailed without mishap.'

'No, my love, I have told you before I will not have you journeying about at such a time. You must bide quietly at Ewelme and keep John close. Do nothing to draw attention to yourself, while the people still surge against me.'

'But I have such fear for you, William.'

'Dread for yourself, your peril may be as great as mine – greater since I shall be gone beyond the reach of our enemies. Yet I put great faith in your judgment. You will know how to tread surely over the treacherous ground that may lie ahead of you. I would not trust my ultimate fate so readily to any other, as I leave it now in these beloved hands.'

All that night he had held her tenderly in his arms. Together they had outfaced the last wretched hours before their long separation, and in the morning she had waved him out of sight from the boundaries of their manor.

One brief letter reached her, dated the last day of April, in which he related how he had called together the gentlemen of Suffolk and sworn to them on the sacrament that he was innocent of treason. They in their turn had vowed to observe his property rights and stand fast by Alice in his absence.

'Mine heart fails at the distance I must now set between us, but the wind promises true and I can delay no longer. Almighty God have you and our son in keeping until we meet again.'

Alice lingered over the last words of the letter. Then she folded it with a sigh and locked it away.

CHAPTER TWELVE

'MOTHER! MOTHER! See what I have found!'

John's voice. Pure as birdsong, it sounded to Alice as she stood brushing her hair in the early morning sunlight. She opened the window of her room and looked down into the pleasaunce.

'You are about early, my sweeting! I will come and see your treasure when I have arranged my hair.'

'No leave it as it is. I like it all tumbling down.'

'You are very flattering, my lord! But your mother cannot be tripping about like a slattern.'

She saw that John was holding some small creature in his hands. Then, even as he lifted it up towards her, his persistance was lost under the sound of hard-pressed horses approaching up the manor ride. Recognising the leaders Alice felt the smile fade out of her. She had deceived herself into thinking they had come through the worst of the storm, and might take some respite.

The next minute she was running along the gallery and down the stairs, heedless of her unbound hair streaming behind her. The riders were already dismounting as she reached the doorway.

'Flint Hawthorne, what has happened? Why do you return? Why have you left my lord? And Will Bylton! I do not understand how you are come together.'

But their faces told her what she most dreaded to know. With a desperate calm she led the way into the hall and took the great chair at the head of the table, motioning the two men to sit beside her.

John ran in crying eagerly. 'Mother see this is what I found – a baby owl!'

'Not now, my dearest child. I . . . I cannot see it just now.'

'What is the matter, mother? You look so strange. Why is Master Hawthorne come? Is it news of my father?'

'Yes, my son. Now go to your room and wait for me there. You may take your owl and I will come and see it soon.'

When John had gone she looked levelly at Hawthorne. 'I understand that you are come to tell me my lord is dead. How was he killed?'

Will Bylton leaned across the table. 'Alice you will not like to know –'

'You are mistaken, Will. I want to know everything,' she put in sharply. 'Go on Flint Hawthorne, I am waiting.'

'He was murdered, lady. Beheaded.'

Alice clenched her hands determined not to let the horror overwhelm her before she had learned all.

Her voice sounding husky and strange in her own ears, she asked: 'Where was this done?'

'At sea. We were lying off the Kent coast when we met with a mighty ship. Its captain sent a boat to us asking what business we travelled on and who was aboard. Suffolk spoke to them. He told them he was sent towards Calais by the king's command. They persisted that Suffolk must himself go with them and tell this to the captain.'

'God have mercy! And could he not sense it was a trap!' Alice cried.

'He did not seem to fear any treachery, although I urged him not to go.'

Alice understood how it had been. William had never come alive to danger until it was too late.

She listened like one in a trance as Hawthorne's story unfolded itself, translating in her mind from mere words to reality. She was with William in the boat, pulling away from his own ship to the stranger who challenged him from the stronger vessel. With him she scaled the net, felt the shifting deck under her feet, heard the canvas snapping in the breeze, and with sudden alarm the coarse voice of the captain shouting: 'Welcome, traitor!'

They had imprisoned him in a cabin then, thrusting Hawthorne and two others who attended him into the hold. Now she could not see William, did not know what he had suffered or how he had borne it, for Hawthorne had not seen him for two days.

'One of the crew who brought us food said he had been tried again on the charges the king dismissed and that this time he was found guilty. I know not who was the captain nor by whose orders he laid hands on Suffolk. But the ship was well armed and carried one hundred and fifty men at my guess.'

On the second day of May, William was taken off the ship into the long-boat and there a makeshift block had been set ready. One of the roughest of the crew had struck off his head.

'Was it quick, was it merciful?' Alice seemed to plead.

Hawthorne hesitated and it was too late for him to lie. She saw in his eyes that it had been neither.

'Why did none of his men come to save him? Two ships against one and they dared not attack . . . ' Her voice broke off and she pounded her fists on the table in helpless anguish.

'Lady, I cannot say. There was some false tale sent them and without my lord to lead them they knew not what to do. Moreover Suffolk's chief officers had gone ahead to Calais in the spinner to see how he would be received and knew nothing of what happened.'

Alice was silent for several minutes. 'Where is my husband's body?'

'At Dover, lady. The sheriff of Kent helps our men to guard over him, never fear.'

'What's left to fear? They have done their worst.' She spoke bitterly and Will, watching her eyes harden and her mouth take on a resolute line, wished that she would weep.

'Alice, this tragic news has come upon you suddenly. Let me call your ladies to attend you and . . . '

'No, Will. I have no time to spare for the tears and crooning of womenfolk. Though I am but woman myself yet I must

197

wrastle over our property with men. My lord warned me they would prowl like wolves about our boundaries while he was in exile. Now he is dead they will begin to savage us.' She rose and began to pace the room, twisting the thick coil of hair which hung over one shoulder. The feel of it stirred a memory and she said, halting abruptly: 'I must don the wimple. I have said that once before. Somehow I never imagined I would say it a second time.'

She walked back to the table and gave Will her hand across it. 'My good friend. My thanks for coming to shoulder some of the pain of these tidings. I conclude that Hawthorne, knowing of our old companionship fetched you away from your own business to bring me comfort. You may go now with an easy mind.'

'No, Alice I will stay. There may be some service . . . '

'In truth, there is none,' she interrupted him firmly. 'There are matters I will discuss with you later, now I would as leif be alone.'

When Will had taken his leave, Hawthorne would have gone also. But Alice barred his path.

'Now my lord is dead, do you serve me, Flint Hawthorne?'

The man looked uncertainly at her, fingering the hilt of his dagger. 'Have you any use for me? I am not a man suited to the silken attendance of a woman's chamber.'

'I have always some use for a man who can be trusted. Say! Will you give loyalty to me, or if not me, to my son?'

'What would you have me do?'

Alice moved close to him so that her eyes blazed up into his. 'I want to know the name of my husband's murderer and I want him struck down.'

'Lady, I do not know. The captain of the *Nicholas of the Tower* was a rough man. He could have been a pirate. Some believed so, who can tell?'

'*Nicholas of the Tower?* Was that the name of the ship which overtook you? Then the prophecy that my lord should beware the Tower was fulfilled.'

'I do not understand, lady. What prophecy is this you speak of?'

'No matter. It is nothing. But I will have that man's life

198

who captained the ship, aye and he that was executioner. You must seek them out wherever ships put in along the southern coast. It should not be difficult to find out the port to which this vessel belongs. Succeed and I will reward you so well that you need never serve any man again.'

'It shall be as you say. I will set out tomorrow.'

'Good. And now I must order Masses said for my husband and break this evil news to our son.'

Alice moved towards the stairs giving her hand to Hawthorne who knelt to kiss it as she passed. The rustling of her skirts sounded like ghostly whispers in the deserted hall.

* * *

There was little time for mourning in the days that followed. Alice called together the chief officers of William's household from the boundaries of their land and assembled her own men, so that urgent business might be dispatched and the property consolidated.

Her financial advisers, whose fathers had served her father, came from the City to watch with jealous eyes lest their interests be usurped by those who had managed the property of the late duke.

Now that the two households would become as one under Alice's control, there were two officers for every major post, a surfeit of stewards and secretaries, of butlers and captains of horse. The most important among them, soberly robed to match the occasion, roosted upon benches in the manor hall and waited for their mistress, who was now their overlord.

When she came among them, descending the stairs with a calculated stateliness, they stood and bowed low. Her grey gown was simply devised as befitted her widowhood but the cloth was of extravagant workmanship. A neat, round hat was set like a crown above her still beautiful face, and tier upon tier of veiling floated behind her as she glided to take her place.

The effect of her entrance was calculated to impress. Here was no faint-hearted woman, quailing before the responsibilities which would face her during her son's minority and looking

199

for a strong arm on which to lean. Her officers exchanged knowing glances and resolved to tread warily.

The table was littered with bundles of parchments but the first matter to which they must give their attention was the Will. Alice motioned to John to stand close at her right hand while it was read to them.

' . . . my wretched body to be buried in my charterhouse at Hull where I will my image be made and my best beloved wife by me.' But it was not fitting that William should be buried in Hull, Alice thought. Far better he should rest where she had decreed in the collegiate church of Wingfield, close by the seat of his family and his own county.

' . . . and only ordained my best beloved wife, my sole executrix, beseeching her at the reverence of God to take the charge upon her for the weal of my soul for above all earth my singular trust is most in her . . . and last of all with the blessing of God and of me, as heartily as I can give it, to my dear and true son I bequeath between him and his mother, love and all good accord and give him her wholly. And for a remembrance my great belays ruby to my said son.'

Alice turned her head to look at John. She saw that he was moved by his father's words and bit his lip to hide the fact. When their eyes met she smiled encouragingly at him.

It was hard to play the part of a man when one was scarce eight years old. But he stood very firm and there was an assurance about the way he held himself which made her proud.

She beckoned to her personal treasurer, Richard Brodoke, who stepped forward with a small silver-gilt casket upon a satin cushion. Alice opened it and drew out the ruby ring. The stone was as big as a man's knuckle – 'red as a Lancastrian rose', William had once said.

'This is yours now, my son.' She drew a second ring from the casket and weighed it reflectively in her hand. It was very heavy. 'Your father's seal ring will also be yours when you come to man's estate.'

She added, loud for the entire company to hear: 'In future you will take as our authority in all matters relating to our dukedom, my personal seal bearing the leopards' faces and the

200

lion queue fourchee. In this neighbourhood I shall continue to use my father's seal wrought with the Roet wheel.'

Later, when all but her closest advisers had made their obeisances to her, received their instructions and been dismissed, Alice took counsel on the terms under which she should hold her son's inheritance in trust. It was necessary to estimate the cost to her own estate of administering John's vast fortune until he came of age. And the men soon fell to arguing the terms, each anxious to prove his diligence on her behalf.

Alice permitted her attention to wander. On the table before her lay the king's grant dated six days after William's murder. It was a significant document, a token of Henry's regard. Addressed to 'our dearest cousin Alice, Duchess of Suffolk', it gave her custody of 'all lordships, castles, hundreds, manors, lands and tenements which belonged to her husband'. Normally these would have passed into the hands of the Crown until the end of John's minority. Instead Henry had offered them in trust to Alice on any terms she chose to arrange with the royal treasurer. Generous, she thought, but no recompense for the pain she must suffer every time she thought of William's body cast upon Dover sands by his murderers. And his head set upon a pole beside it.

Now, as always, she grew taut with horror as the scene took shape in her mind. Who had brought her husband to such a shameful end? Was it the Duke of York reaching out to pluck down the man between him and the throne he wanted? No doubt that with William out of the way Henry was less secure. If York had no part in the murder, had William been a victim of one of the extreme factions at present rending the country, or simply the unlucky prey of pirates? Had he paid with his life because he stubbornly declined to pay ransom?

When her counsellors at last reached their decisions and the meeting ended Alice had not resolved any of her doubts. She took John by the hand and led him to the old winter parlour.

'My father would always bring me to this room when he had some important matter to discuss. Now I, who must strive to be father and mother both, bring you here,' she told him.

'I have one more task to perform in this day's business. It is to give you this letter.'

William had set down this last message to his son in a moment of disillusionment and self-doubt, urging John to a pious humility he himself had lacked, but which he had come to believe, in that despair, was a man's best armour against 'all the great tempests and troubles of this wretched world'.

Alice could not bring herself to withhold the letter yet she delivered it with reluctance. If in time it superseded John's memory of the man his father had been it must give him an untrue impression.

In the early, promising days William had not thought the world wretched but glorious and in his hour of triumph he had lived and talked as though every inch of England was the flower-strewn path of his personal conquest.

'Mother I cannot read this word.' John tugged her wide sleeve to capture her attention. She looked over his shoulder. 'Furthermore,' she said. 'It reads: "Furthermore I charge you in any wise to flee the company and counsel of proud men, of covetous men and of flattering men . . ." '

'Yes I have it now. That line was close-written and I could not make it out.' He frowned. 'I do not quite understand it either.'

'What do you not understand?'

'Why my father says I should have nothing to do with proud men. I thought he wanted me to be proud. At least he used to say I must take pride in our name and the achievements of our forebears . . . And what is a covetous man?'

'Surely you understand what it is to covet. You know from the Holy Commandments that it is a sin to covet your neighbour's property.'

'Yes. Only I would not because we have so many houses that are better,' John said candidly. 'Does he mean I should beware of men who might covet what we own?'

'No, that is not quite what he means.' Alice was careful to conceal her amusement. 'Your father wants you to be virtuous. You will understand his letter more easily when you are older.'

'I understand what he says about obeying you,' John said heartily.

'I am reassured to hear it.' They smiled at one another. 'Now go to Sibilla. It is past your supper hour. You may leave the letter with me and I will keep it safe for you.'

She rolled the parchment slowly as John left the room and then unrolled it again and read the words ' . . . love and worship your lady mother, obey always her commandments and believe her counsels and advices in all your works, the which dread not, but shall be best and truest to you.'

She closed her eyes wearily. 'Pray God I am equal to this trust. Oh! do not let me fail. Do not let me fail!'

*　　*　　*

In the weeks that followed Alice dared once more to believe that the danger to John and his inheritance had passed. It seemed wise that they should continue to live quietly in Oxfordshire for the time being. But she had retained the services of William's special relay couriers, who brought her news of events throughout the country.

By this means she heard for the first time the name of Jack Cade. Soon it was known to everyone. What had begun as a minor stirring in the county of Kent turned into a dangerous rebellion, with Cade at the head of a considerable army. Nor was it an ill-equipped peasant force that encamped on Blackheath and began to issue threats and demands against the government. Men of widely differing social status were rallying to Cade's banner. The name of Sir John Cheyney was prominent upon the list, and there were other gentlemen of good family, as well as merchants whose commerce in the Cinque Ports had been hit by the French wars. Some even believed the Duke of York was encouraging the uprising, for there were well-known Yorkist sympathisers in the rebel camp.

The court was at Leicester, where parliament was in session, when news of the rising reached it. Hastily gathering a force from among his lords, the king returned to London and ordered Cade to disperse his army.

The next news that reached Alice in Ewelme, was of an encounter at Sevenoaks where the rebels had managed to defeat the king's soldiery. Disaffection was encouraged throughout the south. There were demands for the heads of ministers, and most of all for the heads of Lord Saye and Sele, the Treasurer, and his son-in-law William Crowmer, Sheriff of Kent.

'This man Cade seems to have bewitched England!' Alice exclaimed when Thomas Stonor rode over to tell what he had seen while visiting London on business. 'Whatever he demands suddenly becomes the will of the people.'

'Aye, if he takes London we must dread the outcome. There is considerable support for him. In every tavern men echo his cry that the Duke of York should be recalled from Ireland and given a prominent position in the government. They seem to think York can set every trouble in the country to rights.'

'Well it is my belief York will return without waiting for a summons. But he is not like to want Cade for an associate!'

Thomas Stonor shook his head doubtfully. 'In these times one can be sure of nothing. Men further their fortunes by means they would once have shunned and think no disgrace. What we shall all come to, I know not.'

Alice laughed out loud. 'Dear Thomas! You sound more like an old greybeard deploring the rising generation than a man with scant twenty-six winters to his account. Ah, but I have a fondness for you – and Jeanne. And that splendid godson of mine! How is young William? Tell me of him and let us speak no more of Cade.'

But before many more days had passed Alice discovered that she had been wrong to dismiss Cade so blithely. First came the news that his rebel agent had stirred up the people of Salisbury so that they seized Bishop Ayscough while he was saying Mass and dragged him from the chancel to a brutal death. Ayscough had performed the marriage between the king and Margaret of Anjou and he had acted as confessor to the king. Moreover he was known to have been closely associated with William. The bishop's death had a grim significance for many people.

Then on the fourth day of July – the king being at Kenilworth – Cade entered London and contrived by treachery to occupy the city.

Crowmer and Lord Saye and Sele, who had been placed in protective custody on the king's orders, were dragged out of ward by the rebels and summarily put to death. The heads were displayed on London Bridge. On the same day, Alice learned, she had herself been the subject of an indictment of treason lodged at the Guildhall.

Loyal Oxfordshire friends hurried to assure her of their service in need. Soon the village had the news and reacted with a mighty indignation and alarm.

'Such a love as they have for you, Alice!' Will told her.

'Do you know, the men were loath to take the cress to market this day, for fear Cade's men should come and carry you away in their absence.'

'But how nonsensical! They know I have my men about me. I cannot understand why everyone should be in such a pother. After all, I am a woman – they will not take my head, I imagine.'

'Cade is a ruthless enemy to have at your heels, though, and I doubt he can control his followers.'

'Cade will not come here.' Alice's voice was firm. 'However I must speak to our people and strive to reassure them. I understand their fears. If John and I should perish and the property be seized there might come a lord here to make them sweat and bleed to his profit.'

'You had better have married me.' Will spoke fiercely, out of a sudden anger at the contemplation of her peril. 'You could have lived happy and untroubled then. I wonder if, when the end comes, you will think it has all been worth while.'

Alice looked at him strangely. 'If you are by me then, perhaps I will tell you.'

CHAPTER THIRTEEN

JACK CADE'S triumph over London was short-lived. He had failed to capture the Tower and, finding himself unable to discipline his army in the narrow, crowded streets of the city, agreed to withdraw and negotiate with the government.

In exchange for a general pardon and the promise of redress for some of their grievances, Cade disbanded his main force. But he had kept his closest confederates with him and within two days had violated the truce by attacking Queensborough Castle in Sheppey. He was killed trying to evade capture.

Home from Ireland, to a country seething with the events of that thunderous summer of 1450, came the Duke of York at the head of four thousand armed men. All knew that he returned without leave and pondered the outcome as they watched his purposeful progress towards Westminster.

On reaching London, York announced that he had returned to help restore good government. But the timing of his arrival and the vast number of men he had brought with him seemed to the Lancastrians to menace the throne itself. They retaliated by recalling Edmund Beaufort, Duke of Somerset, from France, and the implication was not lost on the country. It was possible Somerset's claim to the throne could be held superior to York's. For although the illegitimate Beaufort line had been excluded from the succession, such a ruling might be revoked, and his descent was from the fourth son of Edward III while Richard of York descended from the fifth son, in the male line.

The queen, well-pleased with the effect of her party's counter-challenge, mustered Lancastrian strength in the capital.

Early in September Alice was among those to receive her majesty's affectionate greetings and a kind enquiry as to when Margaret might once more have the pleasure of welcoming her at court.

'And the devil of it is I must go,' Alice confided ruefully to Will. 'So far the king has kept faith with me and I cannot fail him.'

'But it is not the king who has called you to court. I dare swear he knows nothing of this message. He would never invite you into the midst of your enemies. I beg you, do not act in ill-judged haste because honour prompts.'

'It is a question of necessity as much as honour. If I stay away from court, those who want to see the de la Pole blood declared corrupt and our estates forfeited, might eventually have their way with the king. My presence will strengthen his resolve to give me justice.'

When Alice reached Westminster Palace, Margaret of Anjou was already waiting to greet her.

'Magnifique!' she cried. 'No woman save a queen can ever have ridden at the head of such a formidable company. I had word of your coming but I never dreamed you could gather so many men in a short space.'

'It has not seemed prudent to deplete the force kept by my lord. My position is not . . . '

'No, no! Indeed you must keep them! We may have need of them,' Margaret interrupted emphatically. She steered Alice towards her apartments and as soon as they were alone began to rage against York.

'That man! Not only has he virtually invaded our city with his army, but he shouts at the king and insults me to my face. Make no doubt of it, he intends to seize power in this land.' The queen clasped and unclasped her hands in her agitation. 'Dieu! Is there no good Englishman who will strike him down.'

'Madame I beseech you to calm yourself,' Alice soothed.

'How can I be tranquil? Lady Alice you do not know . . . Why when my lord, the king, granted him an interview he came striding into our presence as though he walked in his own palace and all but turned me out of the room. "Madame, I decline to inflict the tedium of my communication upon so beauteous a lady," he says. To think of it – that devil bowing me out with a sneer as though I had no right to hear his business!'

As the days went by Alice learned that York had tried to press the king into making a number of reforms. But Henry had withstood him. While promising to submit the recommendations to a special council, he had resolutely declined to act on the advice of one man.

When parliament reassembled in the first week of November, however, it began to appear that York had voices enough in the Commons to urge his will upon the nation. Members opened the session by electing as speaker, Sir William Oldhall, a Norfolk landowner, who was known to be strong for what men were now freely calling the Yorkist cause. If any further evidence were needed to show where the predominant sympathy of the assembly lay, this was soon forthcoming.

A petition was put forward asking that twenty-nine persons be banished from the king's presence and their property forfeited. The Duke of Somerset headed the list and the only woman included was Alice, Duchess of Suffolk. The accusations against them were that they had misappropriated property, tampered with the process of the law and disturbed the peace of the kingdom.

Henry, outraged at this attempt to remove half his court from him, replied that he was 'not sufficiently learned of any cause' for their banishment and declined to part with those accustomed to be in close attendance upon him. Nor would he listen when members petitioned him to declare William de la Pole, a traitor, his blood corrupt and his property forfeit.

Finally the Yorkist element over-reached itself and so brought the session to an end. Thomas Yonge, the member for Bristol, proposed that as Henry had no children the Duke of York should be officially named his heir apparent. To the Council and the lords, however, a Yorkist succession threatened the coming to power of the families of Neville, Mowbray and Vere to form a solid alignment, and even those who had cause for dissatisfaction with Lancastrian rule dreaded still more the prospect of new rivals struggling to grasp a share of the wealth and acreage of England. They adjourned in alarm.

Yonge was sent to the Tower to reconsider his proposal, which the Council declared rank with treason, and York withdrew from London.

Once again the crisis had been averted. But the people who had lived through it were less innocent. They knew now that there must come a reckoning on another day.

*　　*　　*

Alice went home to Ewelme for Christmas. Castellet halted the column as they neared the village so that she could leave her position of safety in the middle and ride to the head of the men. In this manner, with the chief officers of her household about her, she entered the village.

But although the church bell sounded its customary welcome there were few villagers to be seen. Most of the old folk were there – the dames creaking their bones in painful curtsies, the men tugging ragged grey forelocks. And the children met her in force as they had ever done, waving their hoods and scrambling to touch the silver bells that jingled upon the trappings of her horse. Of their parents, however, there was no sign.

Alice, passing along the main street with her left hand lifted in greeting, concealed her uneasiness beneath a serene smile.

She urged the mare to a quicker pace as she turned into the ride and was relieved to see John waving energetically from the top of the mounting block. At least he was safe. But there *was* trouble. It was there in Cecily's face and Sibilla Berney's hands fumbling with her girdle.

Once she would have swept aside the courtesies her homecoming demanded, to come at their tidings. The years had taught her to value the refuge of custom, however, and only when she had reached her chamber and permitted her women to remove her travelling robes, did she beckon Cecily close.

'You have something you dread to tell me. Indeed everyone I see about me is heavy with the guilt of knowledge. Out with it then!'

Cecily met the steady enquiry of Alice's eyes with reluctance. She said: 'The villagers have hid for fear of your anger . . . and for shame. Yesternight they hunted Adeliza like a hare and stoned her.'

'God forgive them! Is she dead?'

'Yes. Stephen came upon them and whipped the men back. They had tied her to a tree. When he cut the thongs she fell, lifeless, to the ground. He said it was Ben Clutch who keeps the Saracen's Head that led them.'

'God forgive them!' Alice repeated and Cecily shuddered. The pious words sounded like the blackest curse.

'I believe they did it out of love of you. Ben Clutch has been telling them that the misfortunes which have fallen upon you were wrought by Adeliza through an evil charm. It has been thought here that when you were seen visiting her cottage you went to chasten her and that in the end she took her revenge by witchcraft.'

Cecily looked with apprehension at the still face of her mistress and, scarcely aware that she spoke her thoughts aloud, said: 'You frighten me with that look. I have seen it too often upon you this past year. Will you not weep a little for poor Adeliza?'

'You forget yourself, woman,' Alice said curtly. She rose and turned away to look out of the window. 'And shall I, who have had so many taken from me, shed tears for one more of slight account? I think not.'

Alice did not refer to the matter again. But she declined to show herself in the village for several days, taking a circuitous road when she left the manor and making no acknowledgment if she chanced to pass one of the tenants.

Christmas came and she did not break the custom of feasting the villagers in the manor hall, nor deny them the time-hallowed gifts of firewood and game. She refused them only her company, keeping her own feast in the enlarged winter parlour, and sending John down with Will Bylton and Cecily to do the honours of the house.

Once the revels of Twelfth Night were passed, however, she began to shed her chilling remoteness and go once more among her people. Thankful to be restored to her pleasant opinion they vowed to each other that never again would they hearken to Ben Clutch. There were many who remembered that he had been leading them into trouble ever since they were children together. A bragging bully, as he had always been, now in middle age he had goaded them into breaking the peaceful tradition of the manor.

Ben Clutch had succeeded to the keeping of the Saracen's Head on the death of his parents. Without appearing to do so Alice watched him over the years, saw him harass a young wife to an early grave because she got no son, and turn a second laughing bride into a cringing drab. She detested his influence upon the men of the village, finding his hand in every mischief, though his attitude in her presence had always been unctuous and ingratiating.

Now he had done this violence and she resolved to find some means of driving him out of Ewelme at the first opportunity.

Then, one morning in mid-Lent, Flint Hawthorne walked his horse quietly into the courtyard and Alice forgot all other preoccupations.

'At last you are come!' she greeted him with impatience. 'It is ten long months since we had word of you. Pray heaven your time has been fruitfully spent.'

But although Hawthorne had travelled from port to port along the southern coast, had frequented taverns where sailors spent their pay, had lingered on quaysides and listened behind doors, he had been unable to discover who had promoted the assassination plot. He had traced the commander of the *Nicholas of the Tower* and revealed him as Robert Wennington, a Dartmouth shipowner and a member of the Commons in 1449 and 1450. Yet it seemed unlikely that Wennington would have had the courage to act on his own authority and, since Hawthorne had been unable to find him, Alice agreed with the conclusion that he was being sheltered by influential friends.

'Will you continue the search? You shall have gold enough for all your needs,' she promised, when Hawthorne had finished the account of his travels.

'You are generous, lady. And I will take your hire.' The answer was prompt and unadorned. The pale eyes considered

211

her. 'You have been in some danger these past months, however. You had better pay me to stay for your protection than to journey about the country in the cause of your dead husband.'

'That is a matter for my judgment.'

Flint Hawthorne bowed to the rebuke but the suspicion of a smile flickered about his mouth as he said: 'I will rest two days and then be gone.'

Four days later Hawthorne left Ewelme a startling event occurred. Ben Clutch was murdered upon the road near Henley. No one knew why he had journeyed there alone. Now they would never know. He had been brought down by an arrow and his purse was gone. That much was sure. The sheriff's men chanced upon the body and brought him home, remarking it strange that an elaborate, silver-hilted knife had not been taken nor the money belt the dead man wore beneath his clothes.

'This robber must have been new to his trade. Most will hack off a finger to take a ring without second thought. They miss nothing in my experience,' one of the officers told Alice. She listened thoughtfully to his report and when he had gone she sent for Cecily.

'Did you talk with Hawthorne about Ben Clutch and his part in breaking my peace on this manor?' She asked the question without preamble and Cecily was no less direct in her reply.

'Yes I did. He asked me if anyone in the village might have reason to play the traitor should there be an attempt against you. At first I said there was no one. But I told him Ben Clutch was a troublemaker and what he had lately roused the people to do.'

'So he proposed to remove the danger for me?'

'Not to me. No surely you do not think I would have fallen in with such a plan!' Cecily countered indignantly.

'No. Hawthorne is a man who likes to think and act alone.' Alice shrugged. 'On this occasion he did well for my purpose.' She saw Cecily's start of surprise and added sharply: 'You need not look so shy at me, woman. Ben Clutch reaped as he

212

sowed. I like that well. It only concerns me that none shall suspect my hand in this.'

'Nay, lady. They would never think you capable of such a thing!'

'Indeed? Then that is strange for death has dealt with me and therefore why should I not deal in death?' Alice saw she was increasing Cecily's alarm and added in a manner more normal to her: 'We will forget what has passed between us here. We know nothing of Hawthorne's doings after he left this place, remember.'

*   *   *

The villagers shared the opinion that the killing of Ben Clutch had a justice about it, little short of divine. In due course, when his widow had taken a stout member of Alice's own soldiery to husband and made short work of producing a thriving boy, they ceased to recall him at all.

By this time Alice had a new problem to face and one which caused her many troubled nights. John was nearing ten years of age and his future education had to be carefully planned. She had engaged a certain Walter Clifford to tutor him and Castellet was teaching him use of arms. But she saw the danger of his continually living in a household governed by a woman, where the only men were in a position of subservience.

'What he needs,' she confided in Thomas Stonor, 'is to serve some time with a man he can look up to, one who can show him how to manage a great inheritance, how to command so that hundreds will obey with ready hearts, how to bear himself with courage, dignity and grace. I see it very clearly yet I am at a loss where to place him.'

Thomas Stonor nodded in understanding. 'Aye, it is hard for you to send him away from you while the temper of the country is still so troubled. Whom can one trust?'

'That is the problem. My lord's brothers long dead and myself an only child, we have no close kinsmen of suitable estate.'

'Well you have no need to be anxious. John is an able boy and if he learns from you, in the end he will not be lacking.'

213

But if she allowed herself to be reassured on the matter of John's education, at least for the present time, Alice continued to look anxiously towards the future. John was William's son and therefore unlikely to content himself with administering his estates like any simple squire.

He would want the satisfaction of high office or perhaps a military command. Also an advantageous marriage must be arranged for him since the contract with Margaret Beaufort had had to be broken to appease their enemies. She must not fail him in her political judgment. The alliances she forged for him must be sound and far-sighted.

It was at this time that the thought came into her mind, unbidden and unwelcome, that potentially her strongest connection might lie where she least wanted to acknowledge it – with the House of York. She recalled her earlier friendship with Alice, Countess of Salisbury, the stepdaughter gained through her marriage to Thomas Montacute. Alice Montacute had married into the Neville family and was sister-in-law to Cecily, Duchess of York.

'If I had to come to terms with York, Alice Neville would act as intermediary for the sake of the love her father bore me,' Alice reasoned. And if she did not like the thought, with its implicit treachery to the House of Lancaster, she did not dismiss it either.

*　　　*　　　*

The queen was with child and the king had lost his reason. It was rumour, it was fact. Simultaneously the two events were relayed through England, and committed Lancastrians trusted that the good news would counterbalance the bad.

But once again they had misjudged the temper of the people. The knowledge that the queen was enceinte was received by many as a calamity. While there was no heir they could afford to be tolerant towards the House of Lancaster in its twilight. The line would end with the death of the king and a new branch, sprung from the great Plantagenet root, would bring fresh hope to a disordered country. So they had thought. Instead, having established beyond question that he had inherited the Valois madness through the blood of his French mother, Henry now promised the kingdom another of the same strain. Only this time there would be tainted French royal blood from both parents.

On the thirteenth day of October, 1453, Margaret gave birth to a son and called him Edward. The following month Alice was among the peeresses summoned to attend the ceremony of the queen's purification at Westminster.

Knowing that the Council had reluctantly allowed York to assume the role of unofficial Regent, she had braced herself for the ordeal of meeting her declared enemy face to face. But she had not anticipated the painful effect which the king's appearance was to have on her. Henry lay back in the great chair of state, unable to speak or move – like a corpse save that he breathed and dribbled, or swallowed when sops were fed into his gaping mouth. In vain Alice kissed the flaccid hands and looked for recognition in the staring eyes which saw nothing.

'Rest yourself, dear lady Alice! You can do no more. He sees, hears no one.' The queen had turned away impatiently, as though she could no longer bear the sight of her husband, and motioned Alice to follow her.

Margaret left the king's chamber leaning upon her women. She had not yet fully recovered from her confinement and was in poor looks. But her spirit was as strong as ever and her determination – so it seemed to Alice – stronger now that she had a son for whom she must fight.

'We had hoped that you might be able to break through the king's trance by calling up memories of happier days,' Margaret confided when they were alone.

'Perhaps you would have me try again another day when he is a little better?'

The queen scowled. 'There is never a day when he is better. He is always the same.'

'If he was struck with this . . . this sickness without warning he may be healed in the same wise.'

'Do you think so?' Margaret brightened. Then she added intensely: 'Indeed, he *must* recover. He shall recover for the sake of our son.' Her voice rose to a shrill cry. 'But if he does not I will drench the soil of England with my own blood before I see York rob my Edward of his inheritance.'

Alice wondered why Margaret of Anjou must always sound as if she was speaking the lines of a Greek tragedy. Aloud she said: 'Madame, you ought not to put yourself in such agitation at this time. You will become fevered.'

*   *   *

When she was not in attendance on the queen, Alice kept to her own apartments, passing the time quietly in dictating matters of business to her secretaries and receiving few visitors. She had hoped in this manner to avoid confrontation with Richard of York. However, she could not deny herself a daily walk in the palace gardens and it was on one of these outings that she had the misfortune to encounter him.

Presuming ill-chance had brought them together, she would have passed by without acknowledgment. But the duke stood his ground squarely in the centre of the narrow path and Alice saw that he had deliberately sought her out and was determined to speak with her.

'The lady of Suffolk walks early!' There was a heavy attempt at joviality in his voice. She saw that he was not at ease and the knowledge calmed her.

'My lord of York does likewise. We are happy that the cares of government leave some little leisure to those who must carry them.'

He considered her, scowling slightly. 'Lady, you and I should talk somewhat, where we are not overheard. Of your goodness, let me accompany you along this path.'

Alice nodded to her women to fall back apace and continued her walk at the duke's side. He seemed to have difficulty in choosing his words and she took the opportunity to observe him with a sideways glance. He was a well-looking man, she supposed, somewhat over forty years of age, but she found the expression of his mouth and eyes formidable. Was this the face of her husband's murderer? As if he had read the thought York said abruptly: 'I want you to know, lady, that I had no

216

hand in the death of your husband, whom God assoil. I did not want his life, only his removal from high office and to this end I opposed him across the Council table.'

'If that be true then it will distress you to know of a vile rumour that has reached me. I heard that you were not content with the grim price my husband paid, but were urging that I, too, should be attainted of treason and my property confiscated.' Alice spoke in a detached manner, even while she trembled within the shelter of her cloak.

'Some speak in my name that which I do not approve,' York shrugged. 'What would you? One cannot control the tongues of free men. But you and I have common kin and there is no call for enmity between us.'

Alice sensed the implied question. 'None, my lord. I am no longer young and being a woman alone want only to live my days in peace.'

'And your son, lady, what of him?'

'He is an innocent child,' she answered firmly. 'You have a son of the same age and must know they think of nothing save horses and hawks. I am not raising John to avenge his father's death.'

York seemed satisfied that she spoke the truth. 'It is well!' She thought that he had done and made as if to call her women about her, but he spoke again. 'We have all a duty to teach our children what will serve them best . . . to reverence peace and the law of the land and to give their loyalty to . . . the symbol of the crown regardless of . . .'

'Regardless of who wears it?'

'Men are but mortal.' He turned his eyes towards heaven inviting approval. 'Some are strong, others frail. Death come to all.'

The words were conventional enough yet they had both lowered their voices aware of the significance behind them.

Alice understood then that if he could be assured of her neutrality in a final conflict between the houses of Lancaster and York, he would spare her from further persecution. Moreover if he gained the throne there could be a place for John in his favour. And looking at the unyielding face before her she

217

felt certain that as long as Richard of York lived Henry's son would never wear the crown.

Realising that it was in her best interests to remain uncommitted as long as possible, Alice contrived in the remaining weeks she was at court, to persuade York of her readiness to come to terms without actually binding herself in any way.

CHAPTER FOURTEEN

THE STONORS had ridden over to Ewelme on a bland morning in the last week of May, 1455, and the laughter of children filled the blossoming gardens of the manor.

John had set up a quintain to show off his prowess at the tilt and sturdy William Stonor, barely six years old, was clamouring to be allowed a try.

'No, no! You are too little for this man's play,' his mother protested, catching him about the waist, while Alice laughed at his endeavours to free himself.

'He has spirit, this godson of mine, and that I like to see.' She shielded her eyes against the sun as John cantered up and saluted with his lance. 'That is enough now, John. We are going into the pleasaunce. Food has been set out for us there and at least William can take part in eating, can you not, mon enfant?'

They moved off in a carefree procession, plucking scented leaves as they dawdled through the herb garden and crushing them in their fingers to inhale the fragrance.

'My lady, a rider here brings fearful news!' Cecily hurried across the grass towards Alice, followed by a man, whose dusty face was streaked with sweat.

'Let him come forward! Whom do you serve, stranger?'

'May it please you, lady, I rode for my lord Somerset.'

'My cousin Edmund Beaufort? What of him?'

'Dead, lady. Slain at St. Albans.'

'Heavenly Father receive his soul! ... How came this about?'

'The king was on his way towards Leicester, and my lord Somerset commanded the royal troops . . .'

'Yes, we know this well! Make haste with your tale for pity's sake!'

'The Duke of York was waiting outside St. Albans. He wanted to speak with my lord the king. I do not know what passed. We were told to dismount and take our ease and for three hours there was much coming and going and parleying and arguing. Someone said my lord Buckingham would not give Richard of York leave to approach the king. But I am only a simple trooper, ma'am, and cannot vouch for the truth of that. Then before we knew what was happening we were engaged . . .'

Thomas Stonor interrupted incredulously: 'You mean a *battle* was fought?'

'Well, so it seemed to me,' the man growled. 'It lasted scarce an hour, yet there was my lord Somerset dead and Henry Percy of Northumberland, aye and Buckingham's own son, Lord Stafford, was sorely wounded and like not to live. Warwick came on our flank, you see, and we had never a chance. Besides we were outnumbered.'

Alice said quietly: 'You have done well to bring me these tidings and shall enter my service for your recompense. Can you tell us what befell the king?'

The man looked gratified. 'The king is safe, lady. I saw the Duke of York kneel to him when all was done and their majesties agreed to ride back to London with York. But some of Warwick's men were dispatching those who wore the livery of my lord Somerset when they could come at them, so I thought best to leave the field. Having no master to serve I bethought me of your connection with my lord.'

Alice nodded. 'And was there much turmoil in the country you came through?'

'Aye, that there was. People ran out at every village and shouted to me to own whether I was for the white rose or the red. In truth I knew not which answer would be best received.'

'Bah! This talk of roses – as though gardening parlance could hide the ugly truth of civil war,' Thomas Stonor broke in impatiently.

His wife clutched her child to her crying in alarm: 'Civil war! Oh Thomas, my love, we must return home at once.'

'Nonsense,' Alice said sharply. 'It is nothing of the kind. Fie, Thomas Stonor! Confess you would not know a civil war if you were standing in the middle of it. You are putting Jeanne in a fright and all on no account.'

Thomas acknowledged the rebuke but persisted: 'No one can predict where an affray of this kind may lead. The king has been slipping in and out of madness this past five years and each time York has taken over the government he must have increased his appetite for it.'

Alice looked round quickly and was relieved to see that Cecily had wisely shooed the servants away. John was listening attentively, however. He was thirteen now. So very nearly a man.

Chiefly for his benefit she said: 'York certainly has somewhat of right on his side in this instance. He made no bid to take the throne while the king was out of his wits. And he has not deserved to be thrust out of office by the queen the instant Henry recovered sanity.'

'That is true,' Thomas Stonor agreed. 'Had he been allowed to keep a prominent place on the Council we would have been spared this wanton blood-letting.'

Alice sighed: 'Alas for Edmund Beaufort. He had no talent for war. In London he spoke to me as one who feels death overtaking him.'

* * *

The next month it became known that York had assumed Somerset's title of Constable of England, and Warwick, his nephew, was made captain of the vital garrison of Calais. Even in the seclusion of the Oxfordshire countryside Alice did not escape the effects of the new régime. As Constable of Wallingford Castle she had been instructed to receive Henry Holland, Duke of Exeter, as a prisoner being transferred from Pontefract. But with Exeter came the Earl of Worcester, bearing letters which gave him such wide authority in Alice's own castle that, reading them, she grew alarmed. If she permitted this encroachment, how far would York dare to push her in future.

'I see how it is!' In controlled fury she crushed the stiff official papers to a ball, while Worcester stood uneasily before her examining the hem of his travelling cloak caught over one arm, and regretting the assignment which had brought him into conflict with so unexpectedly awesome an adversary. 'You have been sent here because I am not trusted. The lord of York thinks that because Exeter is a Lancastrian I will instruct my guards to leave him their keys one night!'

'No, indeed, lady,' Worcester protested feebly, 'I believe the order was given that I might relieve you of some responsibility.'

'I do not wish to be relieved of responsibility in mine own castle, I thank you. I keep it for the king and if Exeter is his prisoner I will keep him safe. However we cannot resolve this matter here. I will write this day to my sovereign lord, and while we await his decision – his, mark you, not York's – you may stay here at our manor.'

Alice wrote so forcefully of her objections to Worcester's supervision that she got her way and York recalled the unhappy earl. She did not, however disregard the significance of the attempt upon her rights. York might not move directly against her but he did not trust her and if he chose to whittle away her power, she could no longer look to the deranged king for protection.

At last she resolved upon a course to which she had given long thought. Well-rehearsed words flowed easily from her pen as she directed a letter: 'To the Lady Alice, Countess of Salisbury – Right heartily well-beloved daughter, greeting ... Knowing as you do the grievous afflictions I have undergone ... in the name of any love you have towards me I ask now for your good offices on our behalf ... My lord of York hath a daughter, the lady Elizabeth, of whom I have heard excellent report ... and should it please him to consider the mutual advantages of such an alliance you may make known to him my readiness to listen to the terms of such a contract as he would approve ... '

When she had set her seal in place Alice called for her chaplain, Symond Braillis, and bid him prepare for a journey.

'You will give this into Alice of Salisbury's own hands if you please and urge her to read it straight. Watch how she receives my message. I would know if she seems well pleased by it or in doubt.'

Braillis nodded his understanding as well he might. Had he not skulked for days about the household of Cecily, Duchess of York, spying upon the Lady Elizabeth Plantagenet to see whether her nature be pleasing, her wits sharp, her health good and her person comely and well-formed. It had not been easy. But in the end the details of his conscientious report were completed. He was able to assure his mistress that Elizabeth was without blemish – unless excessive resolution of character be a fault.

Proud of the confidential mission entrusted to him, Braillis entered wholeheartedly into his next assignment, bringing back not only a dutiful, affectionate letter but information that the countess had received Alice's words with ill-concealed triumph and hurriedly dispatched messages to Richard of York and to Salisbury, her husband.

'So!' Alice's eyes narrowed with satisfaction. 'You have done well, Symond Braillis. This knowledge will strengthen my hand in the negotiations which lie ahead.'

*   *   *

That autumn the king's mind again gave way and York, backed by an enthusiastic Commons, became Protector of the realm. Hardly had everyone accustomed themselves to this state of affairs, however, when Henry recovered once more and the queen bore him off to Coventry. There in the centre of Lancastrian influence, she encouraged him to dismiss a number of prominent Yorkists from office.

York and Warwick continued to hold their appointments but it was made known that Henry wished them to endow a chantry at St. Albans, where Masses could be said for the souls of those who had fallen in the battle they had waged against him. The country waited to see how this provocation would be taken, and was a little surprised that a solemn service of reconciliation should shortly be arranged at St. Paul's, with

Henry and Margaret leading a procession of representatives from opposing parties to pray together in seeming accord. Velvet-gloved hands dropped purses of gold into the offering plate and proud men knelt in prayer. Yet many of them came direct from secret assemblies where tongues had shaped the syllables not of worship but of war.

*   *   *

'John, the time has come to arrange a suitable marriage for you. I have many times worried my head where an alliance might best be made, and always I reached the same conclusion. Though we have reason to mislike it there can be no other.'

'You mean with York?' His voice was expressionless and Alice looked at him warily before she hurried on.

'Of course we both know York has been our bitter enemy in the past. He feared the strength of the force we could field in alliance with the queen and I think he is honest in his belief that by opposing her influence in this land he serves his country well. Now, recalling that we are kin by marriage, he has come to see the advantages of a match between you and his daughter, the lady Elizabeth Plantagenet.'

John asked hesitantly: 'Did York murder my father?'

'I do not believe he did,' Alice frowned thoughtfully. 'It is an action that would be out of character to him. And no evidence could be found to connect him with it.'

Their eyes met and held in a long look that conveyed the trust and understanding that was between them. Then John nodded his head slowly.

'Let it be as you think best, then. I do not forget that my father's last message urged me to follow your counsel in all things.'

'I believe you will be well-suited with the lady Elizabeth to wife. She is fifteen years old – two years younger than you are – healthy and well-formed,' Alice assured him. But he only nodded absently, hardly listening to what she said.

'Just one thing troubles me mother . . .'

'Speak then!'

'The king restored me in the dukedom and I know you

love him well. Yet we are breaking tryst with him and . . . '

'Oh John, John, do not ask me to debate this matter with you. The king is sick in mind and there are many who say the prince is not his son. I cannot tell you if this be true or false. But I know the queen and it does not seem impossible. Moreover when I went to Westminster after the king had lost his reason I saw that he did not rave or chatter nonsense but looked like one who had withdrawn from painful reality. He gave no sign of madness ever before and this came on him when he knew the queen was with child.'

'If this be so it were a shameful thing! By the Mass I will never bend the knee to the misbegotten son of an unchaste queen and her mignon!' John said indignantly.

'Well spoken! And if you yet feel any unease about this match, take comfort in York's assurance that no harm will be done to the royal family. Henry will be permitted to live out his time as king and surely with this sickness of the mind he cannot reach great age.'

*　　*　　*

Queen Margaret had grown tired of living in fear of the menace of York. She began to call loyal supporters to the king's standard, showing those who answered her summons a scale of hospitality she could ill-afford and bestowing on each man a livery blazoned with a swan, as a gift from her son.

'Wear it and let me trust in your strength to see our son be king after his father.' It was an inspired gesture that captured the admiration of the men who knelt before her.

When Margaret saw her charm take effect, she came at her true purpose. She urged the lords to advise the king that he should resign his crown in favour of Edward, promising that if they appointed her Regent she would rule with their counsel.

The suggestion was coolly received. It was one matter to rally about the anointed king and quite another to conspire with his French wife to dethrone him. Nor were the ambitious tempted at the prospect of power wielded through a queen regent. They knew Margaret to be a woman of resolute determination and feared to give her an authority which she would misuse.

The report that the queen had failed in her bid for the regency was a relief to Alice, poised as she was between camps – too far committed towards York to turn back with impunity, and uneasily aware that Margaret's suspicions must have been aroused when John failed to rally with other prominent Lancastrians. Yet that summer of 1459, some instinct outweighing other considerations deterred Alice from concluding the marriage contract. And York, watching Lancastrian leaders crystallise themselves into an army about the king and queen in Staffordshire, was too occupied to press her.

Letters and travellers brought confused tidings to Oxfordshire from the north and the midlands. It was said that York had called Warwick home from Calais and this was soon confirmed for the earl had indeed landed in England and was marching towards his own county. Salisbury was on the move too, with a mighty force including hundreds of the duke's tenants, armed and drilled to perfection. They headed for Ludlow where York himself waited to meet them.

It would be war. It must be civil war. But the people had lived as though on the eve of battle for a long time and were unable to recognise that the sun had finally risen on a day of bloody endeavour.

Determined to stop Salisbury reaching York, the queen directed Lord Audley to intercept him. The two forces closed at Blore Heath – and a victorious Salisbury continued his march. It began to look as though nothing would stop the now united Yorkist force, which turned towards Kenilworth, where York intended to confront the king.

*   *   *

On the night of the twelfth of October a furious storm broke over the neighbourhood of Ewelme, claiming among its victims the weather cock on the manor stables, the proudest and strongest of the elms from whence the village took its name, and the old, half-ruined tower which had stood across the courtyard from the manor-house for so many years, brooding over every happy arrival and sorrowing departure Alice could remember.

The next morning she was dressed at first light and went out to view the damage. A number of her household gathered silently upon the scene, and John came scrambling over a pile of broken stones to assure her no harm had been done to either the stables or the dairy.

'The lightning seems to have struck over the top of the house and been somehow directed by the weather cock upon the turret. The top half of the tower has fallen away from us, by good fortune, and the lower part subsided inwards.'

'That is a blessing, then.' Alice sounded more cheerful than she felt. 'I have always been intending to have that old ruin pulled down. Now it is gone the approach to our home will be much improved.'

But Will Bylton, galloping in among them with the news that his roof had collapsed in the storm, was more concerned by Alice's loss than his own.

'It seems like an ill-omen – that tower to fall now when it has withstood so many tempests in the past,' he shook his head gravely.

'Devil take you, Will, with talk of omens! Time and weather have weakened what is under your thatch in more ways than you know! Here comes nothing but good to me, for now I shall not have to pay the labour of knocking it down.'

'You would never have done that,' he scoffed. 'Did we not as children love this old place? And your father, he let it stand even though he thought it a danger.'

'Peace to your tongue, peace! What do you say, Cecily?' She turned at the familiar step. 'Shall we give shelter to this homeless stray? Upon my faith I believe he has allowed his house to fall in pieces a-purpose so that he will be invited to live here. But I warn you do not listen to him. He is full of foreboding and makes gloomy company.'

Before nightfall Thomas Stonor had arrived to tell them of the rout of the Yorkists at Ludford Bridge.

'I have received a communication that York has fled and is making his way to Ireland, while Warwick, Salisbury, and

227

York's son, Edward, Earl of March are on their way to Calais. They have lost the day!'

'Lost the day!' Alice repeated incredulously. 'But how was this defeat brought about?'

'It was not a defeat on the field. I understand men of the Calais garrison brought over by Warwick doubted his assurance that they would not be forced to use their arms directly against the king. They deserted and confusion and panic spread through the Yorkist ranks.'

'I knew it!' Will Bylton strode fiercely about the hall and returned to stand directly in front of Alice. 'This failure will be your undoing.' He kept his voice lowered so that only those standing close to her – Stonor, Cecily, John and Symond Braillis – could hear. 'I begged you not to commit yourself towards York. I knew this country would never tolerate a move against the king.'

'You speak and know nothing, Will. We have a patient ear for you because of the love you bear us, but John and I comprehend very well what we are about. York made his move before the time was ripe. He will not fail next time.'

'You think they will invade?' Thomas Stonor asked sharply.

'I am sure of it. York is a man who will never be beaten until he be dead.'

*   *   *

Ironically it seemed that having driven York from the country, the queen and her ministers were bent on converting the population to his cause. Throughout the early months of 1460 they hunted out suspected Yorkist sympathisers with unrelenting savagery. Confiscation of property, the rope and the axe – the weapons of government officers who were being encouraged to terrorise a rebellious people – became commonplace.

In April a letter was brought to Alice by a courier, who wore no livery to identify his master. He came from the Duchess of York and had travelled by little-used ways, avoiding towns and villages where he might be stopped and questioned by Lancastrian scouts.

The contents of his communication were simple. The duchess had instructions from her husband to complete the arrangements for the marriage of their daughter to John, Duke of Suffolk. 'My lord writes to me that it will not be long before he returns to England and that when he does he will be glad to find the number of his sons increased.' The words were gracious but the message was direct. York was no longer content with verbal tokens of support. He wanted to be sure that the de la Pole banners would unfurl at his command – and not the queen's – on the morning of the great confrontation which must now be close at hand.

'If we withhold any longer we may have cause to rue it,' Alice warned John when she showed him the letter. 'York is not a man to forget that you waited for his victory to declare yourself.'

'And if he is defeated?' For an instant the wry curve of his mouth reminded Alice of her father.

She shrugged. 'If he is defeated I do not believe it will matter where you stood to watch him fall. Margaret of Anjou is no fool. She will have guessed why we have not been to court.'

'You mean it would only be a matter of time before she turned upon us?'

'We have a large property, tempting as a prospect for confiscation. And they may like to have our heads also.'

'Then let us go to claim my bride.'

*   *   *

The wedding took place with scant celebration. It was an affair of women. Cecily, Duchess of York, had a simple good sense which put the secret ceremony through with efficient dispatch and Alice was pleased to have an opportunity of meeting her stepdaughter again. The significant absence of the menfolk of the bride's family could not fail to cast a gloom upon the party, however, and everyone was relieved when the formalities were completed.

So John brought his wife home to Ewelme, not triumphantly with the pomp appropriate to such an occasion, but quietly, almost furtively. Yet despite the circumstances of the match, the young couple seemed well pleased with each other.

And Alice, watching them together, felt a sudden sadness for her own lost youth and love. Now she was the dowager Duchess of Suffolk. The new title seemed to belong to someone else, someone incredibly old who was only waiting to die.

* * *

On the twenty-sixth of June, 1460, York's son, Edward, Earl of March, landed at Sandwich with Warwick and Salisbury. They made first for London, where they were given a mixed reception by the populace and, leaving Salisbury to beseige the Tower, March and Warwick set out to meet the Lancastrian army which was at Northampton.

There, on a rain-drenched battlefield, died the Duke of Buckingham, Shrewsbury, Viscount Beaumont and Lord Egremont. Casualties in the royal army were heavy, though the fight lasted barely half an hour, for its defence had rested on entrenched guns, which quickly became flooded and useless in the downpour.

The king was escorted back to London, the queen had fled to refuge in Denbigh, and the scene was set for York's return from Ireland.

He landed at Chester and rode through Ludlow and Hereford towards Abingdon. There he halted and called for trumpeters and soon it was seen with amazement that his banners were the royal arms of England blazoned without diversity.

So, with his sword of state borne upright before him, he rode at the head of three hundred armed men to Westminster Palace.

Parliament had been opened two days earlier by the king and was in session when the duke arrived. The lords sitting in Westminster Hall heard the measured tread of York's approaching bodyguard and the metallic ring of armour. Warily they watched him enter following him with their eyes as he paced slowly towards the dais. At the foot of the steps he halted, and appeared to contemplate the empty throne as though he were seeing it for the first time. Then with a heavy deliberation he laid his arm upon its cushion and turned to look at the assembly.

If he had hoped for acclamation, however, he was to be disappointed. The lords were uncertain what the extent of his demands would be and most of them were in no hurry to set up a strong king in place of a weak one. They stared back at him in silence.

The Archbishop of Canterbury, finding himself unable to countenance the lack of respect towards the symbol of the throne, stepped forward with a gesture of rebuke and demanded to know if York wished for an audience with the king.

'I know of no one in this realm who would not more fitly come to me than I to him,' was the trenchant answer.

Now there were no more doubts in the minds of those who heard him. Soon they were asked to consider the substance of his claim to the throne – a genealogical statement asserting his true succession to Richard II. This posed an involved legal question, but one that could not be dismissed lightly since Henry IV had taken the crown from Richard on the grounds that he himself was rightful heir of Henry III. Moreover York had the additional claim of right by conquest.

After lengthy debate it was resolved that the king should retain the crown for life, while York should be invested with the principality of Wales and recognised as heir to the throne.

On the twenty-eighth of October, Henry gave his assent to this settlement, telling his lords in sad bewilderment that he did so to further their content and avoid any greater bloodshed. Under the burden of this grave decision, and in no little dread of Margaret's reaction when she learned that her own son had been finally disinherited, the king's mind once again became confused and York resumed the role of Protector.

While legal arguments had been occupying the Yorkists and the neutral lords in London, Lancastrian leaders in the north had had time to regroup their forces. Hearing that they were maltreating his Yorkshire tenants, the duke collected a modest army and marched north to restore order. It was a serious misjudgment. Too late, he discovered that he had underestimated the strength of the rebel troops and in an engagement at Wakefield he was defeated and killed.

On the last day of the year, the head that everyone had believed was destined to wear the crown, hung instead upon the walls of York surmounted by a paper cap. Alongside was the head of Salisbury, who had been taken alive on the field and slain amid the jeers of his captors.

Suddenly the country which had had two kings to choose between, had none. Henry gibbered and knew nothing. Margaret was with her son in Scotland and the mighty York was dead.

Margaret, having arranged a marriage between her son and the sister of the Scottish king, in exchange for the surrender of Berwick, lost no time in returning to England. She did not scruple to bring with her a motley invading army of ferocious Scots and men of the border country, accustomed to keep their own law by the sword and bow. And her popularity was not increased when rumour spread that French and Irish contingents were on their way to support her.

But to reach London, she would have to pass the armies of York's eighteen-year-old son Edward, Earl of March, and his cousin, Warwick, who both knew they would share the fate of their fathers if they failed to stop her.

CHAPTER FIFTEEN

THE VOICES of the Westminster choristers climbed jubilantly to a final bell-like note and Edward of York had become Edward IV of England. Peers and peeresses prepared to take their places in the procession leaving the abbey. Alice was near the head of the column which inched its way towards the great doors. Outside, enthusiastic Londoners roared their acclamation in the bright sunlight.

There had been an almost sensual magnificence about the ceremony. The swooning breath of incense and burning wax, the voices soaring and intoning, the brilliant embroidery of vestments reflected in softly gleaming gold plate. And, startling the senses, a sudden blaze of jewels, a shout of trumpets, the instant when Edward had rent open his robe to bare his breast for anointing. He was so beautiful, so splendid in height and proportion, that it seemed as though the most perfect of the race offered himself for sacrifice.

But now the ritual was over and the paeans had ceased, Edward would have to justify his claim to sovereignty. Men would expect more of him than they had ever required of Henry.

For her own part, Alice believed they would not be disappointed. Some might insist that it was Warwick who had held together the Yorkist army after the calamity of their leader's death, and swept Edward on in his father's place, through the bloodied fields of Mortimer's Cross, St. Albans and Towton to the throne. It was Edward who had been victorious at Mortimer's Cross, however, and Warwick, who had been defeated by Margaret's uncivilised north countrymen at the second battle of St. Albans, while the final desperate struggle at Towton had been a united effort. Edward could surely claim due credit for the victory there, where his outnumbered army had fought on through a blinding snowstorm to assert his cause by staining the white drifts red. Old soldiers who survived, said they never saw men fight with such desperate fury. But then, Alice reflected, perhaps Englishmen had never met such stubborn opponents as when they fought each other.

So Edward had won and London opened her gates to him, calling him king. Margaret of Anjou had managed to free her husband and together with her son they escaped into Scotland. It looked as if the deposed royal family might play beggar in foreign courts for the rest of their days.

When Alice arrived in London for the coronation she was pleased to find John among those newly distinguished by the young king's favour. He had been appointed Steward of England at the coronation and was to be made a Knight of the Garter at its next chapter. It was clear that Edward had a great affection for his sister, Elizabeth, and would go to extravagant lengths to show it. But Alice thought, too, that he was an adept enough judge of men to appreciate John for his own sake and not merely as his sister's husband.

Viewing John objectively, and seeing how he conducted himself among his fellow men, Alice was well satisfied with the son she had raised. True he lacked both the phenomenal vitality and devastating eloquence of his father. But if John could not beguile he could impress. He was a thoughtful young man speaking only plain, good sense and that in few words. Always mature beyond his years, he had grown up with a natural dignity of manner which did not fail him even in anger. Men might never know John well enough to love him, but Alice doubted if they would be able to withhold their respect.

Superficially John and the young king were not unlike each other. Born in the same year, they were both tall, both possessed of a golden, manly beauty. It was John's nature, however, to be grave, while Edward showed himself pleasure-loving, and self-indulgent, affable to all men and greedy for women.

Yet some talked who had known Edward in other moods. To them he was a man of determined action, a soldier of high courage and quick wits, a potentially great king who was already making energetic plans to bring order and justice to every Englishman, from the high-born to the lowly.

Alice, intrigued by what she heard, and looking forward to her first audience, had been quite unprepared for the reception she was given. John had led her into the king's chamber and there was a burst of laughter from the young man reclining upon the throne.

'Holy Trinity! Never say this is your mother, Suffolk? Did you not tell us her first husband fell at Harfleur? Nay, pardon, madame!' In a bound he had met her half-way across the room and seized her hand. 'Our manners must affright you. But we are astonished, for we had imagined you an old, old crone!'

Alice curtsied deeply, uncertain whether she was amused or displeased.

'My son, Suffolk, spoke truth. I was wed at the time of Harfleur. I was then eleven years of age. You may calculate thus that I am not quite in my dotage, although I have left youth far behind.'

'Ah lady, you do right to reprove our impertinence. You are one of those blessed women permitted to carry her beauty along the years and should never be required to name their number. Madame, we give you a hearty welcome to our court.'

Alice curtsied again. 'It is a joyful day for me, when I can kiss hands with my sovereign lord.'

'I must not fail in a promise to my little brother, Richard. Madame, he loves you well. It seems you met him on the occasion of that happy marriage which made our families one. To his great delight you made him the gift of a book and now he is proud to have a present for *you*.'

Alice smiled in warm remembrance of the eight-year-old boy with lively intelligent eyes, who had told her he wanted to own more books than anyone else in the world. This eleventh child of Cecily Neville had been born with a deformed shoulder which drew one arm up shorter than the other. But it did not deter his mettlesome spirit. What was it he had said? . . . 'I do not have so much time for reading now as I must practice the skills of war to aid my father and my brother, Edward.'

'In sooth I should like to see Richard again,' she told the king.

'Then pray, good Suffolk, bring him hither.'

As John left them, Alice felt a warning jolt from that wide-awake instinct for danger that had protected her all her life. She looked at Edward and saw his eyes harden upon her, although his mouth still smiled.

'We are pleased to have this opportunity to speak with you, alone, lady. There is a need of truth and trust between us and we would know what ambitions you have for your son!'

'Sire, I have none save those which it is within your power to further. If my son finds favour with you, I hope he may serve well where you have most need of him.'

'You are content that he should serve? And what do you say of his blood and his title?'

So there it was, Alice thought. The dusty bones of a scanda-lous rumour were still rattling. Had she the blood of John of Gaunt? Edward must have learned the old tale from his father, who perhaps heard it from his mother. Yet none of them had ever known the truth.

She shook her head with a bewildered air. 'Sire, I do not understand. There is naught to shame us in our blood and as to his title my son is Duke of Suffolk, by your grace.'

Edward snapped his fingers impatiently. 'We do not speak of shame but of pride, lady.'

'By my faith then, aye, we have pride in our blood!' Alice allowed herself to show a little irritation. 'We are proud to be English born, and proud of the loyal service our forebears have rendered to this country!'

The suspicion gradually faded out of Edward's eyes, and at last he nodded with restored good-humour.

'We have made you angry. Does that mean you fail to comprehend our questions?'

'Indeed I am confused. You give me a place of honour at your coronation, welcome me with kindness and then interro-gate me as though I have offended. I beseech you, sire, recollect that I am but a woman, unskilled in men's affairs.'

The door opened and Richard bounded into the room, followed by John and a tangle of wriggling puppies.

Alice had just time to overhear the young king's softly-spoken reassurance and then Richard was claiming her attention.

'See, Lady Alice! I have a gift for you. Do you know what it is?'

'Why, yes! It is beautiful, very beautiful! Have you seen this John, my son? It is a finely wrought copy of Geoffrey Chaucer's Balade de Bon Conseyl. I love these verses well.'

Richard smiled broadly: 'Good, then I have pleased you.'

'My child, you have pleased me before this time. But I will prize this token and think of you whenever I look at it.'

*   *   *

As the years passed and Alice watched John turn the corner from youth into parenthood she knew that he must sometimes be troubled by questions which remained unanswered. Though no man would now be so foolhardy as to remind the king's brother-in-law that his father had been called traitor, John could not have forgotten those overcast days of his boyhood, when they had both lived with danger. It had been necessary then to tell him many bitter truths for his own safety. Now, in his manhood, he would want to understand how such tragedy had befallen their House.

She had expected the questions and they came. One quiet evening John sought her out alone to ask: 'What manner of man was my father?'

She did not pretend any astonishment. She had never pretended with John.

She said: 'He was a great man. He had a bold, adventurous spirit and a high courage. I loved him very much, as you must surely know.'

'There was never any truth in the accusation that he loved France better than England? I mean . . . '

'I know what you mean. No, he was no traitor even in his heart. Your own wit should tell you that is just the kind of slander his enemies would use to bring him down.'

'Yes, I see that. Indeed you have given me the same answer before. But I wanted to hear it again, for now that I am grown to manhood I believe you will speak straight to me.'

'So I will. What else do you want to ask me?'

John hesitated, scowling at his own thoughts.

Alice believed she knew what was in his mind. She said sharply: 'You have heard it told that your father had a close association with Margaret of Anjou. You wonder if perhaps he was her lover?'

John nodded unhappily.

'Mother of Heaven! The unlikely scandals some people spread and others will believe. No, I swear to you there was never any impropriety between them. You do your father an injustice to think him capable of it. Only consider how Henry trusted him. Your father would never have cuckolded him! The queen was young and anxious to learn all she could about politics. Her strength in this country rested on your father's support and his influence was extended through her favour. Mark you,' she smiled slightly, 'I do not deny that he may have enjoyed tutoring so fair a scholar. Margaret was glorious to look at in her bride-days.'

John's face cleared. 'I am glad I have asked you these things. I have wanted always to think best of my father, but sometimes it has not been easy.'

'No, not easy when a man's good name has been so ruth-lessly slandered. Well hear this of me, your father may not have been as skilful a statesman as he liked to believe. He dreaded the voice of the people and closed his ears to it when he should have listened. But this country's turmoil was not of his making and at least it may be said that as long as he held power, the throne was secure and civil war was averted.'

*　　*　　*

'You are very quiet this evening, are you in low spirits?' Cecily Bowman directed the question accusingly across the expansive hearth of the manor hall at Ewelme. Her fingers were busy setting small delicate stitches into a tapestry, but she kept her eyes upon her mistress and when she received no answer added sharply: 'Do not think to keep it from me if you are ailing! And in truth you deserve to take a chill, insisting we sit in this great, cold place of a winter's evening, when we could be comfortable in the parlour!'

Alice continued to gaze into the pulsating heart of the fire but replied at last: 'You know I am never ill. I am thinking.'

'You might think just as well in the parlour,' Cecily muttered bending her head once more over her work.

'If I choose to sit in my own hall I shall do so. You have my permission to withdraw, lady.'

'Nonsense, you know I will not leave you before you retire.'

'Well stay then and be silent! I sit in the hall because it is here my people know to find me when they have need.'

Cecily was not to be deterred. 'You need more rest at your age and ought not to keep such late hours.'

Alice laughed softly and at last raised her head to look at her waiting woman. 'I am sixty-five years old and can have but a little while longer upon this earth. Shall I spend the time in sleep when I go soon to a rest that lasts for eternity? No, no, Cecily. We are a pair of old women you and I. We have both earned the right to do and say as we please. That is why I permit you to wag your tongue, like the scold you are, and also why I pay no heed to it!'

'Bah! I should have married when I had the chance, for it seems I am not appreciated here.'

Alice, firmly believing that the sport of baiting Cecily was good for both of them, said in a tone of deep reflection: 'Yes, you might have had Castellet, I fancy . . . if I had bestowed a fat dower upon you!'

Cecily subsided into an indignant silence. 'But she is right,' Alice thought. 'I am weary. Just a little weary. Only it is not the number of one's years which is significant, it is the range of experience. I am fatigued by the tumults I have lived through.'

A log split open in a shower of sparks and settled itself more comfortably upon the bed of glowing ash. Now a fresh flame began its hopeful dance where the wood had sundered. In her mood of drowsing fancy Alice invested it with a symbolism of the overthrow of the House of Lancaster. The new flame might be Edward IV in his hour of triumph – and triumph he had, despite old Lancastrian sympathies which still haunted parts of Wales and the north. He had managed to bring a better measure of justice to the country, and there was a new confidence in the economy and the export trade as a result of his policies. She frowned, wondering just how much of a threat Warwick had become to England. She had never liked that saturnine, ambitious son of poor Alice of Salisbury. He had thought because he helped to put Edward on the throne that he would be able to govern him once he was there. But under an amiable exterior Edward of York had a will of his own that was every bit as relentless as Warwick's. Ironic, thought Alice, that it was a woman who had come between Edward and his powerful cousin. Warwick had wanted the king to marry Bona of Savoy, sister-in-law of the French king, Louis XI. Instead he had secretly married Elizabeth Wydeville, a widow whose husband had died at St. Albans fighting for Queen Margaret. The trouble with Elizabeth Wydeville was her family – too many brothers greedy for power. People resented their elevation – Warwick most of all.

He was in France now and there were rumours that he had met with Margaret of Anjou and was plotting with her to invade England and restore Henry to the throne. It seemed an improbable alliance. Warwick and Margaret had hated each other for years. Yet perhaps ambition, and the diplomatic cunning of the French king playing his own deep game, had indeed brought about the uneasy union.

Reluctantly, Alice was reminded of Henry, a prisoner in the Tower since he had been recaptured hiding in the north of England. Not that he was treated unkindly by his keepers. Still, she who seldom wept could find tears of pity for the man, now bereft of all dignity, who had once been king of England: Henry, who had worn his crown with an infinite humility, striving to do good by all men, and so selfless that he had given away more than he had ever owned; Henry, who since infancy had been so hedged about by strong, ambitious men that his own will was emasculated; Henry, receiving a deputation of his lords come to tell him Edward would be king in his place and crying out in humiliation and bewilderment, 'But you have called us king for more than thirty years. Our grandfather, and our father before us, ruled this realm and now, after long continuance of our House, you say we are no longer king. How can it be so?'

Alas for Henry, that he had married a woman so rapacious for power she would bring in the Scots and the French, aye, and any other enemy who would follow her, relishing to slay Englishmen on the very threshold of their homes if they would not call her queen. Alice considered Margaret grimly, unable entirely to condemn her for the sake of happier days, when they had listened together to strange tales of the Indies told by travellers bringing voluptuous perfumes and hot spices to the Palace of Westminster. For a moment the image of Margaret softened from distant enemy to laughing companion, and they were once again in the woods of Windsor, following the hunt on a mellow day. She could almost hear the huntsmen urge the hounds forward, 'Sa, sa, cy avaunt, sohow' until they sighted the quarry with a triumphant ringing cry 'Illoeques! Illoeques!' Ah, but it was hard to forgive Margaret for what she had done to Henry, dragging him about the country when he was too sick in mind to know what he was at and treating him as if he were merely some necessary currency to procure arms and men . . . arms and men . . .

'Arms and men!' Alice spoke aloud startling Cecily who had begun to drowse over her skeins of wool.

'Wh-what did you say?'

Alice stood up suddenly: 'I said arms and men have marched through all my days.'

*   *   *

It was told that Margaret of Anjou had kept the mighty Warwick on his knees for a quarter of an hour before she would give him yea or nay to an alliance. But in the end they had clasped hands and Warwick's daughter, Anne, was married to Margaret's son. With the bond sealed in this fashion, Warwick invaded England in September, 1470.

Edward IV, underestimating the Franco-Lancastrian alliance, had been ill-prepared. When the Marquis of Montagu, on whose troops he had been relying, defected, he saw he might be taken by Warwick and withdrew, with his brother Richard, to Burgundy.

A confused England had witnessed a brief Lancastrian restoration. Warwick triumphed over London, waiting for Margaret of Anjou to join him with her son and daughter-in-law. But Margaret had been in no hurry to put herself in danger. She wanted to be sure that the Lancastrian revival was a complete success before she crossed from France. Meanwhile Henry VI, enfeebled by the lack of his wife's support, was a pitiable, lonely figure, bewildered to find himself called king again by Warwick, yet struggling to perform the kingly duties this fierce, loud-voiced man demanded of him.

Retribution was treading on the heels of the treacherous earl, however. He had boasted that as he had set up a king so he could pluck one down. But Edward was not a man to give up anything readily, let alone a crown. He returned to England and in the ensuing battle at Barnet on Easter Sunday of 1471 Warwick was slain.

Too late to put heart into the Lancastrian revival, Queen Margaret made an ill-timed landing at Weymouth on the same fateful Sunday. With unflagging courage she had marched to the south-west, hoping to gather an army along the way. Then, at Tewkesbury, on the fourth day of May, Edward had caught her and inflicted his final irreversible defeat. He had killed her son.

Margaret was discovered hiding in Little Malvern Priory and was taken into custody.

On the twenty-first of May, London once more welcomed Edward IV as king and before midnight Henry, last of the House of Lancaster, had been put to death.

*　　*　　*

For the first few months after Edward's restoration, Margaret, 'some-time called queen', was kept under close guard in the Tower and later at Windsor. Then as the danger of any further Lancastrian rising receded, the king ordered that she be taken into custody at Wallingford Castle.

As Constable, Alice could not avoid the ordeal of a meeting. She went, dreading the emotional display which a long acquaintance with Margaret of Anjou warned her to expect.

Outside the heavy door of the royal prisoner's quarters, she waited to be announced, then entered with her head held high.

Margaret jumped up dismissing her attendants with agitated hands and gazed at Alice with staring eyes.

'Well, lady!' Her voice was husky, threatening.

Alice replied soothingly as she had always been accustomed to do. 'I have come to see after your comfort and to enquire whether there is anything that I can furnish to make your life here more supportable.'

'Ah, you want me to be comfortable do you?' Margaret laughed wildly, pointing a shaking finger. 'Treacherous woman, be gone from my sight. You might have saved me, saved my husband, my child . . . ' Her voice trailed off and she covered her face with her disordered hair.

Alice, struggling with her own self-control, said firmly: 'Madame, you misjudge the matter. I could not have saved you. I could only have chosen to see my House perish with yours.'

'But I had a son . . .!' Margaret's voice was a shriek of agony. And, reacting violently under the stress of the painful meeting, Alice cried out: 'And I *have* a son and by God's grace he lives . . . he lives.'

'Aye, lives as a Yorkist! Never think I failed to see his banners arrayed against me at St. Albans! What a bitter hour that was, when those leopards on their azure field, which I once loved to greet, broke forth to witness your defection! How could you do this after you had known the bounty and protection of my kingly husband?'

Margaret's expression had grown almost inhuman, as she spoke and it seemed that in another minute she might lose the last remnants of control and strike Alice.

But Alice's own anger had driven her beyond intimidation and she answered fiercely: 'Lancaster! York! These names mean nothing to me, madame. Men make a game of life and take sides to give their play significance. What matters this to women, who must see that life goes on? Aye, we had a dukedom at your hands, and many other gifts, which I do not forget. But they were dearly bought with the head of my beloved lord.'

She stopped, her anger spent, and for the first time since she had entered the room, recognised the appalling changes which suffering had worked on Margaret of Anjou.

'Madame, what use is it for us to rage at one another? We have each followed the path of our duty where we thought it lay, and cannot retrace our journeys, nor erase those tracks we left upon the dust. Come, I see you are not well! Let me lead you to this chair.'

Margaret did indeed look as if she were about to swoon, as she clung to a corner of the table and appeared to struggle for every breath.

'It will pass, it is nothing,' she muttered, but she suffered Alice to support her to the window-seat. When the fresh air had revived her a little she said bitterly: 'You are right, however, I am sick – sick unto death.'

'I fear you try your own endurance even more severely than destiny has done, madame.'

Margaret lifted dull eyes to look at her. 'You speak of destiny . . . but I know better. It is God who has punished me and will go on punishing me.'

'Let me fetch your confessor then to bring you ease.'

'Very well . . . but stay a moment, Alice of Suffolk . . . You will come to see me again? I swear I will be calm.'

'I will come whenever you send for me.'

Alice curtsied deeply and as she backed slowly, bowing from the room, was answered by a smile which still retained some of its once familiar glory.

*   *   *

The troubadour was anxious to take a well-filled purse with him when he left the manor-house of Ewelme next morning. But his voice was thin and unsure and Alice decided that he had extolled the beauty of her daughter-in-law long enough. As he paused for breath she clapped her hands.

'We thank you for entertaining us. You may take your ease now.'

John smiled, waiting until the young man had taken himself off, with his half-finished verse still ringing about his head. He said: 'Time has mellowed you mother. Once you would have made that young man wish he earned his bread another way.'

'Perhaps it would be better if he did! But enough of that. I want to hear your tidings – it is a long while since you came to Ewelme. And I must know from Elizabeth,' she nodded towards her daughter-in-law, 'how my grandchildren do.'

'They are in good health, thanks be to God. Edmund walks sturdily now.'

'Aye, and plagues us beyond endurance!' John growled.

'What! He is scarce out of swaddling bands.'

'John speaks truth though,' Elizabeth frowned. 'He has ungovernable rages. I wish he were more like his brother.'

'Humph!' said Alice. She knew Elizabeth doted on her first-born, John, who was ten years of age and had been Earl of Lincoln since he was two. 'You must take care not to show Edmund how you favour his brother or you will make him more unbiddable than ever.'

Elizabeth murmured: 'As you say, lady mother,' and her lips compressed into a thin line. Alice saw John smiling behind his hand. Elizabeth would leave them now, as she always did when she felt she had been criticised.

When they were alone Alice said: 'Tell me, my son, is all well in Suffolk?'

'Nothing is ever well in Suffolk! By the Trinity, I hold our tenants and neighbours there to be the most unruly on earth. Would they were more like your people here in Ewelme.'

'John, they are the same people. It is being treated badly that makes folk intractable. We have not done well by our Suffolk property.'

'It surprises me to hear you say so. You have fought over every inch of our boundaries there, and I mind well how you wrangled with the Pastons for months over the manor at Cotton.'

'The Pastons enjoy litigation! And I have never gone into

245

Suffolk with force of arms. You and Elizabeth have made yourselves very unpopular by sending hired bullies to intimidate those who contest your rights.'

John scowled into the fire.

She rose and poured him wine with her own hands as a gesture of placation, and he accepted the goblet, saluting her over its brim with a reluctant smile.

'Hey-ho! I suppose you will always be putting me in my place, mother, even when I am an old, old man.'

'Not much longer, I think,' Alice replied quietly. 'I have reached my three score years and ten.'

'Impossible!'

'There speaks the tongue of flattery!'

They were companionably silent for a while and then John shifted in his chair uneasily.

'Mother, it is a subject of which I do not like to speak – but I feel I must ask you if you have writ down any directions for me when the times comes for . . . '

'What! For my burial you mean? No I have writ nothing down. Naturally I wish to be laid in my church, here. But as to the tomb, why I care not for that. Ewelme itself is my happiest remembrance. The alms-house, the school, the church, they are well provided for and I would like to think they will endure.'

'It shall be as you desire.'

'Good! Now you had better follow Elizabeth or she will be in the sulks tomorrow.'

'Yes, you are right. Shall I call Cecily?'

'No, I will set here a while longer.'

John kissed her hand and then her cheek.

'Pleasant rest, my son. And John . . . you are thirty-two-years-old, live long and die in bed . . . that too will be a memorial I should like.'

*   *   *

An hour passed and the fire sank low. Cecily would have gone to bed now, and the other servants were accustomed to their mistress keeping late hours. They had their instructions not to wait up, for she could not tolerate them dull and heavy about their work.

'All gone to rest,' Alice thought and she sighed thinking of others who had gone from her through the years. Her father was gone, long, long ago. And yet sometimes when she looked at the familiar chair where he had so often sat in the firelight, she fancied he was still close to her. Will Bylton had gone, suddenly, when he was happily employed listing the items in her library. Dear, devoted Will. There should be such a man in every woman's life.

Thinking of Will called to mind the strange, elusive spirit which had been trapped in the twisted body of Adeliza. Perhaps the evil hands which had sped that spirit like a freed bird were more merciful than they knew.

Other familiar faces were missing, too. Thomas Stonor had died – last April was it? He had not made a very good age, just fifty. And three months ago, Cecily's brother Stephen had been gored and trampled to death by a bull.

Unbidden memory set off at a gallop, plunging her back without warning through the years until she was in France again with Salisbury. Salisbury, who was so accustomed to command that he was unable to ask for anything – even love. And sweet-natured Anne of Burgundy, who left her laughter echoing behind her, had not known how brief a time there was to dance.

William! Alice closed her eyes in sudden pain. It was in France that they had first met. But she had been Salisbury's wife and could not imagine how fateful that encounter was to be. She had yearned then for a life at the centre of great events, and later, when William took her hand, she followed him gladly into the maze woven by men and women of conflict around the destiny of a nation.

With a start of surprise she remembered Flint Hawthorne and wondered what became of him. He had ridden out of Ewelme and disappeared for ever. Perhaps some old enemy found a chance to catch him off his guard . . . or maybe he had met a comely widow and hung up his weapons behind her cottage door.

Alice's thoughts turned to Margaret of Anjou. Over the

past two years she seemed to have found some consolation in religion, and looked forward to the day when she might be ransomed by the king of France. So like Margaret to be wanting something other than she had! And she would not listen when Alice warned her that the charity of kings was sometimes not nearly so bountiful as that of old friends. King Edward allowed a pittance for her keep as a royal prisoner. The elaborate furnishings with which she was surrounded, the elegant clothes and good food – to say nothing of the upkeep of her servants and the diversions provided for her – were almost entirely paid for out of Alice's own purse. But Margaret had never understood the value of money. She seemed to think that she would be given an honoured place at the court of Louis XI. Privately Alice doubted it.

Now the thickening shadows in the hall seemed to harbour all the people she had been conjuring up in her mind, whispering, watching . . .

'Waiting for me are you? Soon now, quite soon.'

She pushed a log with her foot so that it fell across the glowing centre of the fire, and lit a candle, preparing to climb the stairs grown curiously steeper in latter months.

Alice took a last look about her, to see that all was well and smiled contentedly . . . 'Those who come after must do the best they can . . . I leave to them my house . . . secure.'

EPILOGUE

IT SEEMS appropriate to leave Alice de la Pole, Duchess
of Suffolk, in the manor of Ewelme – where she most delighted
to be – on a night in March 1475. She died there two months
later, on the twentieth of May, and lies in an elaborate alabaster
tomb, built to her son's directions, in St. Mary's Church.
Close by are the alms-house and the school, modernised but
structurally unchanged, and still serving the beneficent pur-
poses for which, together with William, her husband, she
designed them.

Alice's son, John, did not reach old age. He died in 1491 –
but at least he died in bed in full enjoyment of his rank and
fortune. That his end was peaceful seems, however, to be unlikely. Inevitably he must have recognised that his sons had
inherited those qualities of ambition unallied to guile, and
courage untempered by caution, which had proved fatal to
earlier generations of his family.

On the death of Edward IV in 1483, Alice's eldest grandson, John de la Pole, Earl of Lincoln, became an ardent supporter of his uncle Richard III. In 1484, when Richard's only
son, the young Prince of Wales, died, he named John heir
to the throne, and for a time it seemed as though Alice's descendants might one day sit on the throne of England.

The conquest and accession of Henry Tudor decreed otherwise. Yet all might have been well, for Henry VII, seeking to
placate rather than antagonise his nobles, showed no enmity
either to Suffolk or his son. But the young Earl of Lincoln
refused to be befriended. Instead he rashly joined Lord Lovel

in promoting the Lambert Simnel plot. He was killed in battle at Stoke-on-Trent in 1487.

John, Duke of Suffolk, contrived to live down his eldest son's betrayal of the new régime and Henry VII appears to have trusted him. But Tudor patience with the de la Pole family was to be ill-repaid.

Mercifully John did not live to see what became of his second son, Edmund, nor to know that his title, great estates and vast wealth would not carry beyond another generation.

Edmund de la Pole could never forget that he had once been second in line of succession to the crown. Bitter, envious and restless he spent a number of years wandering about Europe, hoping that some foreign prince might gamble support on his claim to the throne. Eventually he fell into the hands of Philip of Castile and was returned to England, where he was imprisoned in the Tower. Exempted from the general pardon on the accession of Henry VIII, he was executed in 1513.

Margaret of Anjou was ransomed by Louis XI and returned to France in January, 1476. She was forced to sign over all her possessions to Louis, including rights to inheritances from her father in Anjou, Bar and Provence, and from her mother in Lorraine. In return she received a meagre pension and lived out her days, lonely and neglected. She died in 1482 at the age of fifty-three, begging Louis in a Will to pay her few servants what was due to them and settle her debts.

Margaret Beaufort, who had so narrowly missed being the wife of John de la Pole, instead married Edmund Tudor, Earl of Richmond, in 1455, and bore him the son who later became Henry VII.

SELECTED BIBLIOGRAPHY

Bagley, J. J.: *Margaret of Anjou, Queen of England*, 1948.

Bennett, H. S.: *Chaucer and the Fifteenth Century*, 1947.

Bennett, H. S.: *Life on the English Manor*, 1937.

Bishop, W. J.: *The Early History of Surgery*, 1960.

Chaucer's Major Poetry, edited Albert C. Baugh, 1964.

Marchette Chute: *Geoffrey Chaucer of England*, 1951.

Coulton, G. G.: *Chaucer and his England*, 1937.

Edward, second Duke of York: *The Master of Game* (c.1410), edited W. A. and F. Baillie-Grohman, 1904.

Green, V. H. H.: *The Later Plantagenets*, 1955.

John Harvey: *The Plantagenets*, 1959.

Jacob, E. F.: *The Fifteenth Century* (Oxford History of England), 1961.

Napier, the Hon. and Rev. H. A.: *Historical Notices of the Parishes of Swyncombe and Ewelme in Oxfordshire*, 1858.

Austin Lane Poole, ed.: *Medieval England*, Vol. II, 1958.

The Paston Letters, edited John Warrington, 1956.

Marjorie and C. H. B. Quennell: *A History of Everyday Things in England*, Vol. I, 1918.

Edith Rickert, compiler *Chaucer's World*, 1948.

Rossell Hope Robbins: *Secular Lyrics of the XIVth and XVth Centuries*, 1955.

Sidelights on the History of Medicine, 1957. Sir Zachary Cope, ed.

The Stonor Letters and Papers: edited by C. L. Kingsford (Camden Society, 3rd series): 1919.

Trevelyan, G. M.: *Illustrated English Social History*, Vol. I, 1949.

Ethel Carleton Williams: *My Lord of Bedford*, 1963.

Wylie, J. H. and Waugh, W. T.: *The Reign of Henry the Fifth*, three vols., 1914–1929.

REFERENCES

The Complete Peerage.

The National Dictionary of Biography.

The Defection of A. J. Lewinter

ROBERT LITTELL

'The most entertaining and intelligent spy-story for a long time. Lewinter, an engineering professor working on nuclear warheads, applies at the Soviet Embassy in Tokyo to defect. Nobody knows what to make of him. Is he mad? A plant? Has he got anything really vital stored away in his tape-recorder-like nut? In New York and Moscow intelligence men, behaving with a naturalness rare in spy stories, pore over his Comprehensive Personality Profile and discuss him in bed with their girl-friends' –
The Observer

'Excellent writing, clear narrative, great knowledge of the way espionage really works' – *Daily Mail*

'Full of thrills' – *Evening News*

A Hot Property

JUDY FIEFFER

At thirty-five Faye Oppenheim – former starlet and
one-book author – was keen to get the blood stirring
again. At fourteen, her daughter Esther, simply
wanted blood. Their twin desires took them to the
same boudoirs, left the same scars, received the
same buffettings. And in the meantime husband/
father stayed at home and hoped that they were
both looking after themselves . . .

'Judy Feiffer measures out her characters' lives in
punch lines. They're good punch lines . . . this is a
funny, raunchy book' – *New York Times*

The Raj

DONALD A. ROBINSON

Against the exotic backdrop of colonial life in pre-war India, the novel spins out the adventures of Mary de Give.

Like so many girls of her age she arrives looking for a husband. But the husband she finds and the man she loves are not the same person. And, torn between duty and passion, Mary finds herself caught in the eye of a storm that smashes against her private life and breaks around the destiny of a nation.

General Fiction from Coronet

MILTON R. BASS
☐ 15850 6   JORY   30p

JOE DAVID BROWN
☐ 17862 0   PAPER MOON   40p

CYNTHIA BUCHANAN
☐ 18065 X   MAIDEN   40p

ROY CLARKE
☐ 18994 0   LAST OF THE SUMMER WINE   35p

GEORGE FEIFER
☐ 18778 6   THE GIRL FROM PETROVKA   40p

JUDY FEIFFER
☐ 18992 4   A HOT PROPERTY   35p

JOHN de St. JORRE and BRIAN SHAKESPEARE
☐ 18787 5   THE PATRIOT GAME   45p

ROBERT LITTELL
☐ 18827 8   THE DEFECTION OF A. J. LEWINTER   40p

ROBERT MARASCO
☐ 18989 4   BURNT OFFERINGS   45p

DONALD H. ROBINSON
☐ 18991 6   THE RAJ   50p

All these books are available at your bookshop or newsagent, or can be ordered direct from the publisher. Just tick the titles you want and fill in the form below.

CORONET BOOKS, P.O. Box 11, Falmouth, Cornwall.
Please send cheque or postal order. No currency, and allow the following for postage and packing:
1 book—10p, 2 books—15p, 3 books—20p, 4-5 books—25p, 6-9 books—4p per copy, 10-15 books—2½p per copy, 16-30 books—2p per copy, over 30 books free within the U.K.
Overseas – please allow 10p for the first book and 5p per copy for each additional book.

Name ....

Address ....

....

....